HIGH JINX

HIGH JINX

A Paws and Pose Mystery

Shannon Esposito

Esposito,
Shannon

This first world edition published 2016
in Great Britain and the USA by
SEVERN HOUSE PUBLISHERS LTD of
19 Cedar Road, Sutton, Surrey, England, SM2 5DA.
Trade paperback edition first published
in Great Britain and the USA 2016 by
SEVERN HOUSE PUBLISHERS LTD

British Library Cataloguing in Publication Data
A CIP catalogue record for this title is available from the British Library.

ISBN-13: 978-0-7278-8602-6 (cased)
ISBN-13: 978-1-84751-704-3 (trade paper)
ISBN-13: 978-1-78010-765-3 (e-book)

This is a work of fiction. Names, characters, places and incidents
are either the product of the author's imagination or are used fictitiously.
Except where actual historical events and characters are being described
for the storyline of this novel, all situations in this publication are
fictitious and any resemblance to actual persons, living or dead,
business establishments, events or locales is purely coincidental.

All Severn House titles are printed on acid-free paper.

Severn House Publishers support the Forest Stewardship Council™ [FSC™],
the leading international forest certification organisation.
All our titles that are printed on FSC certified paper carry the FSC logo.

Typeset by Palimpsest Book Production Ltd.,
Falkirk, Stirlingshire, Scotland.
Printed and bound in Great Britain by
TJ International, Padstow, Cornwall.

ONE

cringed as my 1976 VW Beetle shuddered and belched a black plume of smoke before falling silent in the driveway of the Beckleys' thirty-million-dollar mansion.

'Drama queen,' I huffed.

Buddha, my faithful seventy-pound bulldog mix, licked my arm from the passenger seat. I wrapped him in a full body hug and kissed him between his alert brown eyes. 'Made quite the entrance, didn't we?' Shaking off the embarrassment that seemed to be my fate on Moon Key – a private Gulf coast island for the rich and insanely rich – I grabbed my yoga mat from the back seat. 'Let's go meet our client.'

As we approached, I eyed the monstrous home with trepidation. An elaborate stained-glass front door sat beyond flat marble steps. Royal palm trees stood guard like sentries beside the steps and a half-moon balcony hung over the entrance. It seemed like a good place to ambush visitors. I imagined ninjas falling gracefully from their perch to thwart salesmen, thieves and lowly doggie-yoga instructors.

A short-statured man with a shiny, polished head, clad in a white moisture wicking shirt and red track pants emerged from the front door. Hopping down the steps with the confidence that comes from living in a multi-million-dollar mansion, he approached us. Definitely not ninja material. His smile was too bright, his demeanor too welcoming and there was no place to hide a sword.

'Hello.' His eyes flicked from me to Buddha – who, to my horror, had a sling of drool about to drop on the man's spotless pavers – and then over to my old Beetle slumped behind us. I had to give the man credit for his composure. He only twitched a little as he asked, 'And you are?'

I cleared my throat and tried to exude confidence. 'Elle Pressley. I'm here for a doga lesson with Flavia and Athena. Selene set it up.'

'Ah.' He glanced behind him and then, coming to some decision, held out his hand. The crinkles in the corners of his bright eyes held a touch of humor. 'I'm Michael, Selene's other half. Not the better half, according to her.'

I shook his hand, relaxing under his non-judgmental demeanor. 'Nice to meet you.'

'Well, come on then. I'll take you around to the back kitchen. My mother-in-law practically lives in there while we're on Moon Key. People think I'm obsessed with running, but to be honest I'm just trying to avoid weighing three hundred pounds because that woman is most definitely obsessed with cooking.'

I laughed politely as Buddha and I followed Michael Beckley around the left side of the mansion and down a beautiful, curving stone path that cut through tropical gardens. Mini palm trees provided shade on the path with their lush, full fronds, while other plants had been carefully layered throughout to give texture, color and scent to the walk. Silver saw palmettos, fountain grass, elephant ear lilies and bright pink cordyline; various blooming hibiscus and orange bird of paradise . . . the variety was overwhelming, and I kept stopping to touch or smell each one. Michael was kind enough to wait and not be put off by my awe and reverence of his landscaping. However, awe and reverence quickly turned to embarrassment as I realized Buddha was tugging at the end of his leash, and I turned to find he'd shoved his muzzle into a decorative fountain, helping himself to a slobbery drink.

'Sorry,' I mumbled, giving his leash a tug. 'Buddha, come here.'

Michael chuckled as Buddha trotted happily back to me, his dripping tongue dangling from his wide mouth. I smiled down at him, despite my embarrassment, glad this man had a sense of humor. 'Come on, boy.' I decided not to stop and admire anything more lest Buddha decide that he now needed to empty his bladder on any of the perfectly kept foliage. I imagined alarms would sound and those ninjas would swoop down upon us for such a crime.

The path opened up to an equally amazing backyard, the main attraction being a rectangular pool of sparkling dark blue water in the middle of impeccably cut emerald grass. Four bordered landscape beds filled with date palms, bromeliad, various blooming annuals and ground cover were equally spaced around the pool. Tall, graceful coconut palm trees studded the perimeter of the yard and beyond that lay the seawall and private boat slip complete with a docked yacht big enough to blot out the sun.

A loud crack sounded on the other side of the bushes. Jerking my head in that direction, I could have sworn I saw a head peeking over. It was gone in an instant. I glanced at Michael as he eyed the bushes, his face hardening. *What was that all about?*

I ran my hand self-consciously over my sales rack T-shirt, wiping at the dog hair, as Buddha and I were led to French doors set off to the side of a large stone lanai. Massive pots full of cacti had been placed on either side of the door. *More unwelcoming guardians.*

He opened the door and peeked in. '*Yiya*, you still alive in there?'

A slew of angry foreign words echoed from inside, along with a sharp yipping. I assumed it was Greek since Michael had called her *yiya*, which in my understanding meant 'grandmother'.

Michael grinned at me. 'She's not my biggest fan. Selene was supposed to marry a good Greek boy.' He winked at me and opened the door further, making a sweeping motion with his arm. 'No sense of humor, that one. Anyway, she's all yours. Good luck.'

I smiled back at him. 'Thanks.' I stepped into the kitchen with Buddha by my side and was instantly overwhelmed by delicious smells. A plump Chihuahua wobbled toward us, tiny nails clicking on the floor, yipping a high-pitched warning. Buddha sat down and licked his lips, a sign that the little dog was making him nervous. I rested a hand on his head and tried not to make eye contact with the tiny canine guardian. My rule was not to make eye contact with small angry dogs or large drunk men.

'Athena! 'Nough!' An elderly woman in a wheelchair rolled herself away from her work at the counter and moved toward us, waving a hand at the dog. The dog leapt into her lap and stared at us with the same slightly yellowed, dark brown eyes of her owner.

The woman stuck out a weathered, trembling hand. Her voice also trembled and held a thick Greek accent. 'I am Flavia. Nice to meet you.'

I bent to take her hand but Athena bared her tiny teeth, her ears flattening on her head. I pulled my hand back and heard an immediate rumbled response from Buddha beside me. He'd never been aggressive toward another dog before, but he'd never seen me threatened by one, either. Loosening my grip on his leash to let him know I didn't feel threatened – dogs apparently translate tightened grip with fear energy and get protective – I stood back upright and smiled. 'Nice to meet you, too, Flavia.'

'Sorry.' Flavia wrapped her hand around Athena's chest and pulled her close, chastising the little dog in Greek.

'It's fine. She probably just needs some time to warm to us.' Changing the subject to a more pleasant one, I asked, 'What are you cooking? It smells amazing.'

A smile wrinkled her cheeks as she pushed a lever on her chair and turned toward the oven. 'Dis, I make *spanakopita* for lunch.' She glanced back over her shoulder and eyed me suspiciously up and down. 'You eat, no?'

'Yes, I eat.' I grinned. I liked this woman. 'Maybe we should do a little doga first, Flavia. So Selene doesn't feel like she's paying me to eat lunch.' I slipped off my flip-flops at the door and walked deeper into the massive Mediterranean-style kitchen. The brick floor felt cool on my soles. Now that I was paying attention, I noticed the whole kitchen – from the low-slung double oven to the marble counters with cut-a-ways beneath them – was designed for wheelchair access. The Beckleys must've designed this kitchen just for her.

'Bah,' Flavia motioned with a pot holder, 'I get plenty exercise cooking. My daughter, she worries for nothing.'

Burying a smile, I continued surveying the custom kitchen with awe as I worked to convince her to let me earn my keep. This was my first lesson out of the studio at the Pampered Pup Spa & Resort – where I taught doga classes thanks to my best friend, Hope, getting me a job there last year – and I intended to give Selene and Flavia their money's worth. Especially because Selene had offered an obscene amount of money for a thirty-minute lesson.

'You might, but Selene did tell you I teach doga, right? It's actually yoga for dogs, so really, I'm here for Athena. To help you help *her* get a little exercise.' My gaze wandered up to the thick, exposed wood beams hanging low across the ceiling. They'd been stained a rich chocolate color and contrasted perfectly with the rough-textured white walls.

A loud burst of laughter startled me and I quickly glanced at

Flavia. She had her hands perched on the wide hips spread under a flowered apron. Her grin almost completely hid her eyes. 'Fine. We do this *doga*.'

The look she gave me let me know she wasn't falling for my crap line, but she would humor me nonetheless. I really liked this woman. My heart ached for a moment as I wondered what it would be like having a grandmother, but I quickly shook that thought off. No use wanting something that would never happen. That was a sure-fire way to be miserable.

Flavia untied her apron with precision slowness and tossed it on the counter, revealing a black Mumu and a large round pennant hanging around her neck. It was blue with a wide-open eye painted in the center and it was startling. Athena watched me suspiciously from beneath it. 'What you need me to do?'

'Well . . .' I cleared my throat, trying not to stare at the blue eye in the center of her chest. It was unnerving. *Focus, Elle.* Selene hadn't mentioned her mother being in a wheelchair, but luckily I'd brushed up on teaching chair yoga before I came, since she'd mentioned they'd recently celebrated her mother's eightieth birthday.

'Just follow along as best you can, let me know if anything hurts so we can modify it and just have fun.' Smiling, I slid my mat from my shoulder and unrolled it with a flick of the wrist. Buddha immediately flopped down on it, stretching out his back legs in his version of cobra pose.

I grabbed a chair from the table and slid it beside the mat. 'Let's start with our hands and then we'll move on to Athena's paws. First, roll the wrists like this.' I demonstrated, watching her expression for any signs of pain as she followed along. I led her to switch directions. 'Good, Flavia. Now let's start there with Athena.' I patted my leg and Buddha pushed himself off the mat and came to sit in front of me.

'You can teach Athena to listen like that?' Flavia grunted.

I glanced down at the little dog. As soon as I made eye contact, her lip raised. She definitely considered herself the queen of this castle. Pressing my own lips together, I shook my head and held out my hand for Buddha's paw, which he happily plopped in my palm. 'Flavia, I have a feeling Athena would never let anyone tell her what to do.'

'You are right about that,' she chuckled. She picked up the tiny paw – which I now noticed had sparkly tangerine nails – and followed my lead as I massaged Buddha's paw. 'I think dis is why she live so long. She's twenty-seven, you know.'

My eyebrows rose as I appraised Athena. I knew smaller dogs lived longer, but that was an unbelievably long time. She didn't look a day past ten, though her white face hid any gray that might have crept into her fur. Still, that had to be a record. 'That's extraordinary. You must cook for her, too.' My stomach growled. I was having a hard time ignoring the scent coming from the oven. We switched paws.

She nodded once. 'She eat what I eat. But she is too ornery to die, I think. God knows she would cause trouble in heaven.' Chuckling to herself, she patted the dog's back affectionately.

I laughed. 'I don't doubt it. OK, Flavia, let's stretch our arms and shoulders. Please, don't force anything. Lift your arms only as high as is comfortable.' I led her through a few minutes of stretches and shoulder rolls and then moved to stand on my mat with Buddha seated in front of me. 'The pup's turn. Place your hands right under Athena's armpits like this.' Hinging at the waist, I demonstrated on Buddha. 'Then using your body to support her, pull her against your chest and lift her into a stretch.' I pulled Buddha against me and he rose with me, his two front legs up in the air, his belly exposed. His long, wet tongue caught me on the chin before I could raise my head, making me laugh.

We went through about ten more minutes of stretches with the dogs and then, since we couldn't finish with *savasana*, I tried to lead Flavia in a few minutes of meditation with her eyes closed. She was having none of it.

She waved me off. 'OK. We finished.'

I opened my eyes and watched her twirl her wheelchair around and head back to the business end of the kitchen. 'Time for lunch.'

'Finished,' I repeated, nodding from my mat. I smirked at Buddha. His squinty-eyed pant looked like he was as amused as I was. I stood and moved the chair back to the table. 'Anything you need help with, Flavia?'

'You can come get the Caesar salad,' she called.

My stomach rumbled in anticipation as I retrieved the large

wooden bowl of creamy, crouton-filled salad. Flavia had dispersed Athena from her lap perch and replaced the little dog with a tray full of steaming *spanakopita.*

'This is really lovely of you, Flavia.' I hadn't had authentic Greek food since Hope had taken me to The Greek Garden in Clearwater two years ago. And even then, I'm not sure that was entirely authentic. There was no feta to be found.

Flavia plopped a piece of the spinach pie in a dish by the table – which Athena proceeded to gobble up with little growling sounds – and waved her hand at me as she rolled by the table with another piece of the pie on a dish. 'Is nothing. Everybody has to eat.'

When I realized where she was headed with that dish, I tried to stop her. 'Oh, Flavia, he doesn't do well . . .' Too late. Buddha only sniffed the piece of spinach pie once before woofing it down in two bites. '. . . With people food,' I finished under my breath.

I smiled and shoved a forkful of salad in my mouth. I would pay for that later. As I chewed, Flavia maneuvered her wheelchair to the table and made the sign of the cross over herself before picking up her fork. She rolled her shoulder. 'Ah. Much more loose. I like this doga.' Her smile lit up her eyes.

Nodding, I grinned and held up my fork. 'And I like this food. It's as delicious as it smells.'

Flavia chuckled. 'We have *baklava* for dessert, so save room.'

I shook my head, wondering if I'd be able to walk out of here or if I'd have to borrow Flavia's wheelchair.

Flavia entertained me throughout our meal with tales of her childhood in Greece, and the time flew by. Near the end of the meal, I wiped my mouth with a napkin and decided we were acquainted enough for me to ask her about her unusual jewelry. 'So, Flavia, can I ask you about your necklace?'

She reached up and rubbed the eye between knotted fingers. 'This is *mataki* – charm to ward off the evil eye.'

'The evil eye?' I repeated, intrigued.

'Yes. You see, the evil eye, it can harm you even when the person does not intend for this to happen, by complimenting you. The eye protects you.' She waved her fork. 'Also, the cactus out by the door is protection.'

She sure felt like she needed lots of protection. I chewed

slowly, trying to work out the logistics of her beliefs. 'So when I complimented you on the food, I could have accidentally given you this . . . evil eye.'

'If I no wear this charm to ward it off, yes.'

'Then what would this evil eye do? What would happen?'

'Many things. All bad. You compliment my food and I no wear this charm . . . I could drop the whole pan on the floor. Ruined, you see?'

My mouth hung open for a second more than was polite. I snapped it closed and nodded as a sudden sense of foreboding washed over me.

TWO

Twenty minutes later, with the divine taste of honey and flaky filo lingering in my mouth, I packed up my mat, clipped on Buddha's leash and waddled after Flavia through the mansion as we searched for Selene.

I held my flip-flops in my hand so the sleek, inlaid marble floor felt cool and heavenly on my bare feet. Peeking into some rooms as we passed, I saw a theatre with a massive movie screen and four rows of leather recliners; a billiard room with two full-sized pool tables and a bar; a library with a living room set in the middle and some kind of massage room. I bet fifty people could live here without ever running into each other. A young, dark-haired girl was picking up towels from the floor. We shared a smile as I passed.

We emerged from the hallway into a grand living area in the center of the mansion. Floor-to-ceiling windows dressed in cream curtains framed the blue sky and water. It was a stunning view.

Flavia stopped abruptly at the sound of voices. I almost ran into the back of her chair but managed to only tilt awkwardly over the top of her. She grumbled under her breath and flicked the lever on her chair with obvious agitation.

Rolling past a curved staircase with a huge aquarium stocked with brightly-colored fish encased in the cut-out, we headed toward the front door where the voices were coming from.

Under an elaborate entrance complete with pillars and a chandelier, Selene was being embraced by a giant with military-cropped blond hair. And by her peals of laughter, whatever he was whispering in her ear was pretty witty.

'Selene!' Flavia barked. The one word was sharp and cutting. It sent Athena into yipping hysterics. 'Enough.' Flavia pulled the little dog tightly into her bosom.

The giant released Selene, who put her hands on her hips and glared at her mother. 'I'm right here, you don't have to yell.' Chloe, Selene's own plump Chihuahua – sporting a pink T-shirt with

'mommy's little girl' embroidered on it – came bounding around
the corner to see what all the fuss what about, her painted nails
trying to grip the marble tile unsuccessfully as she slid into Selene's
leg. During snowbird season, I blamed the out-of-proportion
number of Chihuahuas on Paris Hilton making them a popular
fashion accessory.

'See what you've done, Mom – you've scared Chloe.' Making
little cooing noises, she scooped the trembling dog up and held
her to her cleavage. I noted Giant's eyes lingered there, and I'm
pretty sure he wasn't interested in the dog. Even pushing sixty,
Selene was a beautiful, well-preserved woman. 'Oh, hello, Elle.
Give me a second to see Sven out and I'll get you your check.'

I waved, uncomfortable with the whole scene. Sven's assessing
gaze had swung to me. Two light blue stones in a chiseled face
looked me up and down. This man was a walking vat of testos-
terone. 'You can just bring it to doga on Monday. It's no biggie.'
I mentally slapped myself. Sure, I was temporarily staying with
Devon in his million-dollar beach bungalow, but I still needed
the money.

'I know!' Her face lit up. 'Why don't you come to our
Halloween party tomorrow night? I can give it to you then. We
have the best Halloween party every year, don't we, Mom?'
Before her mother could answer, she turned her attention back
to the giant. 'Sven, you should come, too!' I had a feeling this
was her real motivation for mentioning the party. 'You can come
as my personal trainer.' This sent them both into more fits of
laughter. Apparently it was an inside joke. Very inside.

I squirmed behind Flavia's chair as another burst of Greek
came from the woman.

'Oh, no, Selene, I couldn't impose.'

'Nonsense.' Selene waved me off. 'You must come. I insist.
You can bring a date and don't forget to wear a costume. It's
settled.' She opened the front door. Like a cornered animal, I
saw my opening and took it.

About halfway to the door, Flavia shrieked behind me. I whirled
around, startled. She was clutching her chest. 'You must leave
from the same door, Elle. Come, I take you back to my kitchen.'

'Jesus, Mom,' Selene cried from the door. 'You and your
superstitions. You almost gave the poor girl a heart attack.'

'You want her to bring bad luck to dis family?' Flavia growled.

'It's OK.' I turned to Selene. 'I don't mind. We'll go out the back way.'

'Fine. See you tomorrow evening,' she called, her attention already back to Sven.

I rubbed my temple as I led Buddha back the way we came, suddenly feeling a headache coming on.

Before I could get out the back door, Flavia clutched my hand. 'Do you feel dizzy?'

'No, I . . . I'm fine.'

Flavia's dark eyes searched my face. 'Headache?'

I blinked. 'Well, a little. But I'm fine, really.' Did she think she gave me food poisoning? I didn't understand what she was really asking. Something was definitely worrying her, though. I could see it in her tight lips and narrowed eyes.

She nodded. 'It was that blue-eyed Sven. You see how he admire you?' She squeezed my hand in both of hers. 'He curse you with the evil eye. No worry. You go. I do exercising prayer for you.'

Cursed? Me? I felt my temple pulse as if the pain was confirmation. I didn't really believe in curses, did I? It's not something I'd ever thought about until today. Well, it couldn't hurt to let Flavia do her thing.

Buddha and I had just made it out of mansion row and back onto Moon Key Drive, the main road that runs around the island, when my Beetle sputtered and died.

No. No. No. Are you kidding me? I managed to let it drift to the side of the road, where I proceeded to crank the key to no avail. When that didn't work, I beat the steering wheel and then fell back against the vinyl seat. My headache blossomed with the stress. Flavia's words echoed between the pain. *Cursed with the evil eye.* No, not cursed, I argued back. I just have a headache and an ancient car that should probably be in a museum rather than on the road.

'You can just pay me next time you come to doga,' I whispered, mocking myself. I reached over to soothe myself by stroking Buddha. He repaid me by yacking up a clump of undigested *spanakopita* between the seats.

'Perfect.' I groaned and reached for the towel I kept in the back for when it rained and the convertible top leaked. Buddha shifted to lean against the door, his head lowered. He actually looked ashamed. I scratched his ear. 'It's OK, big guy. That'll cover up the mildew smell.'

I watched a golf cart go by with four women in oversized sunhats and Jackie O-style sunglasses. Their heads turned my way as they passed but they didn't stop. I suddenly felt like a zoo animal, something to stare at and be weary of at the same time. *Now what?* There was no garage and no tow truck on Moon Key. I was probably making history on the ritzy, private island by having the first car ever to break down here. What an honor. We could walk back to the bungalow, I supposed. It was only three miles. It was a nice day – low eighties, low humidity. I watched a sleek white limo cruise by who then beeped at a red Porsche-shaped golf cart that decided to stop in the middle of the road for no reason. Then again, it was the end of October and the snowbirds were here. We might be taking a risk walking on a road where golf carts full of champagne-fueled millionaires were motoring about. Champagne-fueled millionaires with lawyers on retainer who could get them off if they ran us over. But what choice did we have? Devon wouldn't be back on Moon Key until this evening. I couldn't sit here in a smelly, broken-down car. The humiliation alone might do me in.

My chest tightened. I took a few deep breaths, remembering the words of the therapist I'd returned to because of my anxiety, which had been heightened by recent life-threatening events. 'Your yoga practice has given you many tools for anxiety. Use them.' This was right before she added, 'But in extreme circumstances, use this,' and handed me a prescription for Xanax.

As I was packing up all my stuff and getting ready to brave the walk, my cell phone buzzed. It was Hope.

'Hey, Elle, what are you doing?'

I flipped my yoga bag onto my shoulder. 'Just enduring complete humiliation at the hands of my dead car. How's New York?'

'Awful. Not so much New York as Ira's relatives. We decided to come back early. Did you say your car broke down?'

'Yeah, right outside of mansion row. Are you back on the island?' Could I be that lucky?

'Yep. I'll be right there.'

I glanced up at the sky gratefully. 'Thank you! Oh, hey, do you by any chance have a costume for a Halloween party lying around that you could bring? I have to go to Selene Beckley's party tomorrow night to get paid for a session I just did with her mother.'

Hope laughed. 'That sounds like Selene. I'll dig something up and be there in a few.'

'We'll be here.'

Buddha and I hunkered down inside the Beetle and waited for Hope. Ten minutes later, Hope's black Jaguar cruised up behind us.

'You're a lifesaver.' I hugged her. 'Or at least an ego-saver.'

Hope chuckled and helped Buddha into the surprisingly roomy back seat. 'Probably time to put the old gal out to pasture, Elle.'

I feigned indignation as I slid into the passenger seat. 'You don't put classics out to pasture.' The feel of her car's buttery leather seat beneath me did not go unappreciated. 'Besides, I can't afford a new car. I'm homeless, remember?'

'You are not.' She shot me an exasperated look. 'You're living in a beach bungalow with a gorgeous Irishman who is begging you to move in permanently.'

'We've talked about this, Hope,' I groaned. 'Permanently does not mean the same thing to Devon. He'll only be here until he solves his parents' murder and then he'll jet off to do what he loves and be a travel photographer again.' Whereby history will have repeated itself, with another man of my dreams leaving me in the dust to live a life that didn't include me . . . 'That to me is temporary. So, I have to find my own place. Eventually.'

Hope shook her head but didn't say anything more on the subject.

I rolled my head in her direction. 'So, what happened at the wedding?'

This got her going. She entertained me for the rest of the short trip with the groan-worthy highlights of her week that made me glad I didn't have an extended family, including a story about one of Ira's uncles falling into the champagne fountain at the reception.

By the time we pulled into Devon's driveway, we were both giggling hysterically.

I glanced at my best friend in one of those moments where gratitude actually choked me up. I don't know what I'd do without her. 'Oh, Hope, thanks . . . I needed that.'

'Me, too. Oh, I have your costume in the trunk.' She put the car in park and popped the trunk.

While I let Buddha out of the back seat, she retrieved a bag and handed it to me. With a last hug, she grinned and said, 'I think Devon will approve.'

THREE

'I am not leaving the house in this.' I stared at myself in the bedroom mirror in horror while Devon grinned at me from his reclining position on the bed, stroking Petey, his large brown, happy-go-lucky mutt.

'We don't have to go out.'

I ignored his sultry innuendo. 'Seriously, I don't think she bought this at a Halloween store but at one of those shady little sex shops on the side of the road. You know the ones with the papered-over windows and neon signs?' I covered my blushing face as I once again let my gaze fall to the push-up-style top that forced my small assets into cleavage. I whirled around as another burst of laughter came from the bed. 'Maids do not dress like this. Look at these frills on my butt. That is just not practical. And it's not funny!' I threw the pink feather duster at him.

'No, you're right.' Ducking, Devon swallowed his laughter and with one last pat to Petey, pushed himself off the bed. He stood in front of me and tried to be sympathetic, but the gleam in his eyes gave him away. He was amused. 'They don't. But it'll be fine. It's a costume party. Everyone there will be wearing something over the top. Most likely trying for sexy and look, you don't even have to try.' He pulled me against him and kissed my pouty lips. In such a skimpy outfit, I could feel the heat radiating from his body and began to soften like putty. 'Think about it . . . are the women of Moon Key going to be dressed as clowns?'

I sighed. Reaching back with one hand I tugged at the scrap of black material posing as a skirt. 'No. But they're not going to be dressed up in something from a sex toy shop, either.'

He let himself grin. 'You'd be surprised.'

Turned out I didn't have to worry. The first woman I spotted as we pulled up to the Beckley mansion was exiting a limo in nothing but a conch shell bra and G-string 'concealed' by strands of seaweed, fishnets and gold body glitter. Her date slid out behind her.

'Is that man just wearing a G-string and . . . paint?' I whispered, half-amused, half-horrified.

'Yes.' Devon handed his keys over to the valet. 'And I told you so.' He came around to my side of the Jeep and helped me out, helping himself to a kiss while he was at it.

A shiver ran through me. I don't think I'll ever get used to this man's touch. I let my gaze wander over his little black bow tie, black vest and white gloves. My sexy Irish PI was supposed to be a butler to go with my maid outfit, but his unruly dark waves and that mischievous glint in his eyes kind of killed the effect that he'd be willing to serve anyone. 'I think you actually might be over-dressed.'

He nodded, taking my hand as a couple of gray-haired ladies walked by in nude body suits and Playboy bunny ears. 'Come on. I need a drink.'

Inside was a virtual carnival of costumes. We waded into the grand room where a few Vegas-style hostesses balanced trays of champagne and hors d'oeuvres around, offering them to such creatures as an X-rated Snow White, a woman with her partner on a dog leash and a stooped, shrunken Batman. I tried to look away, but it was too late. I would never look at Batman the same way again. Devon plucked two glasses from one of their trays and downed his with one toss. I would've loved to follow suit but the bubbles tickled my nose and forced me to sip.

Scanning the room full of costumed strangers with mounting anxiety, I finally spotted Beth Anne and Violet, two of my regular doga clients at the Pampered Pup Spa & Resort. Thank heavens. I grabbed Devon's hand. 'This way.'

'Elle!' Beth Anne squealed, hugging me and then readjusting her cat-eye glasses and the short, gray wig hiding her long hair. 'Wow, you look amazing.'

I blushed. 'And you look . . .' I eyed her old-fashioned gray dress and pearls, at a loss for words.

'Like Agatha Christie?' she offered helpfully.

'Yes!' Of course. I should have known. Beth Anne's dream was to be a mystery writer, though I had my doubts about whether she actually liked the writing part. 'Just like her.' I turned to Violet, who was sporting a very sexy devil costume and had her arm wrapped around a man half her age with matching devil horns. Her green eyes sparkled with mischief or champagne . . . or both.

She clinked my glass and introduced us to Jarvis, the twenty years her junior, model material man of the week. Each of the ladies I'd gotten to know on Moon Key had taught me something. From Violet I'd learned that money did in fact give a woman a huge advantage when it came to dating. Though I wasn't sure what Violet did would qualify as dating. More like sampling. I bet she was the type of person to take one bite out of each chocolate in a box.

Focus, Elle. 'Nice to meet you, Jarvis. This is just . . . crazy,' I said, wide-eyed as a flirty Minnie Mouse bumped my elbow.

Violet adjusted her horns. 'Yeah, it's getting crowded. Let's move outside.'

We all tagged behind Violet, pushing our way through the noisy clusters of partygoers, finally passing the movie room, massage room, library and then Flavia's kitchen to emerge out into the backyard where more costumed guests lounged around the stone and tiled seating areas and pool deck. I fanned my face. The cool air was refreshing and succeeded in tamping down the anxiety created by the crowd. I glanced around. Silver and black candles floated on the pool surface, their tiny flames flickering in the breeze. It was a simple but stunning effect with the endless moonlit Gulf waters spread out beyond the yard. There was also entertainment out here in the form of a band, belly dancers and fire-eating men on stilts.

It was a beautiful fall evening with a clear night sky bursting with stars, but after a while I migrated to huddle by one of the tiki torches as the air held a bit too much of a chill for my comfort once I'd cooled off – especially in this skimpy costume. Devon moved over to wrap his arms around me from behind as he started a conversation with Beth Anne's husband, who'd joined us. He wore a funny little mustache and top hat and introduced himself to us as Hercule Poirot, Agatha Christie's most famous detective. Apparently his real name was Carl and he was a sculptor.

'You've never met him?' Carl was saying when I tuned back into the conversation.

'Haven't had the pleasure,' Devon replied.

'It would not be your pleasure, I assure you.' They were talking about Oliver White, the Australian art dealer and casino owner who lived next door. Carl's tone suggested foreboding. 'Look up narcissist in the dictionary and there'll be a picture of Oliver.'

Voices suddenly rose at a loud pitch as an argument headed our way. I recognized Michael Beckley, Selene's husband, even though he was dressed as Elvis in a sparkling white jumpsuit with a black wig concealing his bald head. I didn't, however, recognize the girl with spiky black hair and a purple streak in her bangs yelling at him or the thin woman trailing them with her head down, cradling a kitten on a leash.

As they approached, I could see the normally jolly Michael was about to blow a gasket. His face was beet red beneath the wig. He didn't seem to notice or care about the wake of silence the trio was leaving behind through the crowd. Even the band had stopped playing and the fire-eaters stopped shoving flames down their throats.

'You owe me an explanation!' The girl screamed into the stillness. Even the frogs and insects stopped chirping.

Michael whirled on her, his fists clenched. 'I. Owe. You. Nothing. Get off of my property.'

The words were spit with such vitriol, I cringed.

The purple-haired girl stopped like she'd hit a brick wall and slid her arm around the woman with the kitten. Her lips pulled back from gritted teeth. 'We'll just see what Mom has to say about this.'

Michael let out a frustrated growl as the two women trekked off through the backyard hand in hand. The crowd parted to let them pass and they slipped into the house through French doors on the other end of the mansion.

'Sorry about that, folks,' Michael bellowed, regaining his composure. 'Please, continue enjoying the festivities.'

We watched him follow the same path into the mansion as the women had taken. After the low murmuring of gossip began, the band resumed their song.

'What in heaven's name was that all about?' I asked, resting my hands on Devon's arms wrapped tightly around my waist. I suddenly felt the need for reassurance.

'Not sure.' Carl's eyes narrowed in thought. 'But I think that was their daughter, Cali. I haven't seen her here in a few years.'

'His daughter? Sounded like a pretty major fight. I wonder what could make a father so angry at his own daughter?' It may have been selfish and I did feel a bit guilty, but I was secretly glad to see another family fighting, especially one with money. Maybe my relationship with my mother wasn't so abnormal after all.

'I'm sure they'll work it out.' Beth Anne waved off the drama. Her amber eyes sparked behind the fake glasses as they reflected the tiki torch flame at my back. 'I just can't wait to find out what Michael's big Halloween prank is going to be this year.'

'Prank?' I asked.

'Yeah, last year he dropped a hundred tiny mechanical spiders down on the guests.' Beth Anne shivered and adjusted her wig. 'They felt real as all get out. Caused complete pandemonium. Some of the guests even jumped into the pool to get 'em off. It was funny . . . eventually.'

Violet chuckled, turning her attention from Jarvis, though she kept a hand on his hip. 'Yeah, well, Selene forbade him from doing anything that would disturb the party like that again this year.'

Speaking of Selene, I should look for her soon. I needed to get paid so I could fix my broken car, which Devon had so gallantly towed to his bungalow with his Jeep.

When the conversation turned to stories of past Halloween parties and who'd hired which designer for their costumes, I decided to go look for her. Besides, I really had to pee.

I leaned my head back to look up at Devon. 'I'm going to go find the ladies' room. Want me to grab you a drink while I'm daring the crowd?'

'Sure. A Guinness if you can find one.' He kissed me softly. 'Hurry back.'

'Will do.' I slipped from his arms and followed the same path into the house as Michael and his daughter had before. This led me to the opposite wing from the one I'd been in with Flavia. As I entered the wide hallway and rounded a pillar, someone wearing a flowery robe and a wooden mask bumped into me. The tall figure stopped and stared down at me through the tiny slits in the wood. Then he or she kept going, jarring my shoulder violently on the way out. 'Ow.' I rubbed my shoulder. Rude. Or drunk. Or maybe they couldn't see so well through the small slits. I shrugged it off and walked further into the large marble-floored hallway.

It was quieter here. The crowd must all be congregated in the grand room and outside. I enjoyed the silence as I peered into each room I passed looking for a restroom. One room was dark, but I could still see various pieces of art hanging on the walls as cluttered shadows around the room. Interesting, but the important thing was it didn't look like the kind of room that had a bathroom. The pressure on my bladder was getting intense.

A young maid suddenly darted past me. 'Excuse me, sorry,' she said breathlessly over her shoulder. Surely she would know where there was a restroom. I followed her lead, stepping into the kitchen, where chaos seemed the norm with things steaming and clanging and people talking over each other. I glanced at a squat man expertly wielding a monster knife to dice an onion and muttering to himself. Nope, wouldn't ask him. Another woman was sliding some kind of individual portions of what looked like cheesecake onto a tray and yelling at the young maid for not being where she was supposed to be. To my embarrassment, I noted our outfits looked very similar.

'Excuse me?' I said, stepping deeper into the kitchen.

When the maid turned, I realized it was the same girl I'd seen picking up towels on my previous trek through the mansion. She eyed my costume and smiled warmly at me.

The woman's eyes were not so kind. 'Yes?' she barked.

'I was just looking for a restroom?'

The maid seemed to take pity on me. Before the woman could bark again, she cut in, saying, 'My room is just across the hall. You can use the restroom there.'

'Oh.' I felt both relieved and surprised at her generosity. 'Thank you. My bladder thanks you, too.' We shared a smile and I left the kitchen.

I found her room and the large restroom attached to it. When I came back out, I was less focused on my full bladder, so when I passed her dresser I stopped. There was a photo of her with her arm around one of the maids I recognized from The Pampered Pup, a sweet girl named Novia Morales. The resemblance was there. Sisters? Then I noticed a framed photo of the maid with Michael Beckley. They were both sweaty and had huge smiles and a number taped to their shirts. They must've run a race together. I wondered just how cozy their relationship was. Then I noticed the two dolls leaning against that frame, bound together with twine. There was no mistaking their purpose. They were voodoo dolls.

FOUR

As I was stepping out of the bedroom, I ran smack into a lady in a cat costume. I grabbed her shoulders as I saw her toppling over. 'Oh, I'm so sorry. Are you OK?'

Her glassy gray eyes tried to focus on my face. She giggled. 'Yes, yes. Fine.' Then a cat claw came up and pushed into my chest. 'Flavia asked me to come find you. She's supposed to get the semolina cake out of the oven in a few minutes but can't get her wheelchair through the crowd.' She leaned over and I involuntarily jerked away from the assault of whiskey breath. 'Between you and me, I think she just wants to go find Selene, who's disappeared from the party along with that personal trainer she's been glued to all night. Lord, have you seen that man's loin cloth?' Her eyes became unfocused for a moment and then she waved. 'Anyway, they were getting real cozy before they took off.'

'Took off?' I'd never get my paycheck from her at this rate.

She licked her dry lips and poked me again. 'You need to go get the cake out for her in Flavia's kitchen. Brush it with butter and don't forget the syrup.'

'Oh.' I held up a hand. 'But I'm not . . .'

'Now, before it's ruined!' she ordered. Then she twirled around and stumbled back down the hallway, singing what sounded like a mix of opera and someone stepping on her tail at an alarming volume.

I sighed. Well, that's what I get for coming out of the maid's room in a maid outfit. OK, fine. I could handle getting a cake out of an oven and putting some butter and syrup on it. Maybe I'd even find a Guinness in the kitchen for Devon.

I trekked back outside and navigated my way to Flavia's kitchen from there. The French doors guarded by cactus were shut but not locked. I slipped in and immediately squealed and clutched my heart. Hanging from the wood rafters was a body.

My hands flew to my mouth. 'Oh my God!' But then I recognized the blue-tinged face and the Elvis costume and irritation rose to replace the fear. 'Mr Beckley.' The Halloween prank. Of course. My shaking legs barely carried me over to where he was dangling with his arms at his sides, a noose around his neck.

'You scared the living daylights out of me. So, your prank this year is to give your mother-in-law a heart attack?' I crossed my arms, not amused. Though, I had to give it to him. He had done a great job on the make-up.

Moving behind him, I spotted the cable running down the rope and underneath his white sparkly jumpsuit. 'Huh. I always wondered how they did that in movies.' I suddenly smelled the cake burning. 'Crap.' Racing over to the low oven, I grabbed two oven mitts and pulled the door open. A thin layer of gray smoke wafted out. 'Great.' I slid the cake out carefully and placed it on the counter. Staring at the pre-cut pieces, I groaned. I was pretty sure they were not supposed to be black on top. Flavia wasn't going to be happy. And unlike Mr Beckley, I didn't want to be the one to cause her unhappiness.

Sighing, I threw the oven mitts on the counter. No use buttering and syruping burnt cake.

As I passed Mr Beckley to leave, I said, 'You're going to have a while to wait. Flavia's . . .' I looked up at him. 'Flavia's stuck in the grand room.' I didn't want to be the one to inform him that Selene had pulled a disappearing act with her personal trainer and Flavia might be trying to track them down. 'Mr Beckley? OK, you know what. You're doing a great job staying in character but could you just nod to acknowledge you heard me?'

I waited. I moved closer. I got a really bad feeling. The sounds of the laughter and music outside faded into the background as my attention narrowed. 'Mr Beckley? Michael?' I whispered. *Oh, God.* Stepping forward reluctantly, I kept my head tilted up to watch his face as I reached out and grabbed his wrist. If he scared me right now I would kill him. He was warm but there was no resistance. Closing my eyes, I felt for a pulse. There was none. I shook his arm. 'Michael!' I backed away and then stumbled back through the kitchen door into the backyard.

'Somebody help!' I screamed.

'Miss Pressley.' Detective Farnsworth eyed me as he pulled out the patio chair. It made a scraping sound on the stone that set my already fried nerves on edge. He lowered himself into the chair, oblivious. 'Nice to see you again.' He obviously didn't mean it. His gaze slid to Devon, who had his arm protectively around my shoulder. 'I'm going to need to speak to Miss Pressley alone.'

I grabbed Devon's hand, my body starting to shake again under the beach towel he'd wrapped around me. We'd been sitting there for thirty minutes already while the two Clearwater homicide detectives and a slew of officers and crime-scene techs arrived by boat and took over the party. They'd corralled everyone outside into the backyard and ordered us not to leave. Though, glancing around it seemed half the party had skedaddled before the police had arrived. 'Does he have to go?' I pleaded to the detective.

''Fraid so. Sorry.' Detective Farnsworth flipped open his notepad and tapped his cheap plastic pen impatiently on the table.

'It'll be all right.' Devon kissed my forehead. 'I'll just be right over there. Within eyesight.'

I nodded. My head felt like it was floating. As I watched Devon make his way over to join the rest of the shocked partygoers, Detective Salma Vargas intercepted him. I felt a twinge of irritation. He'd been spending a lot of time with her lately since she was helping him with the investigation into his parents' deaths in a boating accident five years ago, which Devon didn't believe was an accident at all. The man driving the boat that had hit them had recently been released, time served, and Devon was more determined than ever to prove the man actually murdered them. As I watched Devon and Salma talk, something uncomfortable rose within me: a sharp dart of pain like a splinter in my heart. Devon should be with me right now, not her.

'Miss Pressley?' Detective Farnsworth repeated.

I blinked and directed my attention back to him. 'Yes. Sorry.' *What was wrong with me?* I trusted Devon, and even if they had dated before he met me – I was still too chicken to confirm that hunch – he was with me now. His choice. It must be the stress. Pushing away the ridiculous thoughts, I refocused on the detective.

'I realize a dead body is a shocking thing to find, especially after everything you've gone through recently.' He squirmed, seemingly uncomfortable with being empathic. 'But I need you to try and remember everything. Details are going to be important here to catch whoever did this.'

'Sure.' I pulled the beach towel tighter around my shoulders, glad to be covering up the skimpy maid outfit, and shook my head. 'But can I ask why you think someone did this? I mean, couldn't his harness system just have failed?'

He squinted his eyes and pursed his lips. 'No.' Then he stared at me expectantly.

'I can't ask? Or his harness didn't just fail?'

'Both.' He continued to stare at me. It was unnerving. I was starting to feel guilty. For what, I had no idea. I thought about confessing to stealing a roll of toilet paper from the Seven-Eleven bathroom when I was thirteen and Mom wasn't in any shape to drive to the store. Luckily, he decided to start asking questions so my petty theft stayed a secret. 'So, let's start from the beginning. Why did you enter the kitchen?'

'Because a drunk lady in a cat costume asked me to get Flavia's cakes out of the oven.'

He briefly looked up at me, a flash of irritation in his eyes, and then continued to scribble in his notebook. 'Go on.'

'Apparently Flavia couldn't get her wheelchair through the crowd so she asked this cat lady to find the maid to get her Salma-something cakes out. Salma . . . selmo . . . sounded like salmonella.'

'Semolina.' Detective Farnsworth scratched his eyebrow, looking impatient, and made a circling motion with his hand. 'Go on.'

Geesh. Touchy. Should I let him in on the cat lady's theory about Flavia going to look for Selene and Sven? I decided no. That was gossip and he wanted the facts. 'I happened to be coming out of the maid's bedroom after she let me use the bathroom in there, so drunk cat lady mistook me for her . . . the maid. It was easier to just go rescue the cakes rather than try to explain I was just in a maid costume.

'Anyway, I saw Mr Beckley . . .' I choked on his name, suddenly realizing he was no longer a person but just a corpse. That was so surreal. 'I saw Mr Beckley hanging there as soon as I entered the kitchen and it scared the bejezus out of me.' My body tensed up at the memory. I held my breath, waiting to feel the wave of emotion. Nothing. Exhaling, I went on: 'For a moment

I thought he was really dead but then I remembered Beth Anne Wilkins told me he pulls a prank every year. So I thought this was his prank. And it was. Only it didn't go as planned, I guess, and he really was dead. He told me Flavia wasn't very fond of him. Guess he was trying to scare her, right? Since he chose her kitchen to do it and must have timed it for when she'd be coming back in the kitchen to get the cakes from the oven. Did you know this place has two kitchens?' I clamped my mouth shut. I was rambling; something I did when I got nervous. I really needed to start carrying my anti-anxiety medication with me. I didn't like the idea of needing medication, but if there was ever a time to give myself permission, finding a dead body would be it. Though I was proud of myself for not having a panic attack, I did feel strangely numb.

'To answer your question, yes, he was trying to scare his mother-in-law. Two servers backed up the maid's claim that Mr Beckley's plan was to scare his mother-in-law by letting her find him hanging. What did you do after you noticed the body?'

Wow, he actually answered my question. I should return the favor. 'Well, I, um . . . I took the cakes out of the oven.'

His mouth worked back and forth and the fat below his jaws wiggled, giving him the demeanor of a bulldog, but he didn't say anything. 'Go on.'

'They were already burnt so I didn't bother buttering them.' I stared at his hand clutching the pen. He had a painful-looking hangnail on his thumb. 'Then I was leaving and I realized Michael hadn't said anything so I asked him to nod or do something to acknowledge he was OK. It was creeping me out. He didn't move so I touched his wrist to find a pulse and there wasn't one. That's when I realized he might actually be . . . you know . . . gone.'

'Do you know what time that was?'

I nodded. I'd glanced at the digital clock on the microwave after pulling out the cakes. 'Twenty after nine.'

He scribbled in his notebook. 'Did you touch anything else in the kitchen?'

I thought through my steps. 'I don't think so. Just the oven, the oven mitts and the cake. I'd been in there yesterday, though. I did a private doga session with Flavia so I touched more stuff then. If you find my fingerprints anywhere, that's why.'

Detective Farnsworth rubbed his temple. He needed a haircut. His hair was hanging over the tops of his ears. 'So you didn't see anyone exiting the kitchen? Passing you on the way in?'

'Nope. You really think somebody killed Mr Beckley on purpose?'

'That surprises you?'

'Well, yeah. I guess. He just seemed like such a nice guy. A happy guy. Who would want him dead?' I thought about the fight we'd all witnessed. 'Except maybe his daughter.'

He glanced up. 'His daughter?'

I nodded. 'They'd just had a huge fight about . . . I don't know . . . maybe half an hour before I found him. We were standing over there by that tiki torch.' I motioned to the area. 'And Mr Beckley came around the corner with his daughter, I think her name's Cali, and some other woman. Cali was screaming at him that he owed her something and he screamed back at her that he owed her nothing and to get off his property. It was pretty ugly. She said she'd see what her mom, Selene, thought of that and then she and the other woman stormed off into the house.'

Detective Farnsworth was very still and his eyes were bright with interest. 'And what did Mr Beckley do then?'

'He apologized to us all and then went into the house after her.'

'Can you point out his daughter to me?'

I pushed myself up on stiff legs and walked out into the yard. He followed. Scanning the yard, I spotted Flavia first. Selene and another couple were seated around her with their heads bowed while an officer talked to them. No sign of the daughter, though. Then I turned and saw her. 'Oh, there she is.' She'd emerged from the house a few feet away from us, escorted by another officer. She was holding the hand of the woman who was with her earlier, and the woman trailed the black kitten on the leash. Cali looked defiant and fuming, not at all the demeanor of someone who'd just lost her father.

'That's her – Cali, the one with the purple streak in her hair,' I whispered. If she was the killer, no need for her to be mad at me, too.

Just then Athena jumped off Flavia's lap and bolted toward us, yipping and running more like a banshee than a twenty-seven-year-old Chihuahua. Chaos ensued as Flavia and Selene started screaming at Athena, and the man who'd been sitting with them jumped up in pursuit of the little dog.

Defying gravity, the kitten leaped into the air, expanding like a furry puffer fish. Its pupils dilated like a coke addict as it twisted around mid-air and did the one thing nature had programmed it to do when danger approaches – climb.

Cali's friend screeched as the panicked kitten stuck to her leg and then used its tiny claws to scramble up her body and hold its ground on her shoulder, where it made the cutest little hissing sound. Blood had already begun to seep from various parts of the woman's stick-like bare legs and arms. Her expression was frozen in pain as Cali tried unsuccessfully to remove the embedded animal. It didn't help that Cali started giggling and had to bend over to catch her breath. Guess grief manifests itself differently for different people.

'I told you not to put her on a leash,' she said between bouts of laughter.

'Athena!' The man grabbed the dog midair as it tried to jump on Cali's friend after the kitten. 'Sorry, Sam.' He held the dog into his chest and, wincing at Cali's effort to free the kitten, quickly pivoted and carried the dog away.

Detective Farnsworth and I exchanged an amused glance before he cleared his throat. 'OK, you can go home, Miss Pressley.' Then he walked over to Cali and the other woman. 'When you're done there with the kitten thing, Miss Beckley, I need a word.'

Relieved his focus was now elsewhere, I went to Devon.

He'd ended his conversation with Detective Salma Vargas and was standing by the pool with Beth Anne, her husband Carl, Violet and Jarvis.

Devon scanned my face and then wrapped me in his arms and pulled me into him. 'You all right, love?'

I nodded, scratching my cheek on a button but enjoying the warmth and feeling of being protected that washed over me. 'Fine. He said I can leave now.'

'So, Elle, *you* found Michael?' Beth Anne's voice held the same kind of awe awarded to a death-defying circus act.

I turned in Devon's arms so I could face them. 'Yeah. Detective Farnsworth wasn't forthcoming about what really went wrong with the prank, though. He didn't seem to think it was an accident.'

'Oh, that's because someone cut the rope to his safety harness,' Violet offered in her casual way of dropping a bombshell.

When we all stared at her in surprise, she just shrugged. 'I know one of the officers.'

'I bet you do.' Beth Anne smirked at her.

Cut his safety harness rope? No room for accidental death there. 'If someone did that, why didn't he call for help? There were enough people around; surely someone would've heard him.'

Violet shrugged. 'Rob . . . I mean, officer Jenkins said he would've immediately become disorientated and his brain oxygen would've been cut off within twenty to thirty seconds. No time to call out.'

Wow. At least he didn't suffer long. I tried not to imagine Michael Beckley's last moments, but unfortunately I had a good imagination. 'Did he say if they have any suspects?'

'No, but I see the detective is talking to Cali. After that fight I'd say she's a pretty good candidate,' Violet said.

Cali didn't seem to be enjoying the conversation with Detective Farnsworth at all. Her arms were crossed and her jaw clenched. The family watched them closely, also.

Now that the band had stopped playing, the night was silent except for the frogs and insects. People were talking but in hushed whispers. 'Who's the couple sitting with Selene and Flavia?'

Beth Anne turned to see who I was talking about. 'Oh, the guy dressed as Peter Pan? That's M.J. – Michael Jr, Selene and Michael's son. Not sure who the cute fairy girl with him is.'

'That's Lulu Dutrey,' Violet offered. 'She owns that Urban Creole restaurant, The Gumbo Pot, over on 10th Avenue. Amazing food.'

'Oh, yeah. I've been meaning to try that place.' Beth Anne stared at the woman with gold corkscrew curls and fairy wings seated between M.J. and Selene. 'That itty bitty thing? Huh, I would have never guessed.'

There was no way I could ask Selene for the money now, but I did feel like I should at least give my condolences. I tilted my chin up to Devon. 'We should go say something to the family and then get out of the way.'

'Agreed.'

'See you ladies in class on Monday.' We said our goodbyes and headed over to the family.

Unfortunately, Detective Farnsworth beat us to them. We stood behind him, unsure what to do as he started questioning the distressed group. My eyes immediately went to Lulu Dutrey. She was mesmerizing up close. The wings fit her perfectly as she had a face like a fairy with mocha skin and striking pale green eyes. Her grief, glittering in her eyes and swelling her already pillowy lips, just seemed to make her more beautiful and fragile.

A strangled wail suddenly came from Flavia and she spat on Detective Farnsworth. I jumped back reflexively.

'Ooo,' she cried. 'I did it! It was me!' *Pt! Pt! Pt!* She then spat on herself three times.

FIVE

'**M**om!' Selene cried out in shock as Lulu turned her head and threw up behind her chair.

I wished I could've seen Detective Farnsworth's face at that moment. Two officers moved in front of him, hands at the ready near their guns. Detective Farnsworth calmly pulled out a handkerchief and wiped at his shirt as he used the other hand to signal to the officers that he was fine. They relaxed and stepped back a few feet.

'What are you talking about?' Selene cried over Flavia's continued hysterics.

Flavia clutched the eye pendant at her chest. 'My curse took away the protection of God! Dis is why he is dead!'

Selene made a noise of disgust. 'Stop it, Mom. Enough with the stupid curses.'

A passionate string of Greek exploded from the tiny woman in the wheelchair. I was impressed.

'*Yiya!*' a pale M.J. cried as he pulled Lulu protectively closer to him. Her eyes were closed and she was very still. It was kind of odd seeing them together. Lulu was so extraordinary and M.J. was so . . . well, normal. He also had a deer caught in the headlights look about him. Probably in shock. 'Let's all calm down, all right? This isn't helping the situation.'

Flavia's hand trembled as she pointed a crooked finger at M.J. 'You young people don't believe. You don't know. The curse of a mother is a death sentence.' She began to weep softly and crossed herself.

Selene rolled her eyes and looked up at Detective Farnsworth. 'Obviously my mother is insane. She didn't kill my husband.' Her face drained of color and she suddenly looked like she'd just been emotionally hit by a truck. Her arms collapsed into her lap. 'Oh my God. He's gone. He's really gone.'

This seemed like as good a time as any to step in. 'Excuse me.' I moved past Detective Farnsworth and gave Selene an awkward hug. It was like hugging a deflating balloon. 'Before we left, we just wanted to say we're so sorry for your loss. If there's anything we can do, just ask.'

I nodded sadly to Flavia and the others and then we made our exit, taking the path around the house, which was illuminated by puddles of yellow light. As we emerged from the side of the house we ran smack into a uniformed officer cradling a roll of yellow crime-scene tape and Alex Harwick, head of Moon Key security. Devon and Alex glared at each other for a second – both of their faces darkening – then Devon grabbed my hand and pulled me quickly around Alex. 'Feckin' eejit,' Devon growled under his breath.

I glanced at Devon as we hurried to the Jeep. What was behind his hatred of Alex? Sure the man was an idiot, but what I saw in Devon's demeanor was fury. I'd have to wait for the right moment to ask him about it and this definitely wasn't it.

My Monday morning doga class at the Pampered Pup Spa & Resort was filled with twelve dogs and their owners. This was my limit on what I felt I could keep control of, which had forced me to add a third class during the day now that snowbird season had arrived. Not that I'm complaining. I get ten bucks per client and while money may not make the world go round, it sure could turn my car from a hunk of junk into actual transportation. Having Devon drop me and Buddha off here in the morning was just not acceptable. He shouldn't be responsible for getting me to work. Maybe I should just move back into one of the suites here until I get my car fixed? My heart sank. I realized how attached I'd already gotten to Devon and sharing routine moments with him, like letting the dogs out and making breakfast together. Yeah, a little humiliation was a small price to pay for waking up in his arms every morning. But it felt wrong that I was technically mooching off him for a place to live after only seven weeks, two days and six hours of dating exclusively. Not that I'm counting. And even though he keeps assuring me he doesn't see it that way and just wants to be with me, it still bothers me. Was I overthinking this? Why did I have to make things so complicated?

I was tired and not in the greatest mood as I stroked Buddha's back and waited for everyone to get settled. I'd given up trying to sleep last night after the third time a nightmare about Michael's hanging corpse had me jerking awake in a cold sweat. I'd also been thinking about Flavia all day yesterday and her staunch belief in curses. I'd grown fond of her and hoped she didn't really believe her disapproval of Michael had anything to do with his death. The only person to blame was the one who cut the rope on his safety harness.

Besides my regulars, there were a few new faces in class. When everyone seemed settled I put on a smile and said, 'Good morning.'

'Morning,' a variety of voices and levels of enthusiasm replied.

'For those of you that haven't been to doga before, I'm Elle and this is Buddha.' Buddha glanced up at me when he heard his name, and I patted the Australia-shaped tan spot above his tail. 'Buddha's been doing this for a while, so don't expect your dog to mimic him. The main thing to remember here is to relax so both you and your dog have a pleasant experience. Don't force them to do anything they don't want to do. It's perfectly fine if they want to wander around the room or rest on the blanket instead of participating. If you didn't grab a blanket from the closet, please do so now.' Budgeting was not an issue at the Pampered Pup, so I'd ordered yoga blankets, blocks and straps for fifteen clients.

I patted the mat and Buddha stretched out, his stump of a tail ticking back and forth. I wondered if he even remembered his life on the streets before I found him five years ago. I sure hoped not. 'OK. We're going to start with just a cross-legged seated pose. If you have a small dog you can try seating them on your lap. If your dog isn't a lap dog, just try to get them to relax on the mat in front of you like Buddha is demonstrating here.' Relaxing was Buddha's area of expertise.

A commotion in the back of the room startled everyone and put all the dogs on alert. 'Hold onto your dogs, everyone!' Jumping up, I navigated over mats, water bottles and oversized Michael Kors handbags. Whitley Moorehead, the cool-headed staple of the group, had beaten me to the brawling dogs and had one of them, a Norfolk terrier new to doga, clutched to her bosom.

'It's all right. We're all friends here,' she cooed. Then she handed the sturdy, wire-haired terrier off to Gwen, the visibly shaken owner, who scolded, 'Naughty, Gilly. That was so naughty!'

'Everyone all right?' I asked through heaving breaths. This was my first dog fight in class and it shook me, too. I was not good with confrontation – human or canine – and would feel awful if a dog got hurt in my class.

Gilly squirmed in her owner's arms, gagging and working her tongue against the roof of her mouth.

'They're fine. She's got a little . . .' Whitley circled her own mouth with a French-manicured finger and smirked at the small brown terrier.

Gwen tilted her head and then, grimacing, pulled some of the other dog's fur from Gilly's tongue.

'Yes, Bristol's fine.' The other owner – a tall woman with her silver hair pulled up in an elegant French twist – stroked her miniature Collie, who was panting hard but showed no other signs of being hurt. 'Her thick fur is like armor. My apologies. I'll keep her leash on.'

'One of you should probably move, too, just so you both can relax.' Whitley put a hand on my arm before going back to her mat and her greyhound, Maddox. 'It happens. No biggie.'

'Thanks.' I gave her a shaky smile. She was one of the few women in here who understood my struggle with anxiety. I appreciated her bringing calm energy to the situation.

Still, I felt very unsettled as I continued the class. My mind kept returning to Flavia's words that I was cursed. Of course, it was ridiculous. I was only noticing all the bad things happening because of what she'd said. I led everyone in a few calming breaths, mostly for my own benefit, and then we continued.

The new class I'd added was right after this one ended so I only had time for a quick restroom break before the next bunch of women and their dogs arrived. Most of these ladies were snow-birds and new to my class, so they would be more of a challenge. I was surprised to see Selene come through the French doors and then groaned as Flavia rolled through the door behind her. Not that it wasn't nice to see Flavia – it was the little devil on her lap I wasn't happy about, especially after I'd already had one dog tussle this morning. Pushing myself off the floor, I went to greet them.

'Selene, how are you holding up? I didn't expect to see you in class today.' I hoped my sympathy showed more than my weariness. 'I see you brought your mom. Hello, Flavia.' I nodded instead of reaching for her hand, knowing that would be greeted by tiny teeth. I wanted to ask her if she'd said that prayer to remove my curse yet, but that would be ridiculous since I didn't believe in curses.

'Ack.' Selene made a noise in her throat. She had her inky black hair pulled back in a tight ponytail, her normally flawless complexion was mottled and bags had settled beneath her chestnut eyes. 'We're staying here at the spa so I figured why not. I'll go crazy if I have to sit in that room today just thinking about Michael being gone.' She rolled her eyes toward her mother. 'Can you believe it? We can't even go home to our own house to grieve. First those detectives keep our guests there until three in the morning questioning everyone and then they kick us out, tape off our house and have police guarding the door. We couldn't even get clothes to take. Nothing. Just, "Get out!" We had to go shopping yesterday for clothes for everybody.'

'Really? I didn't know they could do that.' Besides the legal aspect, the amount of police tape they'd have had to use to secure that mansion probably broke their budget.

'Mm. Apparently they can do whatever they want. We can't go back until they've finished processing the house and they won't tell us how long that'll take.' She rubbed the space between Chloe's ears vigorously, clearly agitated. Who could blame her? 'At least the pups are going to have a good time – this place is doggie heaven. Chloe has a mud bath later and acupuncture. Maybe it will help her arthritis. Ah, here, I brought your check. Sorry it's taken me so long to get it to you.' She pulled the check from her bag and handed it to me. 'When things settle down maybe we can set up a private class for Mom once a week while we're here?'

I went to answer her but we were interrupted by a cluster of ladies vying for Selene's attention to offer their condolences. I caught a lot of 'we can't believe it,' and 'Michael was such a great guy. Everyone loved him.' She accepted their sympathy

with grace, and I had to admire how well she was holding up.
Did Sven have something to do with her resilience? *That would
be firmly in the none-of-your-business category, Elle.*

I quietly slipped back to the front of the room to wait for
everyone to get settled.

By the time class was over, I was starving but I still had some
spa duties to take care of, not to mention Buddha to walk and
feed. I grabbed a protein bar from my emergency stash and took
Buddha out to the 'garden' for his bathroom break. Heading back
through the main lobby to get to the elevator up to the suites, I
almost walked right under a ladder. Stopping myself dead, I went
around it – not that I was superstitious but there was no use in
tempting fate. I smiled up at the worker wrapping a string of
black-lit skulls around the chandelier as I passed by. Decorations
were being hung for the big Halloween bash this Saturday night
and who didn't love a party? Everyone was buzzing about it.
Luckily, the costumed ones at this party would be the dogs. It
wasn't required for people to dress up in costume but it was
black tie, so I needed to go raid Hope's closet this week.

A costume for Buddha was on my mind as I came around the
corner to find Novia, one of the maids and a friend of mine,
crumpled and crying in the hallway. I raced up to her, thinking
maybe she'd run into a spider. She was deathly afraid of the
creatures. I soon realized by the devastated look on her face that
this was way more serious.

'Novia, what's going on? What happened?'

She was clutching a cell phone in one hand and grabbed my
hand with the other. It was shaking. 'Oh, Elle.' A string of Spanish
erupted from her before I could stop her.

'English, Novia,' I gently reminded her.

'*Si*, sorry. It's my sister, Breezy. She has been arrested . . . for
murder!'

I stared at Novia, blinking and trying to process. 'I don't
understand.'

'*Asesinato!* Murder! You have to help us.' Her red-rimmed
eyes widened as she squeezed my hand harder. '*Si*, your boyfriend,
he is detective, no?'

'Yes,' I said cautiously. Murder was serious. I wasn't sure I
wanted Devon getting involved in another murder case. The last

one I involved him in got him shot. Besides, things were really heating up with his parents' investigation right now, so I knew he didn't have time to take on another case.

'*Si, si*, he can help prove she's innocent. Like he did Dr Ira! Oh, Elle, she did not do this, what they say. She would never hurt Michael. She loved him.'

My heartbeat stuttered when I finally understood the connection. 'Michael? Oh, God, Michael Beckley.' *Of course.* The photo of Novia with the Beckley maid on her dresser. That was her sister, the maid I'd met. But why on earth . . . Then I remembered the photo of Breezy and Michael. And the voodoo dolls tied together. *She loved him?* That was not good.

Novia had started to sob hard again. I was probably going to regret this, but how could I refuse to at least have Devon talk to her? Maybe he could recommend someone to help them. I pulled her in for a hug and then made her look at me.

'OK, here's what we're going to do. I'm going to call Devon, we're going to sit down with him and you're going to tell him everything you know. And I mean everything, Novia.' *Were Breezy and Michael having an affair?* If so, she needed to be upfront about it. 'I can't promise you anything because he's very busy right now on another case, but he definitely can't help Breezy if you lie to him.'

She was nodding furiously, her eyes filling with hope. '*Si*. I understand. Everything.' She clutched me again. 'Oh, *gracias*, Elle.'

''Ello, love.' Devon's sexy voice picked up after the second ring.

Closing my eyes, I couldn't help but smile. 'Hey yourself.' I was stretched out on one of the suite beds, my head resting on a three-hundred-dollar, fire-hydrant-shaped pillow. Buddha was rubbing his face with glee on the even more ridiculously expensive comforter. 'Got a sec?'

'For you? Eternity.'

Promises, promises. As much as I hated doing this, I had no choice. 'Are you with Detective Vargas by any chance?'

'No, just Quinn.' Quinn was his friend from Ireland who'd come to Florida in August with some information about Devon's parents he thought might help. He apparently could only stay for ninety days without applying for a visa, so they were spending every spare minute working to try to solve his parents' murder. Luckily for Devon, his parents had retained dual citizenship when they were alive, so he was automatically considered a US citizen and didn't have to worry about how long he was in the US. Lucky for me, too. 'I'll be chattin' with her later though. Did you need something?'

'Yes, actually. I know your priority right now is your parents' case but my friend, Novia, is really upset and asked for your help. Her sister, Breezy, is one of the Beckleys' maids and she's just been arrested for Michael Beckley's murder.'

There was a beat of silence, and then, 'Really? The maid?'

'Yeah, so I was wondering if you could find out from Detective Vargas what evidence they have against her and maybe later come talk to Novia?' He hesitated and I knew it was going to be hard for him to commit to any other cases right now. 'Just one conversation to see what you think. And then you can maybe recommend someone to help them.'

'All right. We'll have a chat when I pick you up then.'

I smiled, knowing he was doing this for me. It meant a lot. 'Thank you.' I rolled my head toward Buddha when we disconnected and sighed. 'Why do I have a feeling I'm going to regret this?'

SIX

The three of us sat on a bench out the back of the Pampered Pup in the gardens. It was enclosed so well-behaved dogs could roam, though Buddha was stretched out in the grass at my feet as usual. Devon had offered to buy dinner at Café Belle, but Novia said she was too upset to eat. She sat on the edge of the bench, twisting a Kleenex. Frizzy hair framed her round face, and her eyes were fixed hopefully on Devon.

'I'm afraid I don't have good news,' Devon said quietly. 'I talked to Detective Farnsworth, the lead detective on the case. They brought Breezy in for questioning because witnesses spotted her runnin' from the kitchen just ten minutes before Elle found Michael. Her fingerprints were also the only ones, along with Michael's, pulled from the waist belt of the climbing harness, which was supposed to hold Michael up but was severed. And though the knife they believe was used to cut the cord was clean, a drop of Breezy's blood was found on the floor beneath Michael. They arrested her on suspicion of murder after she admitted to being with him during the twenty-minute window in which he was killed. Though she explained the drop of blood – she said she was helping him set up the prank and poked her finger on a broken sequin while she was helping him zip up – they believe she was the last one in the kitchen with him.'

'Well, except for the real killer,' I offered. I thought about Breezy running past me in a hurry and how the lady in the kitchen was upset with her for not being where she was supposed to be. Was that just because she was helping Michael with his prank? Twenty minutes? That's a pretty wide window when it probably only took the killer thirty seconds to cut the rope and skedaddle. 'How did they come up with the time of death?'

'Besides body temp, it's the time frame between the time two servers saw him entering the kitchen alive and the time you found him.'

Can't argue with that. I nodded for him to continue.

'They also found the voodoo dolls in her bedroom, bound and leaning against the picture of her and Michael together. They're working on the theory she killed him because of some kind of lovers' quarrel.'

'She did not do what they say! She could not!' Novia's tears burst from her eyes, streaking her face. Her hand made a sweeping motion. 'Voodoo dolls? This is what they say? Yes, she loved him but she only wanted the best for Michael, for him to be happy. Everyone thinks voodoo is for bad intentions. *Ridículo!* She uses these dolls for Mr and Mrs Beckley to fix their marriage. She was concerned because she says Mr Beckley has a mistress. She saw him talking on the phone last week, whispering like to a lover, and he seemed very upset. He hung up quickly when Mrs Beckley came in the room. Breezy, she just wanted to help. She have a soft heart. And Mrs Beckley, well . . . she has her own secrets, you know.' She turned her face away.

Devon nodded and then glanced at me. Worry darkened his eyes. 'That's definitely something your sister needs to tell the detectives if she hasn't already. What else can you tell us about your sister's relationship with Michael Beckley?'

Novia shrugged and glanced up at the sky. 'She's been working for his family for seven years, since she was eighteen. Mr Beckley has always treated her like a daughter. He got her involved in running, took her to her first marathon, but my sister, we have no men in our life, you see? Just me and her and our *madre*. So, she does think she loves him, you know . . . romantically. But she would never hurt him. They need to understand that.' She covered her mouth and closed her eyes. We gave her a moment. When she opened them, she clutched her heart. 'She's so . . . how you say? Sensitive? She cannot survive in a jail. Will you help her, Mr Burke? I cannot pay you much but I will give you all my savings. I beg you.'

Devon stared at his black boots for a hard moment. Then, glancing at me, he said, 'I'm not going to take your money, Novia, because I'm not sure there's a whole lot I can do at this point. They've arrested her on suspicion of murder and they've got thirty days to file formal criminal charges. If for some reason the prosecutor doesn't formally charge her by then, she'll be released. As of now, they'll set bail and she can be released to await formal charges . . . if she can make bail, which will probably be around two million.'

'Two million dollars?' We both watched Novia's eyes widen in horror. My heart broke for the family. I knew they couldn't come up with ten percent of that to get Breezy released through a bail bondsman. They would have no choice but to leave her in jail.

Devon rubbed his jeans roughly with both hands and mumbled something under his breath. 'Does she have an attorney?'

Without looking up, Novia said, '*Si.* They've assigned her one.' The tears came again on a little choke of despair.

I understood her despair but I knew Devon was right. What could he do? His attention and resources were in another place. He reached over and squeezed my hand. 'All right, then. If Elle is willing to poke around a bit and finds something she needs my help with, I'll be glad to see what I can do.'

Me? Poke around a bit? I immediately began to shake my head. Did he not remember what happened a few short weeks ago? He really wanted me involved in investigating another murder? I sat up straighter as they watched me because I suddenly couldn't take a deep breath.

I tugged at the yin-yang necklace beneath my shirt. It felt tight against my throat. 'I'm sorry,' I choked out, staring from Devon to a hopeful Novia. 'I just don't know how . . .' *Don't know how I could put myself in danger again. Was that selfish? Or self-preservation?* 'How I could do anything that the police can't.' I gave Devon a pleading look. *Please don't put me in the middle of this. Saving her from spiders was one thing. But asking me to save her sister by poking around for a murderer quite another.* I felt a touch of anger spark with anxiety as the fuel. 'Devon, you're the one who's trained in investigating. I'd have no idea how to prove Breezy's innocence.'

Wait a minute . . . maybe this was just his way of being able to take the case without taking her money? Maybe he just needed Novia to believe it was me who was going to be doing the poking around so she didn't feel bad about him doing it for free. That had to be it. Otherwise, why would he ask me to be in a potentially dangerous situation again? 'OK.' I glanced tentatively at

Devon, looking for a sign from him that this was what he was thinking. His expression was unreadable. 'I guess I can see what I can find out.'

Novia stood up and wrapped me in a hug. 'Oh, *gracias*, Elle.' Swiping at her nose with the mangled Kleenex, she held her hand over her heart. 'Whatever you can do, we will be grateful.'

As she released me, I felt something fall in my hair. Reaching up without thinking, I grabbed the tiny object between my fingers and felt a sharp bite. 'Ouch!' I shook my hair like a mad woman and jammed my throbbing thumb into my mouth.

Buddha jumped up and gave me an inquisitive gaze that then followed the wasp as it flew away.

Devon glanced over his shoulder. 'You all right?'

I pulled my thumb out of my mouth and stared at the angry red mark and swelling. I mumbled, 'No. Apparently I'm cursed.'

'So, what are you thinking?' I asked as we pulled away from the Pampered Pup in Devon's Jeep. Buddha had his head shoved between the seats so I had to lean up to see Devon.

'About you being cursed?' His eyes shimmered with tired humor.

'You heard that, huh?' I examined my sore thumb. 'Apparently Flavia is very superstitious and she informed me I've been cursed because Sven the giant admired me.'

'Cursed because a man admired you? You should've been cursed all your life then,' he smirked.

'Funny. Seriously, though, what do you think? It sounds like they have some pretty damning evidence against her, but do you think Breezy actually killed Michael?'

His thumbs thumped the steering wheel as he shook his head. 'Well, it's not good that witnesses put her running from the scene of the crime in the short time frame Michael's safety harness was cut, with her fingerprints on the safety harness and her blood at the scene. That's the biggest problem. Nor is it good that she admitted she was in love with him. Detective Farnsworth feels very strongly that with time and pressure she'll crack and confess to the murder, too.'

'But is she even strong enough to cut a rope? She's so tiny.'

'Michael was wearing a typical climbing harness. They've got

nylon rope which isn't too hard to cut through with a serrated
kitchen knife. I've actually had to do it before. It's why they
make it from nylon and sell serrated knifes for climbing gear.
Easy to cut if you get hung up, which is another fact not in her
favor. Obviously this was a spur-of-the-moment crime, a crime
of passion and opportunity, not a premeditated one. Otherwise,
why would someone risk committing murder with so many poten-
tial witnesses around? You heard Novia say Breezy believed
Michael had a mistress. If she was in love with him . . . well,
rage and jealousy are powerful emotions that release all kinds
of chemicals in the body that can give a person super-human
strength and irrational behavior.'

'Like the Hulk?' I smirked, leaning my forehead against
Buddha's neck. His steady rhythmic panting was comforting.

'Who?'

I wanted to ask him if he was joking, but I was too tired.
'Never mind.'

He stopped at a light. I noted we were in a line of five cars
which was odd for the small, private island. Or maybe not during
snowbird season. I wouldn't know. Last season I started working
at the Pampered Pup but I still lived with Mom in the ghettos
of Clearwater.

A white poodle stuck its head out of the back seat of the black
Benz in front of us. Its wet tongue and diamond collar shone in
the moonlight. Buddha's ears perked up as he watched it. The
song 'Gangsta's Paradise' popped into my head. Hope and I had
cruised the beach for hours after she got her driver's license,
blasting that song and singing at the top of our lungs. We were
probably the reason the city passed noise pollution laws. I smiled.
Good times.

'What's goin' on in that head of yours?' Devon asked.

My smile spread. 'Believe me, you don't want to know.' The
light turned green. My mind returned to Breezy. 'OK, so the
other problem is the creepy voodoo doll factor . . . two dolls tied
together and leaning against the photo of Novia and Michael?
That looks pretty bad. But Novia said it wasn't used for ill
intentions, that she was actually trying to help save Michael
and Selene's marriage. Hang on.' I pulled out my cell phone and
did a search for voodoo dolls. Scrolling through the first few

search results, I said, 'Seems she's right. It says here that many cultures use voodoo dolls as a focal point to cast spells but more for blessings and positive intentions. The use of dolls for revenge did not originate with voodoo magic.'

'But she could use it for whatever she wished. Salma seems to think they have a strong case. And the cute young maid being a mistress is not a stretch. Happens all the time with the help.'

'I just don't see it. Michael really seemed like a good guy, not like those over-privileged, rich celebrities sneaking around with their maids and nannies. Besides, what about the daughter, Cali? They don't suspect her at all? That was a terrible fight they had.'

Devon rubbed the back of his neck. 'Agreed. Apparently Michael had recently started the process to cut Cali off from the family fortune.'

'Wow. And that's not motive?'

'Definitely. But Selene is vouching for her daughter's whereabouts during that time frame. She said Cali came to her about the fight with her dad at around eight forty-five p.m. She was really upset so Selene took her up to her bedroom to talk and tried to get her to take her medication.'

'Really? Did anyone else verify that? Cali's girlfriend, maybe?'

'I don't know.' Devon glanced at me. 'Why?'

'Well, it's just the cat-costume lady mentioned something about Selene and Sven disappearing together. How do we know Selene's not lying to give herself an alibi because she was actually having a very personal training session?'

'Cali would've had to back up her story, but I guess people have lied for less. I'll see if I can find out if they interviewed Sven. Find out his version of events.'

I thought back to the Halloween party. Was Sven outside with the others? Surely he would have stood out. 'You know, I don't remember seeing him after the police got there.'

Devon's jaw tightened. 'I don't either.'

We rode in silence for a few minutes. I bit the inside of my cheek as I thought about everything we knew so far, which wasn't much. 'Why was Michael cutting Cali off anyway?'

Devon rested his hand on my knee as he pulled into his driveway and squeezed. 'I don't know. That might be a good place for you to start digging.'

'Yeah, about that.' I turned to him, motioning for Buddha to sit so I could see Devon's face clearly. 'Please tell me you only volunteered me so you could help Breezy without taking her money. Because I know you wouldn't want me getting involved in another dangerous murder investigation, right?'

He shut off the Jeep and glanced at me with a smirk. 'I have no idea what you're gettin' at, Miss Pressley.'

I relaxed. 'Yeah, right. You're a sly one, Mr Burke.' I leaned over and pressed my lips softy against his.

He kept eye contact as he pulled me in for a deeper kiss. When he finally let me go, he said, 'And a lucky one.'

'And a dangerously charming one,' I mumbled to myself as I hopped out and let Buddha out of the back seat. As we all made our way to the front door, I turned to him. 'I forgot to ask: did Breezy tell the police who she thought Michael's mistress is . . . was, I mean?'

'Don't know.' He slid his hand behind my neck and kissed me even more passionately on the doorstep. Our eyes were locked as he swung the door open. 'I will find out tomorrow. But tonight, no more talking.'

I squealed as he swept me off my feet. Petey greeted us happily as Devon carried me through the door.

SEVEN

The next morning I'd finished my sunrise yoga session on the beach and sat in the sand watching the dogs romp through the shallow surf. There was a chill to the early morning air coming off the cooled Gulf waters, but I'd stopped noticing and my goosebumps went away after the first few sun salutations. Petey's ears suddenly went up as his attention turned toward the love of both of our lives jogging toward us shirtless. I let Petey jump all over him with abandon while I sat back and silently admired his well-maintained physique.

'I thought you were going to help me get this mutt under control.' Devon planted a kiss on my cheek as he plopped down beside me in the sand and blocked Petey's enthusiastic jumping kisses with a forearm.

'Give him a break, he hasn't seen you in a whole . . . thirty minutes,' I laughed.

Devon shot me a look. 'He used to go on the morning run with me and still could.' Rubbing the dog's head in both hands, he added, 'But the lazy clown prefers to stay here and play instead. Go!' He waved Petey off, and with a last lick of Devon's hand he was back in the water. 'Listen, Elle, I'm going to be staying with Quinn for a few days at the hotel. Something important's come up that we need to work on together. Can you mind Petey for a few days?'

I bit my tongue and my initial reaction. I didn't understand why he wouldn't give me details on the investigation. Every time I tried to probe, he'd shut down. Did he not trust me? He sure trusted Detective Vargas. *Don't be petty, Elle.* 'Of course, but I don't understand why Quinn doesn't just stay here at your place. It isn't because I'm staying here, is it?'

'No. Of course not. I told you that since Clyde Lynch was released from jail, Quinn's been followin' him. He can't very well do that from a private island that you have to wait for a ferry to exit.'

I nodded and wiped some sand from his forearm. 'I see. This thing . . . it's not dangerous, is it?'

His gaze hung on mine for a moment before it skipped off and moved to the dogs, who'd worn themselves out and were now sprawled in the sand, both their tongues hanging out, eyes squinting in the bright morning light. 'I'll be careful, Elle.'

I did not like that answer at all, but what could I say? Then I had an idea. 'Well, since you're not going to be here for a few days, why don't I take the dogs and stay at the Pampered Pup? With me doing three classes a day now, they'd get way more attention there. I'll set Petey up with some grooming and pampering. And plus, I won't have to worry about getting a ride back and forth.'

'Oh, sorry. Forgot all about your car situation. OK, but why don't you just let me get your car fixed?'

'Because my ego wouldn't like that,' I joked, but it was mostly true.

After our shower and breakfast, Devon dropped me and the dogs off in front of the Pampered Pup. As he wrapped his arms around me and I melted into him, I felt the ache of missing him start in my chest. This is exactly what I was trying to avoid by not dating all those years. Attachment. The cause of all suffering, according to Buddha – the man, not the dog. Pushing back, I looked up into his eyes. 'Please be careful.'

'Or what?' He smirked, kissing the tip of my nose.

'Or Petey will be very angry with you.'

One eyebrow rose. 'Petey, eh?' Kissing my mouth and then my hand, he said, 'I'll call you later and let ya know what I find out about Michael's alleged mistress and the whereabouts of Sven.'

I pressed my nose into his neck, taking in his spicy scent. 'You're very good at changing the subject.'

'I'm very good at a lot of things. That's why you love me.'

'I do.' I sighed, frowning.

'I do, too. See you in a few days.' He gave Petey one last ear rub and kissed him on the nose, getting a lick on the eye for his trouble. 'Be good. Don't embarrass us in front of all these uppity rich folks.'

I crossed my arms. 'You know you're one of them, right?' I teased.

Chuckling, he waved and jumped in the Jeep. I picked up my yoga bag and backpack with my free hand and we all watched him drive away. I really needed to go back to my mom's house and grab some winter clothes. A cold front was coming through this weekend. OK, our cold fronts may not deserve that title since they don't involve ice or snow, and Canadians will probably still be happily frolicking in the Gulf, but everything's relative. I'll be freezing in the summer clothes I'd been wearing. This was the thing on my mind as I said good morning to our security guard, Marvin, and then led Buddha and Petey through the front doors.

Rita Howell, the spa manager, was standing in front of my studio doors with two men in gray shirts and name tags. Her hands were on her hips and her eyebrows were doing that thing where they meet in the middle, signaling her unhappiness. This was something no one working at the Pampered Pup ever wanted to see, since her unhappiness quickly became our unhappiness.

'Morning, Rita,' I said tentatively. 'What's going on?'

Her mouth hardened as she crossed her arms. 'A pipe burst in the wall and flooded your studio.' She moved her hot laser gaze to the two men. 'Well, don't just stand there. Go get the wet-vac or whatever you need to clean that mess up.' I detected relief in their demeanor as they hurried away from her. I fought the urge to join them. 'Of course, part of the wood floor is ruined.'

'Ruined?' I whispered. I felt Buddha lean against my leg, something he does when he senses I'm upset.

'Yes, but don't worry. I'll get someone in here to replace it ASAP. Shouldn't take more than a few days.'

'A few days?' I repeated, trying not to indulge where my thoughts were going . . . straight to the word *cursed*. 'Soooo . . . I guess I could . . .' *Nothing*. I was drawing a blank. I could what? Go lounge on the beach for a few days while not getting paid? Not. An. Option.

Always one to think outside of the box, that's exactly what Rita did. 'It's no problem. You can teach your classes outside in the gardens until it's fixed.'

'Outside?' I repeated. All the energy was quickly draining from my body.

She eyed me closely. 'Are you feeling OK, Elle?'

I nodded slowly as I thought about my pampered clients – who wear three hundred dollar yoga pants and diamond earrings to class – practicing doga outside, on actual grass, with actual uncontrolled air temperature and killer attack wasps.

My eye twitched. My hand moved to rest on Buddha's head. 'Sure. I'm fine. That's a great idea.'

She was still eyeing me closely. 'Good. I'll have Carrie print out a sign to hang on the door directing your clients to meet you in the gardens.'

'Thanks.' What was I going to ask her before this mess? 'Oh, can you also have her open up a tab for dog food and some spa treatments for a few days? I'll settle up on Friday.' Devon had given me his credit card and told me to give Petey whatever pampering I thought he'd like. I thought he'd like a dead fish bath, but he'd have to settle for Dead Sea mud.

'Of course.' She rested a hand on my shoulder as she went to leave and then, snapping her fingers, she whirled back. 'Oh, I almost forgot. I've got two judges lined up for the pet costume contest at the party Saturday night, but I need one more to prevent a tie. You'd be the perfect third judge. What do you say?'

'Sure,' I said, nodding and smiling, because that's what I always say. I was beginning to feel like if you looked up 'yes man' or more accurately 'yes woman' in the dictionary, there'd be a picture of me. Smiling like an idiot.

'Great.' She eyed me cautiously. 'Are you sure you're OK? Because you've been through a lot lately and I'd understand if you needed to take some personal time.'

'No. Nope,' I said quickly, trying to make my face look smooth and unstressed. 'Really, I'm good. Just need to get some coffee and wake up. But I do need to stay in a suite for a few days. That's still OK, right?'

She nodded with a dismissive wave. 'Of course. We're almost full but Suite 306 is open until Friday. You can stay in there. And I'll get that sign up for you ASAP.' ASAP seemed to be her favorite thing to say lately. I wondered if this applied in her personal life as well. 'I'll get those pancakes cooked ASAP' or 'I'll iron that shirt ASAP.' Wait, that wasn't her at all. More like, 'Bring me my breakfast and ironed shirt ASAP.'

'Thanks.'

I looked down at Buddha and Petey, two sets of bright eyes and two dripping tongues, waiting patiently. 'All right, come on. Let's go scout out a place where there's no bees or ants.' The landscape crew did a pretty good job keeping the fire ant mounds at bay but their bites were painful enough that I needed to double-check the area we were moving class to. I didn't want the spa to get sued for my negligence, and I wasn't feeling very lucky right about now.

EIGHT

My morning class went pretty well, despite the added distractions of gnats buzzing our eyes and ears, loud planes flying overhead and a few of the dogs wandering off since there was no door. But at least eight of the clients decided to stick it out since they were mostly here year-round and had some sense of loyalty. The new midday class did not fare so well. Only three ladies and pups decided to attend when they learned they'd be trading an air-conditioned, candle-lit, lavender-scented room for the great Florida outdoors. And by the time my last class at four o'clock rolled around, so did a booming, drenching October storm. The day was a bust.

As I lay in bed that night, sandwiched between the two dogs, listening to the thunder rumble and heavy rain pelt the window, I couldn't help but subtract the money I'd lost today from my budget. I was still giving Mom money to cover her bills, but if I did that this week would I be able to fix my car? I really didn't want to see Devon lying under my old beater in the driveway of his million-dollar bungalow. It was humiliating enough when I parked it there when it was running. I grabbed a bone-shaped pillow and pressed it into my face as I groaned in frustration.

I had just about fallen asleep when something startled me awake. And not just me. As I pushed myself up on my elbows and peered into the dark room, my heart beating like a jack-hammer, both dogs lifted their heads and stared at the door with their jaws clenched and ears alert.

We all listened. There it was. A sharp scratching sound on the door. Buddha growled and Petey lowered his head and glanced at me. Did one of the dogs get loose from a suite? Or the more important question: would a murderer wielding an axe scratch at the door?

'Scooch,' I whispered, nudging Petey off the bed so I could move my legs. I flung the covers off and tiptoed across the shadowy room. As I reached for the door handle, the scratching intensified. I flipped the lock, pulled open the door and . . .

And nothing. There was no one there. No axe-wielding murderer. No loose dog. I stepped out and, glancing up and down the hallway, made little kissing noises in case the dog was scared off by the sound of the door unlocking. 'Here, puppy, puppy,' I whispered. Nope. Nothing.

Shrugging, I shut the door and crawled back under the covers just as a flash of lighting lit up the room like a strobe. Thunder boomed on its heels. 'Yikes. That was close.' Sighing, I got into the position on the side I wanted to sleep on before the dogs pinned me down again. I scratched both their ears as they plopped down against me. 'Guess we're all imagining things. 'Night.'

But we weren't. At least, I didn't think so. The scratching woke us three more times and the last time it was accompanied by a muffled yipping. Each time I yanked open the door to find the hallway empty. I even called to Angel, my deceased childhood dog who sometimes visited me in spirit form, thinking maybe it was her but she never appeared.

The next morning, I dragged myself out of bed with a pounding headache. The storm had passed, but as I led Petey and Buddha into the gardens for their morning potty break and romp, I knew my day was toast. My flip-flops were sinking into the grass with a sucking sound as I walked. The ground was a sopping mess. There was no way I was holding my morning doga class out here.

On my way back in, I wondered if things could get worse. I should not have asked that.

As we came through the doors, M.J. was rolling Flavia and her little devil dog toward us. Petey had been happily bouncing beside me until Athena unleashed her indignation upon us in a fury of yipping.

With a deep bark and gleeful bounce, Petey took off toward the little dog like it was inviting him to play. Petey was not one to pay attention to social cues. I had to give Flavia credit for hanging onto the little demon's harness for dear life, and to M.J. for quickly whirling the wheelchair around to face the other direction. But that didn't stop Petey from bounding toward them, yanking my arms from their sockets in the process. I lost my balance in what would've been comical in a silent movie kind of way if it hadn't hurt so much when I landed on my face. My mouth met the floor with a sickening crack. I didn't have the sense to let go of the leash either as he dragged me across the tiles. 'Petey!' I finally managed. 'No!'

I felt Petey halt and the leash go slack. My world at that moment consisted of a booming in my skull that reverberated through my teeth, a background symphony of panicked voices speaking Greek and the slow realization that the blood pooling on the floor beneath me was mine.

A warm tongue licked my ear. My cheek. My eyelid. I used what little strength I had to push Buddha away. 'I'm OK, boy.' But he moved in front of me, a warning growl rumbling in his barrel chest. Lifting my head up, I saw M.J. standing with his palms out, looking a bit worried. 'Easy, boy. Just want to help.'

'Buddha! No!' I scolded, getting a blaze of pain across my eyes for the trouble. 'Sit.' Ever since he'd seen me in danger at Devon's house, he seemed to have gotten more protective. I'd have to fix that before it got out of hand. Or maybe he just sensed that I was cursed.

M.J. leaned forward and reached for me. This time Buddha let him. With gentle hands, he carefully helped me sit upright and lean against the wall.

'Ow. Ow.' I cringed, gripping the sides of my head. The movement set off the bass drums.

M.J. was frantically pressing a handkerchief into my hand. 'For your lip. Try not to move. I'm going to go get help. Be right back.'

'So sorry, Elle! Dis dog! Ack!' Flavia said before M.J. wheeled her and Athena away with him.

I dared to open an eye as I heard panting directly in front of me. Petey sat inches away from my face, tongue dripping saliva on my thigh next to a spot of blood, tail wagging.

'You're lucky you're cute.' Gingerly, I pressed the handkerchief against my lips. They already felt swollen and hard as a rock. Great. *Ow.* Again, I pushed the word *cursed* from my mind.

No. No. No. I don't believe in any of that. I've always been accident-prone, and I just happened to be having a bad week. A really bad week. One for the record books, for sure.

'Elle?' Marvin, the security guard, came hurrying down the hall, his keys and various security guard duty things jingling. He patted Buddha, who thumped his stubby tail at the sight of Marvin as he kneeled down in front of me with a blue ice pack gripped in his meaty hand. 'You all right? Anything broken?'

I squinted at him through the pain. Petey gave him a lick on the ear for his trouble. 'No. Just my *wips*, I think.' Lips, actually, but he knew what I meant, even if I was speaking like a three-year-old at the moment. I pointed at my swollen mouth.

I watched him cringe as he surveyed my face and made some empathetic noises. 'Looks like milkshakes for you for a few days. Here.' He handed me the ice pack. 'Get some ice on those babies. I've seen prize fighters come out of the ring with smaller lips than you.' He chuckled as I tried to frown at him and almost passed out from the stab of pain above my eyes. 'You'll be all right, I suspect. We just need to find you some aspirin and a soft bed.'

'I'm staying in suite 306,' I whimpered.

He looked up at M.J. 'You mind keepin' her company until I can fetch a wheelchair?'

'Of course.' M.J. hiked up his khaki pant legs and squatted down beside me as Marvin hurried off. I eyed his expensive leather sandals and wanted to warn him about the swamp the gardens were at the moment. He grinned at Buddha, who was lying down against my leg but watching him closely. 'What a good boy, taking care of your mom.' And then he shook his head at Petey. 'I'm not sure you're going to be getting any dinner after that stunt.'

Pulling the ice away from my mouth for a second, I said, 'He 'ouldn't have hurt Athena.' At least, I didn't think he would've. His posture had seemed more playful than anything, plus I've seen him interact with smaller dogs at the dog beach. He's never been aggressive. Of course, we were talking about Athena here.

'Well, that's a shame. I've never been too fond of the Athenas.' M.J. shot me a conspiratorial half-smile.

The Athenas? What did he mean by that? Though he had his mom's coffee-brown eyes, I could see his dad in his smile. It saddened me. I wondered how he was holding up. Should I offer my therapist's name? She was really good. Unfortunately I didn't have the strength to ask.

Marvin returned and they helped lift me into the wheelchair.

Then he fed me some aspirin and water with a straw, picked up the dog's leashes and we were off.

The room was dark, the thick curtains pulled tight as I returned to the land of the living. Someone was knocking softly. 'Hang on,' I mumbled, trying to untangle myself from the sheets, the dogs and my own blurry dream state.

Holding my head steady with one palm, I opened the door and squinted at Novia. Buddha stayed on the bed, but Petey was pushing against my leg to get pets from this new human. I'd have to work on his door manners.

'*Hola.*' She held up a bottle of aspirin and shook it, wincing as she saw my mouth. 'Mr Marvin, he asked me to check on you. Give you more of *dese* and take care of dogs.'

My heart melted. I wondered if Marvin would adopt me. Was I too old to be adopted? Well, I wasn't too old . . . or proud . . . to know I needed help, that's for sure. 'Thanks, Novia.' I opened the door wider to let her in and went to get the dogs' leashes. I saw my phone blinking on the table. The message was from Devon.

I listened to it as Novia retrieved a bottle of water from the mini-fridge.

'*Hey, Love. Just wanted to let you know I had a quick chat with Salma. She says Michael's wife doesn't believe he had a mistress. Selene said Breezy may very well have been in love with him but he wouldn't cheat on her. He's not that kind of man. So, no information on that front, sorry. Oh, also, Sven was not on the interview list. Salma said she'd ask Selene when he left the party. Anyway, I'm sure you're in class now so I'll give you a ring later.*'

Class. Right. If he only knew.

'Is from Mr Burke? Any news?' Novia looked at me hopefully. She was clutching the water bottle in both hands like a lifeline.

I shook my head then gripped the table edge as the room tilted sideways. 'Whooa.'

Novia grabbed my elbow and held me steady. 'You need rest.'

As she helped me back into bed, I took her hand. 'How is 'reezy? Have you talked to her?' B's were impossible with swollen lips.

'No. But our *madre* has visited her. She's very scared.'

I nodded. I couldn't imagine visiting my daughter in prison, especially if she'd been accused of murder. Then I did imagine.

If I had a daughter, I would do everything in the world to protect her. Did that include lying to the police to keep her out of prison? Is that what Selene did when she gave her daughter, Cali, an alibi?

'We're not giving u' until we find out the truth. I 'romise.' P's were not much easier. I was gaining a new appreciation for my lips. I guess they were good for more than making out with hunky Irish detectives, though I was a big fan of that particular skill.

Apparently she understood me anyway because a sheen of tears appeared in her eyes. The hurt and fear were almost palpable. '*Muchas gracias*, Elle.' She squeezed my hand and then went to retrieve the water and aspirin.

I felt bad. What I should've said was Devon would find out the truth. I would cheer him on from the safety of the sideline. But she didn't need to know that – it would just make her feel bad for not paying him.

The bottle was hard to navigate. As I poured more of it down the front of my T-shirt than in my mouth, she cracked a smile. 'Oh. I should maybe have brought you straw? I get you towel.'

'Thanks.' It hurt to smile back as she handed me the towel.

She clapped her hands and picked up their leashes. 'OK, come on dogs. *Vamos*.'

Buddha slid halfway off the bed, stretched his back legs and then dropped them onto the floor. Petey was already turning circles at the door.

'Thanks, Novia. Just let yourself in when you 'ring them 'ack.'

My next foray into consciousness was in the middle of the night, and I noticed I had an extra dog in bed. Along with Buddha stretched out along my right side and Petey pinning me down and snoring on my left, Angel was curled up at my feet. *Great.*

Most people would kill for a visit from their long-deceased childhood dog, and I did love seeing her and knowing she was still around in some sense. I just didn't love what her visits meant: that there would be danger ahead for me. She always showed up to warn me when something was about to go very wrong in my life. She was a bit late this time, I mused. Her shining eyes met mine. 'Hi, girl.' I squinted in the dimly lit room. Was it my imagination or was she more solid than she'd been in the past?

NINE

The next morning Angel had gone and the band in my head had thankfully taken a break. The swelling had gone down some but my lips were still tender. I iced them until they were numb and then gingerly brushed my teeth. After a cold shower I texted Devon, explaining I'd busted my lip in an accident and it'd be easier to communicate by text than to call. He didn't reply back. I pushed away the fear that something might've gone terribly wrong in their investigation. Or that he and Detective Vargas had to stay up all night on a stake-out, sharing fast food and old memories. Or maybe they were undercover at a fancy restaurant, sipping on expensive wine and laughing together. 'Sto' it.' I scolded myself out loud, throwing my toothbrush into the sink. *What is wrong with you?* Sometimes I truly think my own mind is my worst enemy.

After I let the dogs play out in the still-squishy gardens for a bit I brought them back in, wiped down their wet legs and paws then walked them downstairs so I could check on the progress of the studio floors.

The French doors were closed and someone had marked through the 'Classes will be held in the garden' sign and written in black marker: 'Class canceled until further notice.' It was a reminder of how much money I was losing to this stupid . . . I stopped. *Stupid what? Curse?* Good grief, had I really started to believe it? Shaking my head, I peeked through the glass above the sign. Through the dust I could see two people in white jump-suits and white masks working. Some kind of hum was coming from inside, too. Like a generator. I sighed. I wasn't an expert in wood floor repair but that did not look good.

Since I wasn't going to be able to work today, I took the dogs back to the suite for their breakfast. There were some extra treats in a bag on the table next to the two bowls of food, which had been prepared at Café Belle. Probably hormone-free, grass-fed, Harvard-educated free-range chicken. 'Don't get used to it,' I said as I moved the bowls to the floor for the patiently waiting dogs. At least I'd been able to train Petey not to knock me over when I fed him. Trying not to knock me over at the door was next on the training list.

I would have killed for a cup of ginger tea. Instead I texted Hope while the dogs inhaled their food:

Need dress for Saturday night, got anything?

Yah! Girl fun, I need some. Wanna come over after class?

Class is canceled. Come pick me up; explain when you get here.

On my way.

I hung outside with Marvin for a few minutes as I waited. We talked about the coming cold front. Marvin apparently was looking forward to it. I glanced up at the dark clouds still blotting out the sun. To me, it seemed ominous. I'd take a sunny, choking-on-the-humidity summer day anytime over this. But maybe that was just what I was used to.

Hope's Jaguar rounded the fountain. When I opened the door and slid in, she gasped.

'Oh my God in heaven! What happened to your . . .' She paused, fury pinking her cheeks. 'Did Devon do that to you? Did he hit you? I knew that man was too good to be true!'

I stopped her protective tirade with a hand on her arm. 'No. 'Etey, Devon's dog, 'ulled me down.'

She eyed me suspiciously as her anger dissipated. 'You wouldn't lie to me, would you?'

'Uh uh.' I tried to smile as I held up my pinky. ''Inky swear.'

She wrapped her pinky in mine. Pinky swear was sacred. Never to be used to cover a lie. 'All right, then.' She chuckled as she pulled away from the Pampered Pup. 'You know women pay my husband thousands of dollars for lips like that.'

'Ha ha.'

'Do you think my 'om will do anything e'barrassing if I introduce her to Devon?' I was contemplating a black satin dress in Hope's full-length mirror. We'd already gone through half-a-dozen dresses and the stories of my recent string of bad luck. I even told her about Flavia thinking I'd been cursed by the evil eye, which she laughed off. Hope had always been the rational one in our dynamic duo.

'Of course she will. She's your mother.' Hope cocked her head at me from her cross-legged perch on the king-sized bed. 'Are you thinking about introducing them?'

I tugged at the black satin, trying to see if I could get it to cover more of my cleavage. 'Do you have anything with more material on top?' I unzipped the side zipper and wiggled out of the tight dress. 'And yes. She's been bugging me to 'eet him for weeks.'

Hope slid off the bed and sauntered off into her closet, which was big enough to park a camper in. She emerged from the cedar bowels of organizational heaven with two more black dresses – one a short taffeta cocktail number with spaghetti straps and a modest neckline, and a longer one with a slit up each leg to the top of the thigh. 'Here, I forgot your legs are your best assets. One of these should work. Ira prefers me in the plunging neck-line to show off his work. Sometimes I feel like a walking advertisement.'

I laughed and rolled my eyes as she puffed out her chest and strutted around the room. 'You're ridiculous.' I slipped into the taffeta dress first. 'Anyway, I need to go home to get 'y bike and some winter clothes anyway. So, I thought I'd 'ring Devon and get her off my 'ack.'

'Riiight. What's the worst that can happen?'

I glanced at Hope in the mirror. She was sitting on the edge of the bed now, swinging her legs and smirking at me.

'I know what you're thinking. Come zi' me u'.'

'What?' Hope hopped off the bed. Her cool fingers zipped up the dress as she grinned at me in the mirror. 'Surely she would not come stumbling out of the bedroom drunk and naked a second time.' She couldn't hold it in any longer and burst out laughing.

I whirled around. 'As you'll remember that was a 'ery traumatic time in my life so I don't know why you 'ind it so 'unny.' But I was starting to laugh, too. Gingerly. *Was it possible I could really laugh at this?* After all, I half blamed that incident for the reason Tommy Mathers went off and left me without looking back.

I did laugh then as I remembered that day, still so clearly etched in my psyche. Being so excited to introduce her to the love of my life. Calling to her that we were there. The horror as she stumbled out of her bedroom without a stitch of clothing.

The peals of laughter came from me in manic bursts and felt so good, like a release. Clutching my own stomach, I watched Hope wipe at her eyes and try to catch her breath.

I leaned against her dresser. 'Oh, God. I'll never 'orget the look on Tommy's face. He was so horri'ied, so e'arrassed. He just 'olted out the door. I'm sure he 'robably still has nightmares.'

'Wait, wait,' Hope got out between her snorting laughs. She grabbed my hand. 'Did you just say his name?' Her eyes grew round in surprise. Or mock surprise, I'm not sure which.

'Yeah, I guess I'm finally over him, huh? Only fifteen years later.' It didn't even hurt. Not one little bit. Interesting.

She squeezed me in a tight hug. 'Oh my God. You really are in love!'

'Oh, sto' it,' I laughed, trying to squirm out of her grip. 'And ow, ow . . . watch 'y 'outh.'

'I can't believe it. We have to celebrate. I'm taking you to the mainland. You can't work today anyway.' She let me go, hopped away and then whirled back around. 'Oh, and that's definitely the dress.'

I hoped they had straws wherever she was about to drag me to. I turned and gave myself the once-over. Yep. This was the dress.

TEN

The next morning I shuffled the dogs out into the gardens and let them off their leashes in the fenced area to play. I wore my sunglasses, even though a blanket of heavy grey clouds with dark bellies still blotted out the sun. Turned out the place Hope took me last night did have straws . . . stuck in oversized, delicious frozen margaritas. Three of them. I was possibly feeling worse than I've ever felt in my life, except for the time the stomach flu hit me on the school bus and I had to jump out the back emergency exit at a stop light and camp out in a gas station bathroom for an hour before Hope's dad could give me a ride home. That was a pretty bad day, too. My skull took another assault from the bowling ball rolling around inside it. I whimpered.

Someone, presumably Rita, had left a new note on the studio door that said indoor doga classes would resume on Friday morning. That note would be the bright spot of my day. I pressed a flip-flop harder into the grass. Water squished up. Yeah, there'd been no sun to dry out the ground. So what would I do with myself today?

Devon had texted me last night that he'd pick me up after my last Friday class. I felt kind of lost. I watched Petey run around, tossing up a tennis ball he'd found and trying to get Buddha to play with him. There was also an older Lab with a gray mask ambling around, sniffing the edges of the fence. A lady sat on the west side of the fence, busy on her cell phone. I assumed the Lab was hers. I rarely saw anyone bring their small dogs out here and let them run loose. Those lucky pups mostly rode around in golf carts, dressed in their cute little designer outfits that cost more than my whole wardrobe. Who was I kidding? The few clothes I owned didn't qualify as a wardrobe.

Was there something I could do to help out with Breezy's case without putting myself in danger? Probably not much in my condition. Thinking was even a challenge right now.

I decided a long nap was in order. Luckily, the dogs were always up for a nap.

Three hours later I woke up feeling much better. The monster headache had quieted to a tap now and again. I pulled the curtains open, feeling restless. As I stared out at the beautiful dark blue Gulf waters and the edge where they met the city of Clearwater, I held an ice pack on my mouth and thought about Michael's death. I couldn't not think about it. I wished I hadn't been the one to find him. Then I could've remembered him as the happy-go-lucky guy I'd met instead of a blue-faced corpse hanging from the kitchen rafters.

Hope had asked me last night if I thought Breezy was innocent. I had said yes and meant it. So why was I just standing here freezing my face? There had to be something I could do. Whether I liked it or not, I was already involved. I just had to make sure I didn't do anything stupid and bring myself to the attention of the real murderer. I could do that.

Grabbing my phone, I dropped the ice pack in the sink and texted Devon to ask if the police were still processing the Beckleys' mansion. He responded fairly quickly with a yes.

Good! That meant that the Beckleys were still staying at the Pampered Pup. I really needed to meet Cali and get a sense of what kind of person she was. Contrary to how she acted on the night of his murder, was she devastated that her father's dead? Or was she relieved? Does she feel guilt over their fight before he died? Or did she care at all?

Devon had texted me more information about what Selene had told Detective Farnsworth. Apparently Selene had been trying to get Cali to take her medication but Cali wanted Selene to confront her dad first so she wouldn't take it. What exactly did she do to make her dad so angry that he was cutting her off from the family fortune? And I needed to find this out without being obvious about it and making anyone suspicious of my motives. Easy, right?

I washed my face and eyed my mouth. My lips were almost back to normal. Just that pesky cut inside from my teeth still smarted. Pulling my auburn hair in a messy bun atop my head and then slipping into the well-worn black sundress I'd stuffed into my backpack, I kissed the dogs. 'Don't chew up anything while I'm gone.'

On my way down the hall, a new maid, who Rita had hired for the tourist season, was backing her cart out of one of the suites. She had a round, ruddy face under short cropped gray hair.

'Hello.' She nodded and smiled shyly at me.

'Hi, we haven't met yet.' I held out my hand. 'I'm Elle, the doga instructor here. Sorry, I forgot to hang the occupied sign on the door but my two dogs are in suite 306 if you'll be going in there. They're big but friendly.'

'No problem.' She shook my hand with her own, which was warm and dry. 'Patsy.' She chuckled. 'Yeah, I heard about the doggie yoga here. That must be a fun job.' Her accent held a hint of southern roots.

'Most of the time,' I answered, suddenly and happily aware I could make the M sound again. Thank the stars for small miracles. 'Hey, there wasn't a dog that got loose from one of the suites a couple of nights ago, was there?'

Her eyes widened a little and she glanced down the hall. 'No, none got loose that I know of.' Her expression shifted and brightened. 'But Miss Rita did tell us she's been getting complaints from guests hearing a dog barking in the hallway at night or scratching on their door. No one's reported a dog missing, though. Did you hear something, too?'

I shrugged, trying to be casual. Teaching doga was enough weirdness; I didn't want it to get around that I was hearing a non-existent dog scratching at my door. 'No, just heard the rumors and wondered if you'd seen anything. Well, thanks. It was nice to meet you.'

I'd have to ask Rita more details about that later. Right now I was a girl on a mission.

I checked Café Belle first. I couldn't actually afford to eat there more than once a month but it was a favorite hangout for the guests and regulars alike. Also, now that the hangover was receding, my stomach was letting me know it was ready for solid food. I tested the cut inside my lip. Tender but I could at least handle some soup. My stomach rumbled. I did not appreciate the direct access it had to my thoughts.

'Just one today,' I said to Marisol, the hostess/model/actress while I self-consciously pulled at my wrinkled sundress. I really needed to care more about my appearance or less about what people thought of me. This environment wasn't good for what little self-esteem I had.

As she led me through the spacious dining room, which was also in the process of being decorated for the Halloween party in two days, I wondered again why Devon was with me when there were gorgeous creatures such as Marisol roaming the earth.

No sign of the Beckleys. *Oh, but, look at the banyan tree!* As the centerpiece of the dining room it'd always been an interesting feature but now it was simply stunning. They'd wrapped strands of tiny gold and white lights around the branches and hung candle lanterns from some of them. It was beautiful.

'Elle!'

I turned my attention away from the tree. Beth Anne, Violet and Whitley were sitting at a round table by the window, waving me over. Perfect. If I couldn't find Cali, these ladies would be the next best thing: full-time residents who'd grown to be more than just clients to me. Also, always on top of Moon Key gossip.

'Come have lunch with us.' Violet pulled out the chair beside her. Her Weimaraner, Ghost, pushed himself off his cushion to nudge my hand as I took the offered chair.

'Thanks. Hello, boy.' I stroked beneath his silvery chin and his eyes closed in appreciation. He was such a sweetheart. Then I noticed the bottle of champagne on ice. 'Are we celebrating something?'

'Yes!' Violet declared, her smile igniting her green eyes like a switch had been flipped. 'The success of my newest lipstick, Cinnamon Crush.' She signaled to the waiter, who was always fluttering over the tables like a genie hummingbird, ready to grant your every wish in the blink of an eye. 'Glass for our friend, please.'

I knew Violet had made her original fortune through her own organic makeup line – and her still-creamy complexion well into her fifties was a great testament to her products – but that was as much as I knew about makeup in general. 'Congratulations. Forgive my ignorance, but how does a lipstick become successful?'

'When a millionaire talk show guru recommends it as one of the hot new must-have items of fall,' Whitley offered, adjusting her glasses. She'd gotten a new haircut and her silvery hair brushed her shoulders in a modern, slightly layered bob. Reaching up, I touched my own pile of hair self-consciously. It felt dry. Maybe I should get a trim? Or a new style? 'And hard work, of course,' she added with an eye-roll as Violet shot her a disgruntled look.

'To luck and hard work then.' Beth Anne lifted her glass after the waiter returned with mine and expertly poured the bubbly.

'Cheers,' we all said over the sound of clinking crystal.

I hesitated, still weary of my hangover, then took a sip. Hair of the dog and all that.

The waiter took our orders and then flitted off to fill them.

'Do you know when classes will be resumed, Elle?' Beth Anne asked. 'Shakespeare's about to get on my last nerve. He needs his doga.' Despite her annoyed pretense, she glanced down beside her – where I knew her little shih tzu was curled up – and her dimples punctuated an affectionate smile. These ladies loved their dogs and that's what put me on common ground with them. I couldn't relate to paying cash for a Mercedes but I could relate to a dog stealing your heart.

'Well, Rita hopes tomorrow morning.' I had my fingers and toes crossed. 'You'll be getting a call later tonight to let you know for sure.'

'Until then, we have champagne.' Violet raised her glass and then suddenly put it back down. 'Oh, I forgot to tell you what Maddox's costume is for the party. He's going as a William Wegmen photograph!'

'How on earth are you going to do that?' Beth Anne fingered the tiny diamond snowflake nestled in the dip of her throat. It kept catching the light and was mesmerizing.

I pulled my attention away as I thought of something. 'Wait!' I held up a hand and then immediately closed it and slipped it under the table. No use bringing attention to my raggedy, bitten nails. 'Actually, I'm not sure I should know ahead of time about their costumes. Rita's asked me to be a judge for the costume contest and I don't want to have any bias.'

They all looked at me and then Violet laughed, her eyes glowing with amusement under her glossy, spiked red hair. 'Good Lord, Elle, you're too honest. But we'll respect your wishes.'

'Thanks,' I said, suddenly distracted by the fact that Selene,

Cali and M.J. had just walked in. The only color in their ensembles besides black was the purple streak in Cali's bangs. Did they dress that way because they were still in mourning or because it was so fashionable? I watched Marisol lead them to a bistro table under the tree.

Beth Anne followed my gaze and then groaned. Ducking her head, she moved her hand to play with her ponytail and whispered, 'Poor Selene. I wonder when the police are gonna let them back in their house. I can't imagine losing my husband and then being kicked out of my own home.'

'Are they still here?' Violet turned in surprise. 'What in the world are the police looking for? Didn't they already arrest the maid?'

'Really? That little dark-haired maid with the killer figure?' Whitley asked, turning to glance at the Beckleys as if she were there with them.

'The police think she was having an affair with Michael.' Beth Anne was still whispering even though there was no way the Beckleys could hear her from across the dining room.

Whitley stared at Beth Anne for a moment, her gray eyes narrowing behind the wire frames as she processed that juicy little tidbit. 'Huh. Makes sense, I guess. I saw them running together a few times last year around the golf course.' Then she sighed and waved it off. 'Well, I wouldn't blame him if he did, the way Selene and that trainer carry on.'

'Can you blame *her*?' Violet snickered.

'No wonder you're not married,' Whitley retorted gruffly, but her lip quivered as she fought a smile.

'One of many reasons, my dear friend.' Violet winked at me over her champagne glass.

I decided this would be a good time to butt in and get some answers. 'So, do you guys know why Michael was in the process of cutting Cali off from the family fortune?'

'Well, yeah!' Beth Anne said. 'Don't you ever read the paper, Elle?'

'You mean the tabloids?' Violet smirked and fed Ghost one of the sweet potato treats the waiter had brought to the table.

'It's not gossip.' Beth Anne's expression briefly flashed annoyance. 'It's fact. Cali accepted a million dollars for a tell-all story about her family and said some pretty damaging things about them personally, along with stuff about the Beckley Foundation. Why she would put hundreds of millions of inheritance in jeopardy for a measly one mill is beyond me.'

A measly one mill? My throat dried up. I reached for my water.

'Well, she does have some mental health issues,' Whitley offered sympathetically in a low tone.

'Guess everyone has a limit though. Even a guy as easy-going as Michael is . . . was.' Violet cringed and glanced over at Michael's family.

Mental health issues? Is that what she was taking medication for? I tried to be as nonchalant as possible when I asked, 'So, do you think Cali would be capable of harming Michael?'

But apparently I'm not really good at nonchalant because I suddenly had three sets of eyes scrutinizing me. Their combined, focused attention was unnerving. I took another sip of water to cool off my now-burning face.

Beth Anne tapped a hard nail against her crystal champagne glass. 'Elle, do you know something we don't?' Her voice was soft but her focus was intense. She may look like a sweet southern belle with her long, honey-highlighted hair and petite frame, but when she smelled gossip it was like a shark smelling blood.

'No, no.' I shook my head, feeling my messy bun sliding down the side of my head. I reached up and readjusted it. Glancing up from beneath my lashes, I saw they were not going to let this go. 'Fine. It's just after that terrible fight we all witnessed between Cali and her dad . . . I wonder if they aren't looking at the wrong person.'

'All right, spill it, Elle,' Violet said, unconvinced. She folded her arms and leaned them on the table. 'What aren't you telling us? Did your PI boyfriend get some kind of inside scoop?'

I glanced at the door. I could make a run for it but they'd just hunt me down like a pack of Versace-clad she-wolfs. 'No. It's just Breezy, the maid they arrested; she's my friend Novia's sister. Novia's asked Devon to help prove Breezy's innocence, so I'm just trying to see if I can help piece anything together.'

They all shook their heads at me.

'What?' I said, a bit more defensively than I meant to.

'You're one of those girls who likes her lessons with lumps

and bumps, eh?' Violet leaned back as the waiter placed something in front of her that resembled a brown rice volcano with carrot strings as lava.

'Yeah,' Whitley chimed in and then waited a beat until after her soup was served to continue her remark. 'Your last foray into trying to figure out the truth behind a murder didn't turn out so well, remember?'

'Oh, leave the girl alone.' Beth Anne jumped in with a sympathetic glance my way. 'She's just trying to be loyal to her friend.'

'You may need some new friends.' Violet eyed her food volcano like she was trying to figure out the best way to eat it.

'She does have some new friends.' Beth Anne looked indignant. 'Us.'

'No,' the other two women said in tandem.

Ignoring them, Beth Anne's eyes brightened and glowed gold as she smiled at me. 'We'll help you.'

They groaned.

'Whoa, whoa, slow your roll there, Miss Marple.' Violet shook her head at Beth Anne and then turned to me. 'No offense to your friend, Elle, but we think the police probably know what they're doing. After all, they're the ones trained in investigating. We wouldn't know the first thing about proving someone did or didn't murder someone else.'

'No offense taken,' I mumbled as I pulled the wine-soaked carnation petals off my shrimp salad. No matter how trendy this fad was I just couldn't bring myself to eat flowers.

'We don't have to have any training,' Beth Anne huffed. 'We just have to keep our eyes and ears open for anything that could help Elle and Devon.'

We were all staring at Beth Anne now. Her face was flushed and she had a glow beneath her sunless tanner.

'Now we know how you look after a good romp in the sack.'

'Violet!' Whitley shot her a half-amused half-chastising glance. 'Look, Elle, it's not that we don't want to help your friend . . .'

'It's fine,' I tried to say.

'No, it's not fine.' Beth Anne was getting mad now. 'We're all going to keep our eyes and ears open. Period. End of discussion.'

There was a silent stare-off between the three women. Then

Violet held up her hand. My gaze snagged on the giant emerald rock on her ring finger, the same shade as her eyes. I wondered if that was a gift from one of her boy toys or if she'd bought it for herself. Sheeze. I reached up and rubbed the tiny diamond yin-yang symbol on the necklace Devon had won for me at an auction: my one and only piece of diamond jewelry. I would be afraid to wear the jewelry these women wore so casually without bodyguards. Then again, who was going to mug them on Moon Key?

'Fine. We're going to keep our eyes and ears open. Happy?'

Beth Anne nodded once and shot me a victorious smile. 'Yes.'

When we wrapped up lunch, I made sure to walk by the Beckleys' table. They seemed to be just finishing up, too. As I was hoping, M.J. stopped me.

'Elle, right?'

I smiled, watching Cali out of the corner of my eye. 'Yes, hello, M.J.'

'How's your . . .' He made a motion with his finger around his mouth, a look of concern in his eyes.

'Oh.' I touched my lip. 'It's fine. Practically as good as new.'

'What happened?' Selene asked, suddenly looking interested.

'Athena the devil dog happened.' M.J. frowned. I noticed his own nose was raw and his eyes were bloodshot. He must be taking his dad's death hard. Or he had some killer allergies.

'Seriously, Mother, I think this one is meaner than Athena the second.' Cali shook her head and laughed harshly.

'Athena the second?' I asked, trying to size up Cali, who seemed agitated as she wriggled in her chair. Her eyes darted about like two little bees unable to land. Was this how she responded to grief? What was normal for her? Was she capable of killing her own father? I wished I'd met her before this happened so I knew what her normal was.

M.J. glanced at his mom disapprovingly. 'Mom didn't think *Yiya* would be able to handle losing the first Athena. She was having heart problems when the dog got cancer. So Mom replaced Athena when she passed. Twice.'

I blinked, processing. 'So Athena isn't really twenty-seven or . . . even really Athena? And Flavia doesn't suspect that at all?'

'God, no.' Selene laughed. 'But I practically had to scour the planet to find two older Chihuahuas with the same brown spot. I'm done. When this one's ticket is up . . . it's up. No more Athenas.'

I didn't know what to say. Was it admirable or devious to replace someone's dog to save them from grief? It did scream of someone willing to go to extreme lengths for their family. I snuck another glance at Cali, who was biting her already chewed nails. I could relate. Would this family also go to such extreme lengths to protect one of their own from a life in prison for murder?

'I trust our little secret is safe with you, Elle.'

I moved my attention back to Selene. Her eyes were doing that glittering-staring-through-your-soul thing that rich, powerful women do so well. I had to learn that trick. 'Secret?' My heart dropped like a stone. Then I remembered she was talking about Athena, not Cali. 'Yes, of course.' But my flight or fight response had kicked in. Cortisol was flooding my body. Thanks to my therapist thinking I'd feel more in control if I knew the mechanics of a stressed body, I recognized the signs. I felt jumpy and my heart rate was up. Time to go.

'Well, Selene, I hope doga will resume tomorrow if you'd like to bring Chloe again. Looks like they'll be finished with the floors tonight. You'll get a call. Oh, and hope to see you all at the Halloween party Saturday night. There's sure to be some wild pet costumes. I'm one of the judges for the contest so you should bring Chloe there. Also . . .' A Butterball turkey would be the perfect costume. And I was rambling. I pressed my lips together and inwardly cringed as my bottom teeth hit my cut.

'Yes, we'll be there. We couldn't keep *Yiya* away unfortunately,' M.J. cut in quickly, saving me from my own social awkwardness.

I smiled gratefully at him.

ELEVEN

Friday morning I awoke with a renewed sense of hope and excitement. Doga classes would resume today, I finally felt recovered from my tumble and Devon would be picking me up tonight. I was also getting excited about the Halloween party. Some fun was definitely in order after this stressful week. I pushed away the little niggling thought trying to mock my new sense of peace and happiness. *Cursed.* How silly. Everyone has a bad day . . . or week once in a while. I had so much more to be grateful for. No use focusing on the few little bad things that happened. No, every day was an opportunity to start fresh. Today was a new day. A curse-free day.

Classes resumed and went smoothly. Well, fairly smoothly. In the morning Beth Anne looked suspiciously like she was trying to eavesdrop on the other ladies' conversations. The woman was obsessed with helping me. I guess I should be grateful for her snooping. She was way more plugged in to the social scene on Moon Key than I was. Maybe she would find out something that would help prove Breezy's innocence, and I could feel like I helped without putting myself in danger.

The midday class was mostly dogs new to doga, so it was a bit of a challenge. Ranger, a young feisty yellow Lab, insisted on playing tug with his owner's block as she tried to use it beneath her forehead in child's pose. And Elaine, who'd brought three Peekapoos to her first class, became overwhelmed ten minutes in, so to help her out I used Cinderella, her youngest one, to teach the class. Buddha didn't seem to mind. He got in an extra nap. By the time the four o'clock class was done, so was I.

As I waited outside the Pampered Pup with the dogs for Devon to come, I noticed the cold front was announcing its arrival. The wind had picked up and was shaking the palm trees like pom-poms. The sound was soothing though the sky was a bowl of menacing, fast-moving dark clouds. I shivered in my tank top and yoga pants. It suddenly felt like October, and I desperately needed to go get some warmer clothes from Mom's house.

When Devon's Jeep came whipping around the fountain, however, my insides warmed like the sun had come out. As he jumped out and strode over to sweep me up into his arms, I finally let myself acknowledge how worried I'd been about him and how relieved I was he'd come back unharmed.

He held my face in his palms for a moment, looking into my eyes. Despite his smile, I could see the toll whatever he'd been through this week had taken on him. He was tired and sad and he smelled stale and faintly of grease. Then he kissed me deeply, his arms moving to encircle me and held me like I was his lifeline. He didn't ease up his grip until Petey decided he'd been patient enough and jumped up on him, nudging us apart with his blocky head.

Chuckling and finally releasing me to pet Petey, he nodded. 'All right. Let's get home.'

Before we got to the driveway, Devon said, 'Hope you don't mind, I've brought Quinn back just for the night. Figured we could give him a proper meal. The lad's been livin' on fast food.'

Well, it was his house. 'No, of course I don't mind.' It would be nice to meet him finally. Maybe I could get some more information from him about what they've been up to. Every time I asked Devon about it his mood darkened and he grew silent, so I'd stopped asking.

'So this is the lass Devon Burke's broken his own rules for?' Quinn wrapped me in a hug as Devon introduced us. His beard tickled my cheek and he smelled like whiskey. I blushed furiously. The dogs both went on a sniffing expedition of his jeans, tails wagging. 'Hello, fellas.' Quinn grinned down at the dogs without removing his arm from my shoulder.

'That'll be enough of that.' Devon grabbed my hand and pulled me into the kitchen, breaking Quinn's grip. Blue eyes dancing with good humor, Devon dropped a soft kiss on my lips. 'Quinn fancies himself as a ladies' man so you'll be stayin' right by my side while he's here.'

'No complaints from me,' I whispered, getting lost in his eyes.

'Ahem.' Quinn cleared his throat. 'A lad could die of thirst while you two make eyes at each other.'

Devon growled and whispered in my ear, 'Maybe bringing him home wasn't one of my better ideas.' Then, grinning at his friend, he asked, 'Wine or more whiskey?'

We decided on a bottle of New Zealand Sauvignon blanc to go with the crab legs Devon was cooking. Quinn turned out to be quite the charming fellow, though I caught the dark circles and grave expression his face settled into when he wasn't telling me a story. And I couldn't get enough of those. Hearing about Devon from someone who grew up with him, and in that lovely sing-song way Irish people spoke was priceless. So was their banter as they argued and laughed and gave each other grief.

At one point in a story about them getting into trouble over taking a car for a joy ride, I was peeling shrimp for an appetizer when the strengthening wind blew one of the outdoor planters into the sliding glass door, causing me to visibly startle. The dogs both scrambled up to investigate.

Quinn and Devon exchanged a look. Then Quinn grabbed the second bottle we'd opened and filled up my glass. 'It'll take some time but your pots'll settle back down eventually. Was a hell o' a ordeal you went through.'

'Your nerves,' Devon offered when I stared at Quinn blankly.

'Oh. Right. Of course.' I wasn't sure about that since I've never really had settled nerves in the first place, but I appreciated the sentiment. Picking up my glass, I clinked his. 'To good times with good friends.'

He nodded. 'The only times that really matter. *Sláinte.*'

We moved to the dining-room table since the approaching storm kept us from eating outdoors tonight. The dogs followed the plates hopefully, settling at our feet beneath the table.

As we took our seats, the rain came. Sheets of it pelted the wall of glass doors. I closed my eyes. Rain I could handle. 'One of my favorite sounds.'

'The lass likes the sound of rain? You outta bring her to Ireland,' Quinn said wryly.

My eyes popped open and I glanced over at Devon. Much to my relief, he was smiling.

'One day I will.' He winked at me, which melted my heart.

I guess my confession about anxiety keeping me from traveling didn't deter him or make him uncomfortable. I wanted to thank him for not giving up on me. On us. But that would have to wait until we were alone. Between the sheets . . .

I cleared my throat and got my thoughts back on track. 'So, Quinn, is this your first time in Florida?'

'It is.' He cracked open a crab leg and eyed Devon. 'Unfortunately I've only got a few more weeks on my tourist visa and haven't even been to Disneyland.'

From the way his expression darkened, I had to believe he was upset by more than missing out on a day at Disney. Whatever they were doing must not be going very well. I'm not sure if it was the third glass of wine Quinn had poured me or the frustration, but I finally became brave enough to ask.

I put down my own crab leg untouched and folded my arms. 'The investigation isn't going well, is it?' I stared at both of them.

Quinn chewed and glanced up at Devon, who was suddenly very still.

'Comes with lettin' 'em in,' Quinn said softly, addressing Devon.

'Sorry.' Devon sighed and the corner of his mouth ticked up into a forced smile as he rested a hand on my knee. 'I know you're worried. It's just . . . it's a big burden and you're not going to be any less worried.'

I squeezed his hand. 'Honestly, my imagination is probably much worse than the truth.' I watched him cautiously. Was he actually going to tell me what's been going on?

He rubbed the dark stubble on his chin, downed the rest of his glass of wine and suddenly looked exhausted. 'All right then. I think I mentioned Ma was the daughter of a prominent jockey? His name was Colm Carberry. He passed when Ma was nine but she stayed a part of the horse racin' community. They practically adopted her. That's why a few years back, when there were questionable rumors around one of the fellas Da had workin' with his thoroughbreds, Martin, one of the jockeys who'd been like family to them, brought it to Ma's attention.'

Quinn made the sign of the cross here. I kept silent so I wouldn't disturb Devon's story. He continued. 'My parents were here in Moon Key at the time but had to fly back for Martin's funeral shorty after.'

'What happened?' I asked.

He shook his head. 'Don't know. Supposedly an accident.'

'Me arse it was,' Quinn whispered.

Devon nodded in silent agreement. 'Most likely not. From what I've been able to gather, Martin's death only made Ma dig in further tryin' to find out if Martin was speakin' the truth against Rooney. She didn't want to believe it.'

'Sorry, what is questionable activity when it comes to race-horses?'

'Dopin',' Quinn offered with obvious disgust.

'Her da was a big advocate for celebrating the animals as athletes and would not stand for druggin' 'em. She confronted Rooney at the funeral. Said she was gonna find out the truth.'

'Would he go to jail?'

'He wouldn't. But Rooney had just won The Breeders' Cup with November Rain, one of Da's horses in question. It was a big career boost. He'd not only be stripped of that win but also be banned for a few years. His credibility would be shot and his jockey career would basically be over.'

'Don't they test the horses for drugs before the race? Or after?' I asked.

'They can do both. That's what Quinn brought me. A signed confession' – he glanced at Quinn – 'and I do not want to know how it was acquired. But it's a confession from the Turf Club fella who took a lot of money to replace November Rain's blood sample with one provided by Rooney.'

I glanced at Quinn, who was smirking a little. I decided I probably didn't want to know how he'd acquired that confession either. 'So, you told me this guy, Clyde Lynch, who'd been in jail for your parents' deaths, had connections to Dublin. How so?'

'He's a distant cousin of the Rooneys. Was stayin' up in Atlanta until three weeks before my parents died, when he relocated to Clearwater with a brand-new bank account.'

'Feckin' dirtball's been rubbin' it in. Knows we've been followin' him so he's been going to every fancy restaurant in town since he got out of jail. Bought a bloody Corvette, too.'

Ouch. No wonder Devon fell into a foul mood when I tried to ask him about it. Seeing the man spending his blood money must be hard to stomach.

'Lynch didn't care that he went to jail for a few years – he was a millionaire when he got out. He made a mistake, though.' Devon smiled, though it wasn't the one with the dimple and shining eyes I've come to know. This one was fierce and his eyes darkened with the same intensity as the storm outside. 'With the new evidence Quinn brought, Salma was able to get a subpoena for his cell phone records. The night of my parents' deaths, he'd texted another number. A local fella with a dodgy past . . . who just happens to have paid cash for a brand-new fishin' boat soon after my parents were killed. Salma's tryin' to find his old boat to get the GPS data from it, but it seems to have disappeared off the face of the planet.'

'Probably at the bottom of the ocean,' Quinn growled.

'So, the GPS data could prove this second boat, belonging to this sketchy person the guy who hit your parents called, was in the area when your parents died?'

'It could.'

'And that would prove . . . I don't really understand. How would the second boat factor in?'

'Where it happened is a particularly bad blind spot around a small island. My parents were creatures of habit. They took the boat out every Sunday on the same route. We figure the second boat was the lookout. It let the first boat know when they were about to round the blind spot so he could ram them. The second boat could've even helped make sure my parents didn't make it out of the water alive.'

'Wow. That's big.'

'It is.' Quinn cracked a crab leg with frustration and sucked out the meat.

I'm sure Salma would've mentioned this and I hated to bring it up, but it was important. 'But, Devon, isn't there a double jeopardy law that would keep Clyde Lynch from being tried for the same crime again?'

Devon nodded. 'Apparently your state and federal laws are separate here. So, although he was convicted of vehicular manslaughter by the state, Salma said murder for hire is a federal crime and he can be retried in a federal court. Plus we're going after the second fella involved.'

Quinn swallowed a swig of wine and added, 'But this other fella, he's no joke. We've tried to follow him but he's slippery

as a fish, that one. Gone in the head, too. Saw him beat a fella
bloody behind a bar one night for knockin' his drink over.'

'Quinn.' Devon shook his head.

Quinn looked properly chastised. 'He didn't see us,' he added,
like that made me feel any better.

I tried not to react but my heart was pounding. 'But this crazy
person knows you two have been following him?'

Devon shot me a weary look. 'He does. The bartender had
tipped us off that he usually drinks with a guy there in the middle
of the week who owns a boat lot. He showed up Thursday night
so now that we know who he is, Salma's going to see if she can
subpoena his sales records for the year my parents died. Maybe
he bought the second boat. It's a long shot but we've got no
other leads.'

*Don't freak out. Don't freak out. He'll never tell you anything
again.* I busied myself with crushing a crab leg with the plyers.
'So, finding this second boat is the key to proving this wasn't
just an accident. Isn't there some other way to prove their
connection? Someone has to know something.'

'There was a possible witness,' Quinn said.

I glanced at Devon in surprise. 'A witness?'

Devon's jaw clenched. 'Not to the second boat. Just to the fact
that Clyde Lynch was braggin' at the bar about all the money
he was about to come into not an hour before he killed my
parents. When he left the bar, he said, 'Time to earn my money.'

'The bastard recanted though when he was asked to give a
formal statement. Said he was mistaken. It wasn't Clyde after all.'

'Seriously? Did this guy end up with a new fishing boat, too?'

'No. A broken jaw.'

'I'd like to give this Alex Harwick egit a full body cast,' Quinn
said.

My fork stopped midway to my mouth as I gaped at him. 'Alex
Harwick? The head of Moon Key Security? That Alex Harwick?'

Devon's eyes flashed with a mix of rage and frustration as he
nodded.

The pounding rain was the only sound as I processed this
information. Well, that explained Devon's hatred of the man.

TWELVE

Saturday morning we dropped Quinn back off at the hotel and then Devon and I made the drive from the posh beach high-rise inland to my mom's house. It was important to get there in the morning, before her beer and Twinkie marathon began. As his Jeep pulled into the cracked driveway, I couldn't help but see the little cracker box house atop sparse, brown grass and sand from his point of view. What a dump.

This was not a good idea but it was too late – Devon opened his door. I grabbed his arm. 'Please forgive my mother in advance for anything completely embarrassing she may say or do.'

Grinning, he leaned over and planted a warm kiss on my lips. 'It'll be fine. Come on.'

I went against every nerve in my body that wanted me to run and instead hopped down and led him to the front door. He carried the bag of groceries we'd stopped for. They were a peace offering so the monster wouldn't eat us. My idea, not his. He'd had a normal, lovely mother so I knew it was impossible for him to even conceive of the damage a crazy one could inflict.

Using my key to unlock the door, I cracked it open and peered inside. 'Mom? We're here.'

'Come on in,' she yelled from the vicinity of the kitchen.

Taking a breath, I forced my legs to carry me inside and closed the door behind Devon. I left it unlocked just in case he wanted to make a speedy exit.

Trying to rub the chilled, damp air from my arms, I took the grocery bag from Devon and nodded toward the small dining-room table I'd sanded and refinished by hand in high school. There was an unfamiliar smell in the air. Sweet, almost pleasant. 'Have a seat. I'll go see what she's up to.'

Instead, he moved to the photos of my childhood displayed crookedly in dollar-store wooden frames above the well-worn floral couch. 'Is that you?'

'No, that would be my embarrassingly dorky evil twin, of

course.' Turning so he couldn't see how inflamed my cheeks had become, I retreated to the kitchen. *And it begins.*

'What are you doing, Mom?' I put the grocery bag down and eyed her suspiciously. She was standing at the stove in the midst of stacked dirty dishes and empty beer cans. She had on a thin brown dress that passed well enough for clothing, though – I had to give her credit for that.

'What does it look like, silly? I'm makin' pancakes. Thought you two might stay for breakfast.'

Stay? Oh, God. Nope. 'We really can't but thanks.'

She waved a pancake turner at me dismissively. 'Nonsense. Here, grab those and take 'em out to the table before they get cold.'

I stared at the stack of pancakes among the trash on the counter. Then I looked at Mom and deflated. Well, she was trying. Making an effort to be a little normal for Devon. Maybe she was trying to make up for that whole fiasco with Tommy Mathers. 'Fine. We'll stay.' I plucked a cherry pie wrapper off the plate that'd fallen from the stack of trash. 'Moving up to the hard stuff, I see,' I mumbled.

'What's that?'

'Nothing.' Sliding a full trash bag out of the way with my foot, I opened the refrigerator to find the butter. *Oh. Gross.* I shut the refrigerator door while my stomach did a flip. Who needs butter?

'You don't happen to have the number to poison control on speed dial, do you?' I whispered to Devon as I slid the plate in the middle of the table.

He stared at the pancakes questioningly. 'Guess we're eating then?'

I scrunched up my nose. 'Sorry.'

'No need. It's a thoughtful gesture.'

'Devon!' Mom came waddling from the kitchen, out of breath and holding forks and plates and a half-empty, sticky bottle of honey. 'So nice to finally meet you. Well, don't just sit there. Come on up here and give me a hug!' She dropped the plates on the table and held out her thick, wobbly arms.

'Oh. Sure.' Devon rose. 'Nice to meet you, too.' He patted her awkwardly on the back as she squeezed him in a bear hug.

It was so strange seeing him here in this tiny house being squeezed by my mother. He seemed larger than life and completely out of place. He didn't belong here. Did that mean he didn't belong with me?

'Well, aren't you a handsome devil,' she purred. Then she pinched his cheek. She actually pinched his cheek! I cringed. 'Elvis, you didn't tell me what a handsome devil he is. And with that accent? Well, aren't you just a good catch for my little girl.' Was she flirting? It was like watching a train wreck. I couldn't look away. Poor Devon's mouth was moving but no words would come. Definitely a fish on dry land. I'd made a big mistake bringing him here. What was I thinking?

'Mom!' I managed. 'Why don't we eat before these get cold?' Please, God, let the woman release him.

'Right. Right.' She released him with a smack to the behind. 'Go getcha some,' she giggled.

Devon's eyes met mine with a mixture of shock and humor. I pressed my fingertips into my eye sockets. What was happening right now? Was she trying to humiliate me on purpose? This was not the stand-offish, negative woman I'd grown up with. That woman I had prepared myself for. I watched her like an unpredictable animal as she took a seat between me and Devon.

'So, Devon, thanks for callin' me when Elvis landed herself in the hospital doin' God-knows-what that she shouldn't have been doing.' She shot me a disapproving look. I grabbed a fork and stabbed a pancake. 'She's always been reckless.'

I dropped the fork. It made a loud clanging noise against the plate. *Me? Reckless? Did she even know me?* 'I wouldn't consider myself reckless,' I stammered. Who was this woman? It was like the woman was playing the part of a mother instead of being *my* mother.

'See how sassy she gets?' she said to Devon with an air of conspiracy.

He reached over and placed a hand on mine with a wink. His touch took my blood pressure back down from critical. *Breathe*, he mouthed to me while she went on.

'Did Elvis tell you I was a single mother? That's no easy task, let me tell you. Hardest job in the world.' I shoved a piece of dry pancake in my mouth. It was like glue. Perfect for the occasion.

'I couldn't give her much but we always had each other.' I chewed slowly, trying to give her the benefit of the doubt. She wasn't trying to embarrass me, right? She's trying to be nice. Have a conversation. I mean, she doesn't know that the polite thing to do is not to sit there and talk about herself . . . especially a fictional version of herself. She's lost touch with society. Possibly even reality. She probably had sugar-and-alcohol-induced brain damage. Maybe I should just help her out instead of being so upset with her.

'Mom,' I cut in, choking a little as I tried to swallow, 'Devon's a travel photographer. Don't you want to ask him about all the amazing places he's been to?'

'Really?' She lit up. 'Oh, yes, please do tell. You know, I always wanted to go to Italy. See Rome and Pompeii . . . Oh, and that leaning tower, of course. What a disaster that was, right?' She laughed and a spittle of pancake landed on the table.

I watched Devon shove a forkful of pancake in his mouth and nod politely as he tried to swallow it.

'I'm going to get us some water.' Defeated, I made my way back in the kitchen. Washing out two glasses, I tried to talk myself down from a panic attack. I couldn't let Devon see me unravel. It was just so hot and so . . . smelly . . . and I could hear her going on and on about things that were just fantasy. I had to get Devon out of there before she made a durable imprint on his brain. Before he started wondering if I was just hiding my crazy. After all, it is hereditary. I dried my hands and pulled my hair off my neck. 'Just this moment. Just get through this moment.'

'You know you're the first boy Elvis has ever brought home. I think she was ashamed of where she came from. Ashamed of me. But I didn't blame her. With kids it's all about designer this and designer that. They don't understand what's important in life is family. Don't you agree?'

Time seemed frozen as I stood behind her holding the water glasses. Designer what? What was she talking about? I'd been happy to find a halfway decent pair of jeans at the thrift store growing up. There were so many things off about what she was saying, but the one that struck me the hardest was her saying that Devon was the first boy I'd brought home. Forget the whole inappropriate 'boy' comment. She apparently didn't even remember me bringing Tommy Mathers home? She must've been too drunk to even know we were there. So, if she wasn't trying to make up for that whole fiasco, what the hell was she doing with all this fake niceness and pancakes?

Devon was staring at me with a concerned expression. I forced a smile and put the glasses down. Some water sloshed out over my hand. I was starting to feel unsettled and confused. I wiped the sweat off my upper lip. I really needed to get out of there. 'Devon?' My eyes pleaded with him. Thankfully, he got the message.

'Oh, you know, I forgot we're supposed to pick up that . . . package for Quinn.' He took a sip of water. 'So sorry, Ms Pressley, we're going to have to cut this short.'

'Yes!' I jumped back up, almost knocking over the chair. 'I forgot about that, too. Sorry, Mom. I'm just going to grab my box of winter clothes. Devon, would you please get the yellow bike from the garage for me?'

'I will. Thank you for the lovely breakfast.'

I was backing up toward my old bedroom. 'Yank the garage door handle hard. It sometimes gets stuck.'

I snuck a glance at Mom. She looked confused as she sputtered, 'Oh. Well. Sorry to see you two kids go so quick.'

I could still hear her talking, probably to herself, and could barely see with the hot tears burning my eyes, but I managed to find my winter clothes box in my old closet. When I came out with the box, Mom had disappeared back into the kitchen. The dishes still sat on the table. I hesitated. I should clean that up.

I couldn't. I could barely breathe. 'Thanks, Mom. Gotta go.' I hurried out the door before she could see the tears. I hadn't let her see me cry since ninth grade and I wasn't about to start now.

Devon had found the bike and had the Jeep running. When I hopped in he squeezed my leg silently as I swiped a rogue tear from my cheek. 'Want to talk about it?'

I shook my head and slipped my hand under the warm, heavy comfort of his. That was all I needed.

THIRTEEN

Seven hours later I'd managed to put the bizarre morning with Mom behind me as Devon and I returned to the Pampered Pup Spa & Resort for the big Halloween bash. We'd decided to bring Buddha but leave a hyper Petey at the beach bungalow. Buddha didn't seem bothered by the lion mane Devon had picked up for him either, thank goodness.

I was wearing my hair down since it was cooler out and the humidity was low enough it wasn't frizzing up. I'd tried to put on the make-up Hope had bought me but ended up scrubbing it all off and opting for just tinted sunscreen and lip gloss. They were handing out masquerade masks at the door anyway – why torture myself? We exchanged my two complimentary tickets for masks: a black one for Devon and an emerald green one with a white feather for me.

First thing I noticed as we stepped inside was that they'd removed all the tables except for the ones along the floor-to-ceiling windows. A raised runway draped in a white cloth had been placed in front of the banyan tree. Tiny sparkling lights hung from the ceiling in between the hand-blown glass balls, their reflections studding the windows. The city lights of Clearwater beyond that gave the restaurant a 3D effect. It was like walking into a fairy land or prom, not that I would know how a prom looks. I never went to mine due to the expense. It was fine, though. It made events like this as an adult even more special.

We were early so the place was still pretty empty, but I needed to find out more information about the pet costume contest and my role in it. As Devon snapped a few pictures of the banyan tree with the digital camera he'd brought, I spotted Rita talking to a lady setting up a table in the corner. Turning to Devon, I said, 'I need to talk to Rita for a sec and ask her about the costume contest.'

Devon draped the camera strap over his shoulder and ran a

hand down my bare arm, causing me to shiver. His eyes glistened mischievously behind the black mask. Yeah, he knew what his touch did to me. 'I'll run Buddha out to the gardens before it begins then.'

I squeezed his hand. 'Thanks.'

As I approached the two women, I slid my mask up to rest in my hair.

Rita smiled. 'Elle!' She air-kissed my cheeks and then put her hands on her hips dramatically. 'My, don't you clean up nicely. Oh, Elle, this is Wanda, an acclaimed pet psychic all the way from New York.'

Pet psychic? I shook the woman's hand. She looked more like a businesswoman than a pet psychic in her black pantsuit and dark, shoulder-length bob. 'And I thought I had an interesting job,' I said, smiling.

'Elle teaches doggie yoga here,' Rita offered.

'How fun. I'll have to check and see if they do something like that in New York.' Wanda's voice was quiet and soothing – a noticeable contrast to her sharp, businesslike outer appearance. 'I've got two highly strung poodles and a terrier mix at home that could use some zen.'

'Oh, you should've brought them to the Pampered Pup with you, Wanda. We specialize in doggie zen here. In fact, that would be an excellent slogan. I need to write that down.'

'Well, with the *live* ones you may.' Wanda's head cocked to the side like a canary. 'But you've got a couple of restless canine spirits here.'

'We do? You've sensed . . . ghost dogs here?' I couldn't tell if Rita was just being polite or if she really believed her.

Wanda nodded. 'Not just sensed them. I've seen them. Heard them. Last night in the hallway. The veil between the living and dead is the thinnest this time of year, you see. Makes it hard for me not to notice them.'

Rita crossed her arms. 'Well, we have had complaints about a dog scratching on guests' doors at night. Could that be these ghost dogs?'

She nodded, catching my eye. 'I believe it's the Yorkies. The ones depicted in the paintings hanging in the lobby. Don't worry, though, the activity will settle down after Samhain and all but go unnoticed again . . . except for those sensitive to such things.' These last words were directed at me. I blushed. Could she possibly know?

'Good.' Rita seemed genuinely relieved and then she gasped. 'Not there, Julius! Sorry, ladies. I have to go help them place the ice sculpture. They're so late. Excuse me.'

'Wait—' I tried. But she was already scuttling off, her arms waving. I frowned. I'd have to catch her later to ask about the costume contest details. 'Well, it was nice to meet you.' I smiled at Wanda, preparing to head off.

'You have a guardian angel.' I turned back to her in surprise. Her smoky gray eyes were soft and almost unfocused. 'But you already know that, don't you?'

I almost denied it but then remembered who she was. If there was anyone I could admit seeing Angel to, it would be a pet psychic. 'Yes. Can you see her?'

She closed her eyes and then shook her head. 'No. Not at the moment. But her energy is around you like a signature. Protecting you.' Her eyes narrowed. 'You've seen her, yes?'

'Yes. She appears to me when I'm in danger. Ironically her name *is* Angel.'

Her smile widened and she nodded. 'What a gift. Well, she may appear more solid to you right now.'

'So I wasn't imagining that?'

She shook her head and laughed softly. 'No.'

I took her card and went to find Devon, finally spotting him coming back through the door with Buddha. I wondered what he'd think about the whole spirit energy thing? I decided not to find out. I knew if I hadn't experienced it for myself with Angel I wouldn't have believed it either.

The café-turned-ballroom was now filling up quickly with patrons donning black gowns, tuxes and masks, accompanied by their dogs decked out in very imaginative costumes. As I watched a white poodle stroll by dressed as Marilyn Monroe – complete with cleavage – I started to get nervous. How in the world was I supposed to judge these costumes? There were so many fabulous dogs here and their owners probably spent ridiculous amounts of time and money dressing them up. My chest tightened and my heart fluttered. Who was I to say which costume was the

best? At least there'd be two other judges there to balance out
my lack of judgment.

A DJ had set up by the bar and every fifteen minutes or so
he'd call out a raffle ticket number and give away a door prize.
Free mud baths, massages, acupuncture . . . all for the dogs, of
course. I watched with amusement as women worth millions got
excited when they won something. Human nature just baffled me.

'Thank you,' Devon was saying beside me as he removed two
glasses of champagne from a waiter's tray. 'Lovely party.'

'It is, sir.'

I smiled up at Devon curiously as I accepted a glass from him.
'What?'

Slipping an arm around his waist beneath his camera strap, I
allowed myself to focus on him alone, feeling my anxiety about
the contest dissipate. I've noticed there are two kinds of blue
eyes: the kind that are flat and non-reflective like denim and then
the clear-as-glass kind. Devon's were the latter, dark blue but
crystal clear, reflecting both passion and mischief. I held his gaze
and let the world melt away. It was one of my favorite things to
do lately and made all the easier by the mask he was wearing.
'You know one of the things I love about you?'

He chuckled. 'I dare not guess.'

'The way you treat everyone with respect and kindness and
don't dismiss or patronize the servers.'

'Really?' His smile spread, and a wicked one it was. 'I was hoping
you were going to say the way I can never keep my hands off you.'
He moved a palm down to my backside to illustrate his point.

'Hey, you two, get a room.'

Reluctantly leaving the intimate conversation with Devon, I
turned and smiled. 'Hi, Beth Anne.' I gave her a one-armed hug,
trying not to spill my champagne down her back, while Devon
shook hands with her husband, Carl. 'And, oh, don't you look
good enough to eat,' I giggled at Shakespeare, her six-pound
shih tzu. The dog didn't seem amused as his dark button eyes
watched us from beneath yarn ropes and brown yarn balls. It
reminded me of that joke:

'Make me spaghetti and meatballs.'

*'OK,' waves the magic wand, 'poof, you're spaghetti and
meatballs!'*

'I don't think he's too happy with us right now.' Beth Anne chuckled and gave him a kiss on his nose, between the yarn strings. Her long hair was down for once and it fell over her bronzed bare shoulder in a silky pane. Even though she was in a black cocktail dress, her whole being was shades of honey, tan and coffee with heavy cream. Even her nails were beige with white tips. Apparently a color pallet wasn't just about your clothes and jewelry – who knew?

'Have y'all seen Violet yet? I cannot wait to see Ghost's costume. I bet she's waiting to make her big entrance.' Before I could answer, she squealed, 'Oh, heavens, will you look at Miss Prizzy in the Marilyn Monroe costume! I have to go say hi. Come on, Carl.' She grabbed an amused Carl's hand. 'Catch y'all later, Elle.'

'How am I ever going to choose?' I moaned, looking over the crowd. 'I still don't even know anything about this contest I'm supposed to be helping to judge.'

Devon chuckled and lifted his camera as a whippet dressed up in the likeness of Michael Jackson walked by. 'Maybe they'll have different categories like funniest or scariest.'

'That would make it easier.' My worries about the contest came to a screeching halt as the Beckleys came through the door. They were all there, including the third Athena, perched on Flavia's lap in a red sequined Devil costume. Apparently, they were fond of irony. 'Speak of the devil.'

Devon followed my gaze. 'Ah, yes. I haven't had a chance to ask you how your investigation is going so far.'

'You mean *your* investigation,' I whispered, watching M.J. gently slip a gold mask on Lulu at the front door. She beamed and gave him a light peck on the lips for his efforts. The rest of the Beckley family had donned their masks and began to navigate the growing crowd in our direction.

'OK, how's my investigation going?'

For some reason, him taking ownership of the investigation did make me feel better. 'Well, I haven't gotten very far. The only suspects we have right now are Cali and Sven. We really need to get to the bottom of Selene's statement and find out if she really was with Cali during the timeframe Michael was killed, leaving Sven's whereabouts unknown. Or if Selene was secretly with Sven, leaving Cali's whereabouts unknown.'

'Solid plan.' Devon grabbed my hand with the same one holding Buddha's leash. 'Come on then.' He moved toward them and put us smack in their path.

'Mrs Beckley.' He greeted Selene with empathy. 'This may not be the proper time, but I just wanted to say how sorry I am for your loss.' He took in the whole family with an intense gaze which settled on Cali. 'My sympathies to all of you.'

Cali shrugged, her dark eyes sliding to her brother behind a red mask. 'Not much of a loss for me. Maybe for M.J.,' she teased with a smile like a velociraptor. 'He was always a daddy's boy.'

M.J.'s face reddened under his own mask and a white ring appeared around his tightening lips. I would have taken her remark as good-natured family ribbing except for his reaction. He didn't respond.

Selene chuckled as if Cali hadn't just insulted her brother and admitted her father's death wasn't a big deal to her. Devon and I shared a look before she said, 'Thank you, your condolences are appreciated. He's very much missed by most of us.' She finally noticed me standing beside Devon. 'Oh, hello, Elle. We took your advice and came. Last night at this place so why not? The police are giving us our house back in the morning.' Wiggling Chloe in her arm, her mouth softened below her black mask. 'Doesn't she make the cutest Winnie-the-Pooh?'

'She does. It's perfect.' I smiled back, all the while trying to figure out a way to bring up her and Cali's whereabouts at the time of Michael's murder. I watched M.J. pluck two champagne glasses from a tray and hand one each to his mother and grandmother, completely ignoring Cali and Sam.

'*Efharisto*,' Flavia said, accepting a glass. I noticed Athena's lip raise as his hand got closer. That dog just didn't like anyone.

'Hi, Flavia,' I said. 'I love Athena's costume.'

She shrugged. 'I no like it but it fits. She is little devil.' Then she waved me closer with a stiff hand.

I heard Devon initiate a conversation with Selene as I moved to the other side of Flavia's chair. Maybe he could steer the conversation toward their whereabouts that night. He was good at that. As I kneeled down – keeping a watchful eye on the tiny demon in her lap – I noted the evil eye charm bulging under the neckline of her black satin dress. 'Yes, Flavia?'

'I finish exercising prayer for you. Things are good now, no? No more headache? Bad luck?'

'Oh, yeah, well . . .' My mind was involuntarily running through all the bad luck I'd had this week. I must've been taking too long to answer.

She made an 'mmmm' noise and pursed her lips, deepening the wrinkles around her mouth. 'I must get you your own protective eye. I take care.' She sipped her champagne and then smacked her lips together, which got Athena's attention. Her little bat ears perked up.

'Oh, that's really sweet of you but not necessary,' I said. But really, who knew what was around the corner? Angel's visit seemed to indicate nothing good. Maybe it wasn't such a bad idea and what could it hurt? I already knew there were things about this world I would never understand. Who was I to say there wasn't such things as curses?

When the family began to split up, I thanked Flavia and stood. Cali and Sam wandered off together and Devon was still talking to Selene on the other side of where I stood. I was just catching snippets of their conversation above the crowd:

'Breezy was like a daughter.' 'She was so angry.' 'Still shocked.'

M.J. now rested his hand protectively on his *yiya's* wheelchair handle, but his attention was firmly planted on Lulu. Who could blame him? I watched her animated conversation. She was all wild hair, palpable energy and a smile that would be perfect for a toothpaste commercial. I had to meet this fascinating creature.

'Excuse me? M.J.?' They both turned to me, her striking light green eyes settling on me behind the gold mask. It was like being hit with a jolt of electricity. 'Sorry, I just wanted to introduce myself. I don't think we've met.' I held out my hand. 'Elle Pressley.'

'Lulu Dutrey.' Impossibly, her smile rose a few watts. 'Nice to meet you,' she said with a soft, unfamiliar accent. It almost sounded southern, like Mississippi-type southern, but with an edge of something else.

I shook her dry, firm hand. 'I hear you own The Gumbo Pot on 10th?'

'You heard right.' She gave a confident nod. 'Have you been?'

'No, sadly I haven't had the pleasure. I've heard good things about it, though.'

'Well, if you're a fan of Cajun come on in and ask for me when you get there.' She winked. 'I'll give you a good discount.'

'Cajun? Yes, I'm a fan. Are you from New Orleans then?' This would fit. She had that otherworldly, magical air about her. Visiting there was on my bucket list, or rather my future braver self's bucket list.

'Louisiana, yes, but the north side. But my mom did drag me down to New Orleans regularly for her business. Interesting place.' She turned her attention back to M.J. 'Sugar, I'm going to go scout out a bottled water. Be right back. Nice to meet you, Elle.'

'She seems pretty great,' I said to M.J. as we both watched her navigate the crowd. 'How long have you two been together?'

He didn't pull his attention away from her until she was completely out of sight. When he finally turned to me he had this look on his face, like a guy who couldn't believe his own dumb luck. 'Actually, Lulu and I have been friends for years. But we just started dating four weeks and two days ago.' He smiled sheepishly.

I smiled back. I'm glad I wasn't the only one who counted days. 'Well, friendship is a great foundation for a relationship. And it's obvious you two are deeply in love.'

His face pinked under his mask as dropped his head to stare down at his black patent leather shoes. 'Yes. I'm a lucky guy.'

Devon sidled up beside me, apparently finished with Selene. He clinked M.J.'s glass. 'To us lucky guys.'

M.J. sipped his champagne then rocked back on his heels. 'You know, Elle, since you haven't been yet, why don't I take you two to Lulu's restaurant tomorrow night? My treat.'

'Oh, we couldn't—' I started to protest.

'No, really,' M.J. said. 'She has to work so it'll give me an excuse to be near her.' He leaned in. 'And a chance to get off Moon Key and away from family for a little while.'

'I heard that.' Selene sidled up to wrap an arm around her son's shoulder. 'Go. It'll do you good to be around people your own age for a change.'

M.J. kissed his mother's cheek and then held his free hand out to Devon. 'It's settled then.'

'OK. I guess it's settled.' I smiled up at Devon as he accepted M.J.'s hand.

Devon gave him his address and then the Beckleys moved on, deeper into the crowded room.

We watched them go. 'So, did you find out anything from Selene?'

Devon shrugged. 'She stands by her statement that she went upstairs to be with Cali. Cali was apparently very upset by the fight with her father, but Selene couldn't get her to take her prescribed sedative. She wanted Selene to confront Michael about cutting her out of the inheritance before she did.' He waved to someone across the room and then added, 'Also, she said Sven left the party when she went upstairs.'

I thought about that. There was no way to prove that Sven actually did leave the party at that time. 'Well, at least we know for a fact one part of that is true: Cali definitely wasn't on any kind of sedative when Detective Farnsworth was questioning her. She seemed angry as a hornet. Oh, thank you.' I took a dog treat from an offered tray and gave it to Buddha, who'd sprawled out on the dark bamboo floor safely between our feet. 'I heard Selene mention Breezy's name. Did she say if she believed Breezy is guilty?'

'She said it was a shock to hear Breezy had been arrested. But she doesn't have any reason to believe the police have it wrong.'

I sighed and leaned my head against his chest. None of us had a reason to believe it yet, really. *That was the problem.* Poor girl. She was the definition of being in the wrong place at the wrong time.

Rita finally approached me about an hour and a half into the party. 'It's time, Elle.'

My stomach did a little flip as I bent down to give Buddha a parting scratch under his lion mane, which was not easy in Hope's little black cocktail number. 'Wish Mommy luck.'

Devon pressed a kiss to my lips when I stood up. 'Luck,' he whispered.

FOURTEEN

There were three chairs set up in front of the runway. I recognized Blair, the dog acupuncturist in the chair on the left, but I stopped in my tracks when I saw who was occupying the one on the right. Alex Harwick. *Seriously?* That was it. If Flavia didn't get me an evil eye thingy I was getting one myself because I was definitely cursed. What was he even doing here? He knew nothing about dogs . . . other than how to act like one. I forced myself to keep walking. Would it be childish to ask Blair to trade seats?

'Well, hello there, Elle.' Alex greeted me with his signature glassy-eyed creepy smile.

'Alex.' I swiped the stapled papers off my seat and plopped down in a very unladylike fashion. I began to flip through the pages of contestants. Leaning away from Alex, I addressed Blair. 'So, we check off these little boxes?'

'Yep,' she said. 'Score them one through five for originality, level of detail, difficulty and audience score. Which means how much the audience loved it, basically.'

'Got it.'

'Vera McNab is giving us ten grand to let her dog win,' Alex whispered.

My attention moved from the paper to Alex's face. I expected him to be laughing but he was serious. 'What?' I jerked my head to see if Blair had heard him. She nodded.

'You guys can't be serious!' I whispered. 'We can't take a bribe to fix a pet costume contest. Who would even bribe the judges at something like this?'

'People with more money than sense.' Alex shrugged his college football-player shoulders. I noticed his tux was straining against them. Probably the tux he wore to his high school prom. He seemed like the type of guy who'd get stuck in the glory days of his past. 'She wants to win, and people with her kind of money get what they want.'

Blair swept a blonde bang off her red sequined mask and out of her eye. 'Yeah, the grand prizewinner gets an Alaskan cruise.'

I looked back and forth between them. Did they even know how insane this was? Vera McNab's vacation house was on mansion row. She could buy a hundred cruises to Alaska . . . probably even her own cruise ship. I shook my head. 'Well, I'm not going to be bribed.'

'Suit yourself. Me and Blair'll split the money, and she'll still win 'cause there's two of us.' Alex winked a bloodshot eye.

'Congratulations, you can count.' Seething, I dropped the papers on my lap and crossed my arms. This gave me a pretty good indication of his character, not that I needed another one. 'What are you even doing here?'

Alex stretched out a long leg that ended in scuffed black dress shoes. 'Rita told me yesterday how she was in a bind because one of the judges backed out and everyone she knew had a dog in this fight. I told her not to worry, I'd save the day.'

'Lucky us.'

The DJ came on, announced the contest would be starting in five minutes and asked everyone to gather round the runway. Good, this couldn't be over soon enough.

Alex leaned a bit too close to me for my comfort. His breath smelled like beer and onion dip. I twitched. Did he just sniff my hair? 'So, still hot and heavy with Devon Burke, I see.'

I tried to unclench my jaw but it wasn't working. 'We're dating, yes.'

'Well, when that doesn't work out, you just give ol' Alex a call. I know we're meant to hook up, Elle. But I'll wait till you figure it out, too.'

Yeah, because a guy who refers to himself in the third person just lights me up. I had to look at him. I didn't want to but I had to know if he was mocking me. Unbelievably he looked completely serious. At that moment I realized he had no idea that he creeped me out on a level even I didn't fully understand.

Then I thought about how he had important information for Devon's parents' case. How he'd told the police about Clyde Lynch bragging at the bar the night Devon lost his parents and then recanted. Maybe I could use his affection for me to our advantage. I couldn't put it that way to him, though. *Hey, Alex, why don't you do me a favor and help out the man who looks like he wants to punch you in the face every time he sees you?* I bit my lip. I'd have to think about that, but meanwhile I'd better not burn any bridges with him.

'Yeah, sure. I'll keep that in mind, Alex.' I didn't sound sincere at all, and I'm sure I grimaced, but Alex just nodded sagely. Like Petey, social cues were not his thing.

There was a drum roll and a spotlight suddenly lit up the runway. Here we go.

'Ladies and gentlemen, it's time to get this party started. Y'all have been very patient so we're just going to jump right into the contest. Without further ado, may I present our first contestant, Sissy Berry and her little Shark, Bruno! Give 'em a hand, folks.'

We watched as Sissy coaxed her little white dog onto the stage. Everyone clapped and whistled as the dog peered out from the blue felt shark mouth. Sissy sashayed down the runway and made it almost to the end, where Bruno turned a nervous circle and then peed.

'Oo!' the DJ laughed as Sissy shook her head and held up a hand in a helpless gesture. 'Well, hopefully the judges won't take too many points away from Bruno for that. When you gotta go you gotta go! Am I right, folks?'

The crowd laughed good-naturedly as Rita hustled over and laid a linen towel over the yellow stain. Sissy picked up her little wiggling shark and took a bow. A few whistles followed her off the stage.

My attention moved from them to Devon, who was standing at the end of the runway with Buddha, where he had a good angle to take pictures. His camera was raised but he was staring at Alex beside me. He was not a happy camper. Nothing I could do about that right now, so I kept my focus on the contest.

'Next up, we have Miss Lilly Founders and her two golden retrievers, Lacey and Lex. Aren't they adorable, folks? Anyone have any rice to throw?'

More clapping, hooting and whistling as Lilly led the canine bride and groom down the runway. They trotted happily alongside her, tails high like flags, grinning in the typical happy-go-lucky golden fashion.

I marked their scores on my sheet, giving them extra points for a happy marriage. You see so little of that these days.

'Next up we have an amazing work of art! Give it up for Violet and Ghost.'

I watched Violet sashay through the kitchen doors to the delight of the crowd. Ghost didn't seem so sure of himself and kept glancing up at Violet with those expressive, pale blue eyes. His head was perfectly placed in the mounted photograph to replace the head of the Weimaraner Cinderella in the famous William Wegman print of the same name. Ghost had a black velvet sheet draped over the rest of his body so he looked like a walking photograph. It was quite effective and the crowd obviously agreed, cheering so loudly they scared him. Poor Ghost kept trying to back up into Violet's legs. She eventually got him the full length of the runway, though, and took her bow at the end. I ticked off all high marks.

Right after that it was Vera McNab and her golden-doodle Parker's turn on the runway. Parker's tail waved from the back-side of a pink gown while her tongue dangled in front from an orangutan costume complete with stuffed furry arms. An orangutan in a prom dress? Well, I'd have to give her high points for originality and Parker was adorable. I couldn't help but feel put off by Vera's bribe, though, so I didn't applaud on principle.

Alex nudged me. 'Not too late to share in the dough.'

My body stiffened as his breath tickled my ear. 'No, thank you,' I said as politely as possible through clenched teeth.

'Suit yourself.'

The rest of the contest went pretty smoothly, barring the occasional costume mishap or the few rambunctious dogs who wanted to bark along with the crowd's cheers. When this happened it just seemed to wind the crowd up more. Everyone was having a good time. I glanced at Rita. She seemed very pleased.

'OK, ladies and gentlemen. That was our last contestant. Time to go fill up your plates and your drinks while the judges collaborate and figure out the winners.'

As the knotted crowd began to disperse, I went to find Rita. I didn't mention Vera's 'gift' to the judges, but I'd decided Devon's idea was a good one and would at least balance out the fraud that was about to go down. She agreed to give out more than one prize package, so I went back to address my fellow judges.

'All right, here's the deal. I know you two are going to give Vera McNab the grand prize, but Rita's agreed to give spa packages to three other winners. Those will be chosen by adding up our points as intended.'

This seemed to make everyone happy, especially Violet, who won one of the packages.

I couldn't get away from Alex fast enough and went to find Devon. He was standing with Violet, Jarvis, Beth Anne and Whitley.

I ignored Devon's irritation for the moment. 'Hey, Whitley, I saw you and Maddox were crossed off the contest list. Is he all right?'

She nodded, her black mask with black feathers a startling contrast to her pale skin and silver hair. 'Yeah, he's got some kind of stomach bug . . . or he swallowed another sock, which he usually yacks up if that's the case. Either way, I left him at home so Gary could keep an eye on him tonight.'

'Poor baby. Hope he feels good as new tomorrow.' I turned to Devon. Time to let him vent. 'Speaking of which, I think Buddha probably needs a potty break.'

The night air hit me and I shivered. The cold front had officially arrived and the warm, humid air had been swept away and replaced with crisp, clean air with a bite. The heavy clouds had also disappeared. Now the sky was just an endless, clear midnight blue filled with stars.

Devon must've noticed me shiver because he removed his tux jacket and draped it over my shoulders. 'Wimp,' he teased. He led Buddha into the grass with his head bowed. I followed.

'So, what did Alex have to say?' I could hear the shape edge of anger in his voice.

'Not much. Just stuff about the contest.' I wasn't about to give him another reason to hate the man.

He grunted. 'I don't like the way he looks at you. He's arse over kick for ya.'

I glanced up at him, stifling a smile. 'He's what?' I noticed Devon used more Irish slang when he got emotional about something, and it was very endearing.

He started fussing with his camera, not looking at me. Snapping a picture of Buddha, he sighed. 'He's just . . . he likes you. And I don't trust him.'

While his jealousy made me secretly happy, I knew it would only hinder my plan. 'Yeah, about that . . . I was thinking maybe we could use that fact to our advantage. Maybe I could get him to give the police his statement again.'

Devon jerked his head up. 'Absolutely not, Elle. I'll not allow you to use yourself as bait.'

Of course, I knew this would be his initial reaction. He needed time to think about it, to realize he had few options. Alex's testimony could really help. I wrapped my hand around his arm and gave him a reassuring squeeze. 'I know how you feel about Alex and I don't trust him, either. Just a thought.' Then I changed the subject. 'Did you happen to notice how Selene seems to favor Cali over M.J.? I don't think I could do that if I had kids.'

We followed Buddha's lead through the gardens as he gave each spot in the grass a good sniffing and marking. Devon nodded, looking disturbed. 'I did notice. Seems like the girl could get away with murder in the eyes of her mother.'

Maybe that's exactly what she did. 'I wonder if Selene was even mad when Cali took that money for the tell-all story about their family?'

Devon angled his head and pressed his lips against mine. The warmth that suddenly flowed through my body was welcomed. Then he ran the back of his index finger across my cheek. 'Good question. Let's go find out.'

I pressed myself fully against the solidness of him and had a sudden urge to head back to the beach bungalow. Instead, I asked, 'How do we do that?'

'The way people have been findin' out things for centuries . . . we'll ask.'

Turned out Selene and company had headed back to their suites after the contest was over. But that was OK. We had a date with her son tomorrow night.

FIFTEEN

We rolled up to The Gumbo Pot in the white stretch limo M.J. had picked us up in about nine thirty Sunday evening. I wouldn't normally venture out this late but apparently the restaurant closes at ten and Lulu wanted to be able to sit down and join us after she was done cooking for the night.

'This place is beautiful,' I said to M.J. as we stepped into the cozy restaurant. And it was. The front of the place was all windows covered in gauzy white curtains and strings of pale pink lights. The back wall was brick with shelving housing hundreds of bottles of wine. The chair backs were heart-shaped scrolls and fresh wildflower bouquets sat in the center of every table. I don't know what I'd been expecting. Maybe checkered tablecloths and Mardi Gras beads hanging from the ceiling? I ran a hand over a jeans-clad hip, hoping I wasn't too underdressed as the hostess led us to a table by the window. Too late to worry about it now. There were only three tables occupied at this late hour anyway. No one to judge me but myself.

'I'll let Lulu know you're here.' She smiled pleasantly. 'Enjoy.'

'Everything looks delicious,' I cooed, reading the menu.

'Thank you and hello, hello!' Lulu was suddenly standing by our table, glowing in a chef's hat and apron despite the sweat beaded up around her hairline and the dark circles beneath her eyes. M.J. stood to greet her but she held up her hands. 'Oh, you don't want to do that, trust me. I smell like a crawfish bath.' She blew him a playful kiss. 'Sit, sit. I'll go wash up and join you in about twenty minutes. Porter's agreed to cook for us after hours. I'll have Gerard bring you out a bottle of wine, and I've already made a special appetizer.' She clapped her hands and held them together in front of her like she was about to pray. 'Devon, Elle, so glad y'all could make it. Be back in a bit.'

M.J. watched her go with a dreamy smile plastered on his face. 'Well, feel free to order whatever you like. She makes a mean crawfish pie and the best chicken and andouille gumbo on the planet. There's also the classic alligator bites if you're feeling brave.'

Brave? Do they bite back? 'It all sounds so good.' My stomach growled as the waiter approached our table with a plate of fried oysters and a bottle of wine. I probably should've had a little snack earlier this evening to hold me over, but I hadn't wanted to ruin my appetite for tonight. My stomach complained louder.

'Good evening.' Gerard's mouth curved beneath his mustache as he began to work the cork in the wine bottle. '*Monsieur* Beckley, you would like to do the honors?'

M.J. nodded and Gerard poured a splash in his glass. After M.J. sniffed, tasted and nodded his approval, Gerard filled up the rest of our glasses.

I eyed the fried oysters. Tiny wisps of heat rose up from them, carrying their delicious scent straight to my nose. I think I made a little whimpering noise out loud. Either that or I was drooling, because Devon mercifully reached out and put a few on my plate.

'*Bon appetit, ma cherie*,' he whispered in my ear. Then he kissed my cheek and loaded his own plate.

'These should be illegal. So, how are you holding up, M.J.?' I asked around a mouthful of the sweetest, most buttery oysters I've ever had.

M.J. shrugged. 'Fine, I guess. Though I think it'll be easier once we have closure, when we can have Dad's service and burial. They're still holding his remains at the coroner's office.'

Devon nodded and wiped his fingers on a cloth napkin. 'I know how that is. I went through that with my parents five years ago. They were killed in a boating . . . accident.' There was a catch in his voice when he used the word 'accident'.

'Oh, yeah, I remember hearing about that. That was your parents, huh?' M.J. sat back in his chair, abandoning his oysters and blew out a breath. 'I couldn't imagine losing both parents at once. Losing Dad has been hard enough.'

'Your sister indicated you two were very close,' I chimed in, mostly so Devon wouldn't have to talk about his parents but also to get M.J. talking about his sister. Actually, she'd said he was a daddy's boy but I wasn't going to put it that way.

M.J.'s jaw clenched as he ripped a roll in half. 'Cali had always been jealous of our relationship. To say she has daddy issues, besides her other obvious issues, would be putting it mildly.'

Should I keep prying? He seemed awfully upset. Maybe just one more question. 'Forgive the assumption if it's wrong, but it seems Cali can do no wrong in your mom's eyes.'

Sighing, he leaned forward and balanced his butter knife contemplatively on the edge of his plate. 'No, that's fair.'

I watched him cautiously. Was I making him more upset by these questions? I hoped not – he'd been through enough. But Breezy didn't have much time. I decided to go for it. 'So, I heard about Cali taking money for a tell-all book about your family. How did your mom handle that? She wasn't furious like your dad was?'

M.J. chewed a piece of the buttered bun slowly. When he swallowed, he glanced up at me and shook his head sadly. 'No. She wasn't. Mom's always let Cali use her mental illness as an excuse for her behavior. And besides, she believes family forgives each other no matter what they've done.'

So if Cali killed her father, Selene would forgive her?

'But Cali went too far this time. All the stuff she fed that disgusting tabloid was lies. Well, except for my mother's string of affairs but that's between her and Dad. It didn't need to be splashed around in public as news. And Cali went after the Beckley Foundation, telling all these fantasy tales of money laundering and theft. We used to do good things with that foundation but her lies really hurt us. Donations stopped coming in. We lost the faith of some key people.' He stopped to sip his wine. 'Anyway, Dad was a good guy. One of the best. He just wanted to do decent things in this world and she spoiled it for him.'

Devon's low voice cut through the silence that followed. 'Your da sounds like he was a stand-up fella, not the type to have an affair with the maid.'

M.J. glanced up at Devon, his mouth ticking up into a grateful smile. 'No, he wasn't. I mean, it's unfathomable to me what the police are saying. That Breezy killed my dad because of a lovers' quarrel? Ridiculous. She may've had a little crush on him. He had a big heart and was easy to love. But Breezy is no killer. She's a sweet girl and practically part of our family. And Dad is . . . was no adulterer.'

I glanced at Devon for any sign that I should lay off the questioning. He didn't seem to be saying that with his body language so I went on. 'M.J., I realize this is a very delicate question, but do you think it's possible Cali and your dad continued the argument in the kitchen and she could have . . . you know . . . killed him in a fit of rage? And maybe your mom is just saying she was with Cali upstairs to protect her?'

His eyes flicked to the window. 'While unfortunately I do think they're both capable of what you're suggesting,' he rubbed his forehead like a headache was brewing and moved his gaze back to me, 'no. Only because the whole story is they were only in my sister's bedroom for about ten minutes. Cali was too worked up and restless so she went down to find Sam in the library and Mom followed her. Mom told me she never left Cali's side. She was afraid of what she'd do. And I know that's true because I ran into them all coming out of the library together when we heard you screaming for help.'

So Selene and Cali had left the bedroom? I tried to calculate the timing. Selene had said she left Sven and took Cali up to the bedroom around eight forty-five. If they stayed around ten minutes, that means they went downstairs to meet Sam in the library a little before nine p.m. Michael was killed between then and nine twenty when I found him. I'd passed the library when Flavia led me through the house . . . the library is fairly close to Flavia's kitchen. Cali definitely had enough time to cut her dad's harness before she met Sam in the library and after Breezy left him. As long as her mom vouched for Cali's whereabouts, though, no one was going to question that.

'I expected those oysters to be gone by now,' Lulu teased as she appeared and kissed M.J.'s cheek. She slid into the chair next to him, wearing a fresh green dress covered in a daisy pattern, her face scrubbed to a shine. 'And what are we all looking so serious about?'

I dropped the whole Cali thing for now. 'M.J. was just telling us there's no way Breezy had anything to do with his father's death,' I said, wanting to get her opinion on Breezy.

'Agreed!' She plucked a piece of the crusty bread from the basket and slathered it with honey butter. 'Breezy and I have been friends for years. She loves the Beckleys like I do, like family.

She'd never hurt Michael. I don't understand why the police are so convinced she did.'

Devon held up three fingers and began to tick them off. 'The trifecta. One, they have hard evidence. Her fingerprints and Michael's are the only ones on the severed harness and a drop of her blood was found on the floor beneath him. Two, there's opportunity. She was seen running from the crime scene and admitted being there during the twenty-minute window Michael's death occurred. And three, they have motive because she admitted she was in love with him.'

'Let's not forget the voodoo dolls she had tied together and leaning against the photo of her and Michael on her dresser. Kind of incriminating,' I added.

Lulu waved her hand. 'She got those dolls from my mother.' She must have seen the shocked look on my face because she laughed. 'Not to keep them bound together forever or anything like that. She told me she saw . . .' Lulu glanced at M.J. 'Sorry, sugar, but she saw Selene getting intimate with her trainer. You know that Norwegian mountain with eyes? And she was worried about Michael having a mistress, too.' I nodded in understanding. 'So she wanted to do something to help their marriage.' She shrugged. 'What could it hurt to send Breezy to my mother? It made her feel like she was doing something and I figured who knows, it might actually help. When you have a mother in the vodun business, you see things. Unexplainable things. Ya know what I'm sayin'?'

I made a note to ask her about those 'things' at another time. Right now I had to keep the conversation focused on Michael's murder. 'Your mother makes voodoo dolls?' I asked.

'Sure, she knows how, though she doesn't do that so much anymore since her arthritis has gotten bad. She owns a voodoo magic shop and dabbles a little. Mostly crystals, books, essential oils, you know . . . touristy stuff. But back home in Louisiana she had a back room with the real deal.'

'Do you think she would talk to us? Give us an idea of Breezy's state of mind when she bought the dolls?' Devon asked.

I knew what he was thinking. Just because Breezy told Lulu she wanted to help the Beckley's marriage doesn't mean it was true. She could've had a hidden motive. Since they both seemed

to think Breezy was innocent though, maybe it was time to come
clean. 'Lulu, we don't believe Breezy killed Michael either.' I
glanced at Devon and he nodded, so I continued. 'Devon is a
private investigator, and he's working pro bono trying to help
prove her innocence and find out the truth about what happened
to Michael.'

'Really?' M.J. said in surprise.

'Really?' Lulu said at the same time. 'That's fantastic. Yeah,
I'll give Mom a heads-up you're coming. Her shop is called
Dutrey's on Garden Street. I'm sure she'd be glad to help.'

'I don't know how to thank you, Devon. Let me know if
there's anything I can do.' M.J. held up his glass. 'To finding
out the truth.'

'Me, too. If I can help, let me know.' Lulu held up her
water goblet. Our clinking glasses echoed through the deserted
restaurant.

Devon took a mouthful of wine and then set his glass down,
addressing Lulu. 'Not a big fan of wine?'

Lulu and M.J. shared a conspiratorial smile then M.J. rested
his hand over hers. 'Why not? Let's celebrate. Tonight.'

Lulu nodded excitedly, kissed M.J. hard on the mouth and
then they both turned to face us. 'We're pregnant!' they said
together.

Devon and I were both stunned into silence for a moment and
then in a rush we both offered our congratulations.

I grabbed my glass. 'Well, another toast is in order then. To
a healthy mom and baby.'

'You're the first people we've told. My mother doesn't even
know yet. I hope she'll be excited to be a grandmother.' Lulu
bit her bottom lip. 'We were going to wait until the second
trimester. Superstition and all that, but I don't want to wait
anymore. I want to shout it from the rooftops.'

The mood had turned to one of excitement as we ordered
dinner and a second bottle of wine for three of us.

'Do you have any names picked out yet?' I asked, getting
caught up in the possibilities. What would their baby look like?
Would it have her amazing eyes and bubbly personality?

'Well, I like Michael if it's a boy. It only makes sense to have
a Michael the third, right?' Lulu tapped her lip thoughtfully.

'Don't know about a girl, but I'm only four weeks along so we have time.'

Wow. Four weeks? M.J. said they'd only been dating for four weeks; they must've started off their relationship with a bang. I smiled to myself at my own joke, but when I moved my attention to M.J. he suddenly looked sad and withdrawn. Was he not as happy as he seemed to be about the baby? Devon must've noticed his mood shift, too.

'Thinkin' about your da?' Devon asked him quietly.

'Sorry?' M.J. came back from wherever he'd been with a shake of his head.

'Your da? I know if I was expectin' a baby I'd want my da around to be a grandfather.'

M.J.'s face paled and he squeezed his eyes shut. 'Yeah. So damned tragic. I still can't believe it's real. He's gone.'

Lulu wrapped both arms around his and rested her head on his shoulder. 'He'll never truly be gone.'

'What about your dad, Lulu?' I asked, changing the subject.

She folded her hands on the table. 'Not around. He passed away two months ago. It was a big mess. My dad's family wouldn't even let us come to the services. They cremated him and held the wake in their big fancy New Orleans house and said they'd call the police if we trespassed. My mom and I were devastated.'

'Why would they do that?' I asked, shocked.

'Because they never liked Mom. Said she was a witch because of her vodun religion. Though if you asked me it had more to do with the color of her skin. They come from Irish and French blood and she's African-American. As far as they're concerned, me and Mom don't exist.'

'That's terrible. So you didn't get to say goodbye to your dad?'

She shook her head while M.J. rubbed her arm, comforting her this time. She swiped a thumb beneath her eye and smiled despite the threatening tears. 'What about you, Elle. Are your parents still alive?'

I squirmed a little. 'My mom, yes. I never knew my dad.'

Steaming plates of food arrived just in time. I'd ordered the gumbo and it came in the biggest ceramic bowl I'd ever seen.

'Now that's a bowl of gumbo,' I laughed. I spooned a big

creamy, seafood-filled pile into my mouth, glad to not have to elaborate about my own parents.

We were all having such a good time, laughing, sharing stories and eating the most delicious Cajun food I've ever tasted, so I hated to ruin the mood by bringing up Michael again but I'd thought of something. If M.J. didn't believe Breezy killed his father, maybe he had his own idea about who did.

While Lulu took her third bathroom break of the evening, I asked, 'M.J., do you know of anyone at the party who would've fought with your dad? Besides your sister, that is.'

He swallowed, wiped his mouth and became very still, eyes wide as if he'd had an internal shock. 'Yes. I do.'

SIXTEEN

He had both Devon's and my attention quickly. 'Who?' I coaxed.

He glanced from me to Devon, his expression hardening. 'Oliver White.'

I'd heard that name before. I looked at Devon, digging in my wine-soaked brain. I couldn't place him.

He helped me out. 'The neighbor.'

'Ah!' I said, focusing back on M.J. 'The art dealer guy.'

He nodded. 'Art dealer, casino owner . . . all-round sociopath.'

'Was he at the party?' Devon asked.

'He wasn't invited, no, but whether he snuck in or not, who knows. He and my dad had a feud going on for years. It started friendly enough with my dad pulling one of his pranks. Only Oliver doesn't have a sense of humor. He threw a couple of boxes of nails in our driveway afterwards so Dad paid the gardener to set the sprinklers off during one of Oliver's girlfriend's book launch parties.' His mouth twitched at the memory. I couldn't tell if it amused him or made him sad. 'Well, you get the picture.'

'Every time I leave, you three get so serious.' Lulu laughed as she returned to the table. 'What are we discussing now?'

'Oliver White,' M.J. said, pulling out her chair for her. 'Elle asked if I thought anyone else could've fought with Dad that night.'

'Oh.' Lulu rolled her eyes. 'Yeah, that man is flat out disturbing. But he wasn't at the party.'

M.J. looked at her thoughtfully. 'How do we know? Everyone was dressed up. He could have easily snuck through the backyard and into *Yiya's* kitchen without being noticed if he was in costume.'

'Why would he do that?' And then they both froze and stared at each other.

'What?' My heartbeat sped up. They'd just remembered something important. It was written on their faces. 'What is it?'

'The mask,' Lulu whispered.

'The mask.' M.J. nodded. Then turning to us, he elaborated. 'Dad has a room in the house dedicated to African art. There's this African mask, once owned by some French poet and worth over a million dollars that Dad had really wanted. Somehow Oliver found out and outbid Dad during a silent auction. Not one to be denied something he really wanted, Dad paid one of Oliver's maids to steal it for him. Paid her well, too. She no longer had to work. I heard she took her family and retired in the Caribbean somewhere.

'Anyway, it became this thing between them. Instead of calling the police, Oliver had it stolen back. Dad had it last, though. Oliver could've used the cover of the party to disguise himself, waltz right in and steal it again. I'll have to check Dad's art room when we're allowed back in the house and see if it's missing.'

I sat up straight, my face drained of blood. 'I don't think it will be there.' I was remembering the man in the mask bumping me in the hallway when I was trying to find a bathroom. 'Someone wearing a brown wooden mask passed me in the hallway right before I found your father in the kitchen.'

Devon picked me up after my last doga class on Monday and we found ourselves headed back over the bridge, merging onto the highway headed to Madame Dutrey's shop in Tampa. With every mile Clearwater receded in the distance, I felt my anxiety increasing. Even though it was only a forty-minute drive, I'd never been this far away from home before. I suddenly wished I'd brought Buddha with me instead of leaving him with Maria for a mud bath and massage. He was my security blanket, my anchor when I felt myself coming unglued. Like now.

Devon had left the top up on the Jeep because of the cold air at highway speeds, but that was just adding to my discomfort and feeling of being trapped. I tugged my sweatshirt collar and tried to concentrate on keeping my breath steady and deep, not letting it get shallow. As I watched the brush and buildings fly by, the feeling of being in a speeding car hurling toward certain death took over. I had no control. My mind flew from one deadly scenario to another. Rationality flew out the window. I saw the Jeep upside down and burning on the side of the road. Who would take care of Buddha? And Petey? My heart rate sped up with my thoughts. Sweat broke out around my hairline. I just wanted to be back in the comfort of the bungalow with my face buried in Buddha's fur. Oh, God. The panic rose like a giant wave.

Then I remembered I had the prescription Xanax with me. With shaky hands, I dug it out of my bag. My focus narrowed down to the act of getting one little pill from the bottle. I stuck it on my tongue and grabbed my water bottle. Here goes nothing. Swallowing, I closed my eyes and rested my head on the back of the seat. My heart was still pounding but I could do this. All I had to do was wait. And breathe. I felt Devon's hand rest on my knee and squeeze. Rolling my head toward him, I opened one eye.

He was glancing at me with concern. 'That bad, eh?'

I nodded and went back to waiting with my eyes closed. Each second ticked by with excruciating slowness until . . .

'Elle?'

Blinking, I came back to awareness slowly. Devon's hand was stroking my cheek. 'We've arrived.'

I pushed myself up and wiped the drool from the corner of my mouth. 'Good thing I wasn't driving,' I quipped. Fighting a wave of dizziness and a general sense of having an out-of-body experience, I nodded. 'Let's go.'

A pleasing chime that sounded like tiny bells announced our arrival. The shop smelled lovely, like incense and spices. A small-statured woman in a white turban greeted us. 'Welcome, welcome!' She came around the counter and clasped each of our hands in her warm, dry ones. Happiness radiated from her, pulling a smile from me even though I was still feeling a bit off from the Xanax. I could see where Lulu got her charisma from. 'You are Lulu's friends?'

'We are,' Devon answered, introducing us and taking in the whole of the shop.

'Thank you for seeing us,' I added. My mouth felt like paste.

'I'm glad to help. That poor girl being accused of murder is just nonsense. Come on.' She led us through the store. 'Ginny, my tarot card reader, is gone for the day. We can talk in the back room.'

It was a cozy store with so much going on I felt overstimulated as I tried to take everything in. There was a wall of jars with various colored herbs and teas; statues and photos of saints; candles, gift baskets and baskets of oils in dark blue bottles; a book shelf; a CD rack; a whole glass cabinet of jewelry; alligator heads and miscellaneous items hanging from the ceiling, like dreamcatchers and wind chimes crafted from tiny wooden heads.

We followed her through a wall of multicolored hanging beads into a room no less stimulating. The statues of saints seemed to be the main décor in here as Devon and I sat on a wicker love-seat, which was well padded with silk pillows.

Madame Dutrey lowered herself gingerly into a chair across from us. A glass table with a deck of tarot cards sat between us and her. 'Have to watch the knees,' she grunted. 'Do not ever get old.'

'The alternative is worse,' Devon said with a touch of humor.

Madame Dutrey chuckled. 'This is a good point, child.' She slapped her thighs with both hands, sending her multitude of bracelets clinking. 'So, how can I be of service?'

Devon glanced at me and nodded. I was still feeling a little loopy from the medication, but also calm so I didn't hesitate. 'The voodoo dolls Breezy had – Lulu said she got those from you?'

'Yes. I don't make many of them anymore.' She held up hands with gnarled, crooked joints. 'You can see why. But she is Lulu's friend, so I helped her.'

'How exactly do the dolls work? I read that they aren't for evil purposes, to cause pain like all the movies lead us to believe.'

'That's true. They work by sympathetic magic . . . like produces like, which really is just a principle of nature herself. How to explain this?' She thought for a moment and then her eyes brightened. 'Take food, for example. Red beet juice is good for the blood. Sliced carrots resemble the eye, complete with the iris, and are high in Vitamin A so good for vision. Tomatoes have four chambers just like the heart and reduce the risk of heart disease. You can look at all kinds of food: cauliflower, good for the lungs; kidney beans for kidneys; celery for bones and see that the concept of like producing like is not magic at all. It is how the laws of our natural world are set up. So, this is how voodoo works. The likeness of a person is created in order to use in prayer to petition the saints on behalf of that person, you see?'

'I think so. When you say saints, you mean like the Catholic saints?'

'Yes. The Catholic saints have also become syncretized with our intermediaries, the Lao. You see, we believe God has delegated responsibilities to the saints and Lao, they are the ones who listen to our prayers and perform miracles on our behalf.'

'So, when Breezy came to you, she was asking for a miracle?'

'Well, not really a miracle, just a way to help the family she loves stay together. She was worried after she heard Mr Beckley speaking to someone on the phone intimately. Binding the likeness of a couple together is a very effective way to petition the saints for help in a relationship.'

So she really did want the dolls to help the Beckleys' relationship? Unless . . . 'How did she seem to you when she came? Was she anxious?'

'She was . . . sad.'

'Did she confess to you that she was in love with Mr Beckley?'

'No, she did not. That poor man.' She ran her hand over the multiple shell necklaces at her throat and frowned. 'But love is love and her intentions were pure.'

'So she couldn't have maybe decided to use the second doll as her likeness instead of Mrs Beckley's?'

Her expression grew thoughtful. 'Was Mrs Beckley's name pinned on the doll?'

I thought back to when I saw the dolls, picturing them leaning there against the photo. 'I didn't actually see any names pinned on them.'

'Hm. Well, she didn't follow my instructions then, but that doesn't really mean anything. Lots of people aren't good at following instructions.'

'This is true.' I nodded and glanced at Devon. Wasn't he supposed to be the one investigating? 'Anything else?'

'I can't think of anything.' Devon leaned up and held out his hand. 'Thank you for your time, Madame Dutrey.'

When she took his hand, she cocked her head and became still, her eyes unfocused. Without releasing his hand, she addressed me. 'Anything else you need, you come back. Ginny is a good reader, too. She gives half price to our friends.' Then to Devon, she said, 'Come, child.' Standing, she made her way gingerly back through the beads and over to the counter. Her expression turned very serious as she once again took Devon's hand. Her eyes studied him with a mixture of ancient wisdom and concern. 'I was led to make this gris gris bag today, and I now believe it was meant for you.' She placed a small white velvet pouch in his hand and closed his fist around it. 'It's for protection. Carry it with you always and think only of being safe when you hold it. Intention is the key to its power.'

Devon seemed speechless. He shuffled his feet uncomfortably. 'Intention,' he repeated. 'Well . . . thank you.'

Once in the car, he tossed the little bag in my lap like it was hot. 'What do ya make of that?'

'Well, for one, it won't bite you,' I teased, surprised at his reaction. As he backed out of the parking lot I untied the little wax string and peered into the bag.

'Madame Dutrey called it a gris gris bag. Looks like some dried herbs, some kind of root and a pink stone.' I stuck my nose in the bag. Smelled like rosemary and something earthy.

He glanced at the bag suspiciously. 'You can keep it.'

'But she said you're the one who needed protection.'

'What is a bunch of herbs and a stone going to do to protect me? That's what I've got a gun for.' Devon seemed agitated as he floored the Jeep on the ramp, merging smoothly with the traffic on the highway.

I was happy to be heading home but not happy with Madame Dutrey thinking Devon needed protection. Even though I didn't understand her vodun religion, I had respect for it, and if Angel's visits had taught me anything it was that there are things in this world I will never understand but that doesn't make them any less real. I put the little bag in my purse.

He hit the steering wheel with his palm. 'Ah, I meant to tell ya. M.J. called me earlier. They got to go home this afternoon and he checked. The mask is indeed gone.'

I stared at him. 'So that means the creepy neighbor was in their house that night! He could have killed Michael. Did you tell Detective Farnsworth?'

He changed lanes to move around a slow pickup truck hauling a tractor. 'He wasn't around, no, but I did talk to Salma.'

Of course he did. *Stop it, Elle.* 'What'd she say?' I kept my tone neutral.

'She's agreed to ask the family to file a complaint about the mask and give her a photo of it. That way she can get a search warrant to look for it at Oliver White's house. I also told her you'd give a statement that you saw someone wearing the mask in the house at the time of Michael's death.'

'Perfect. Hopefully they find the mask in Oliver's possession and then Detective Farnsworth can bring him in for questioning about his whereabouts when Michael was killed.'

'She said Farnsworth is pretty convinced it was Breezy Morales, though. He had another case a few years ago where the maid was having an affair with the husband and sees the same pattern here.'

Well, that's unfortunate for Breezy. 'How long is all that going to take? Filing a complaint and getting a search warrant?'

'She said she'll contact the Beckleys today, tomorrow at the latest, and call the judge as soon as she has the formal complaint for the warrant.'

'OK. Good.'

We stopped by the Pampered Pup to pick up Buddha. Devon had to make a phone call so I went in alone, checking the mud-bath room first. Maria was in there, singing to a tiny mud creature in Spanish. Both their eyes turned to me when I entered.

I waved. 'Hi, Maria. Buddha all done?'

'*Si, si.*' She pointed to the ceiling with a mud-covered hand. 'He upstairs already. He get fat, no?'

I laughed. 'Fat? No, he's just full of love, Maria.' I slipped a twenty on top of the stack of towels and then patted her arm. 'Thanks for taking care of him.'

Entering the suite, I collapsed on the bed next to him and shoved my face into his chest. 'Buddha belly! You smell so good.' I could feel his butt wiggling and he landed a lick on my ear. 'Missed you, too.' I kissed his face and rubbed his belly. OK, maybe he was getting a little fat. Well, I had my bike now. I could run him a bit. 'Come on. Time to go home.' Or should I say our current, temporary version of home. Best not to get too comfortable calling it home. It'll hurt less that way when Devon resumes his real life of being a travel photographer.

When we exited the suite, I heard a squeal and spun around to see Novia coming toward me with a huge grin. She was carrying something wrapped in tin foil.

'Oh my God!' I gasped as I realized the girl behind her was Breezy.

Stunned, I watched as they approached. 'Breezy? You're out of jail?'

Novia wrapped her free arm around my neck and squeezed tight. She was saying something in rapid Spanish. Breezy looked tired, her complexion sallow, but she was smiling, too.

'Novia, English,' I pushed through my choked airway. I could feel her heart beating in my own chest.

'Oh! *Si*,' she squealed. 'Here, these are for Mr Devon.' She pushed the tin-foiled plate into my stomach. 'From our *madre*. She make them to thank Mr Devon, but they wouldn't let her on the ferry so . . .'

'Devon?' I was so confused.

'Is he with you?' Breezy asked from behind her beaming sister. 'I'd like to thank him in person. I don't think I would have made it one more day in that awful place.'

Then it hit me. 'Oh. Devon paid your bail?'

'*Si!*' Novia shouted as Breezy nodded. 'He is angel.'

'Yes, he is,' I agreed. A very wealthy angel, thanks to his parents' fortune. I'm sure they would've approved of his good deed. 'He's also waiting for me outside. Come on.'

The girls followed me downstairs and out the front doors, all the while talking happily in Spanish. I didn't need to understand the words – the excitement in their voices was enough to get the gist of the conversation.

When they spotted Devon sitting in the Jeep, they sprinted to his side. More squealing. More rapid Spanish. Devon glanced at me uncomfortably as I helped Buddha into the car.

'You're on your own, hero,' I teased.

He opened the door to greet them properly and was accosted with the same python-worthy hug I'd been given from Novia. Breezy was more reserved but grateful tears were now running down her face.

I slid into the passenger seat and peeked under the tin foil. Some kind of powdered sugar cookies were piled high. 'Their mother made you cookies,' I said, smiling and holding up the plate.

His hand was clutching the door like he was holding on for dear life. I'd never seen him uncomfortable before and I was thoroughly enjoying the moment. Did that make me a bad girlfriend?

'No thanks necessary, really,' he kept repeating.

'You prove my sister is innocent?' Novia asked, clutching her heart.

'We're working on it.' Devon nodded. He was trying to slide back into the Jeep.

Novia moved her hands to the gold cross at her throat, her face still flushed with gratitude. 'You will. I have faith.'

I grinned at him on the short drive back to the bungalow. He wouldn't look at me.

He finally glanced at me sheepishly when we pulled into the driveway. 'Well, I couldn't very well have let the poor girl sit in prison, could I?'

'Yes, you could have,' I said. 'But you didn't and now it's official. You are the most charming, sexy and virtuous man I've ever met.'

'No, no, no.' He slid his hand behind my neck and pulled my mouth near his. 'Virtuous?' he smirked. 'I'll have to change that.'

SEVENTEEN

After a blissful night, I was losing Devon again for a few days. Now that I had my bike, I decided to let Petey stay at the bungalow – since snowbird season was officially in full swing and the Pampered Pup was booked solid – and ride back at lunch to feed him and let him out. It was only a few miles, and besides, the cold front had lifted and the weather was in the high seventies and sunny, the exact weather people flock here for in the winter. Great weather for a girl and her dog to get some much-needed exercise.

'Welcome, everyone.' I began class when everyone was settled on their mats. Well, the humans anyway. Some of the dogs were still running around being social. I tried not to let the little tiff Bristol and Gilly had gotten into cause anxiety as I watched the dogs sniff each other. I'd gone almost a year without a dog fight. It wouldn't be the norm. Deep breath and let it go.

'When your dog comes to you, we're going to begin with a front leg stretch.' I sat cross-legged and had Buddha sit in front of me. He jumped up and put his paws on my shoulders, licking my mouth. Everyone laughed. 'Yes, he's a little excited this morning. Must be the cooler weather.' I moved my hands to rub under his ears and then rubbed lightly over his sides, which, I had to admit, were wider than they used to be. 'Such a good boy. So, since he's up here, I'll begin. Remember the important part is to get a firm grip under their armpits and support them. Start in a cross-leg position and be aware of your own posture, back straight.' I barely had to put pressure beneath Buddha's front legs and he was already lifting them in a stretch. Such a pro. 'Remember the number one rule: if they struggle or seem to be in pain, don't force their legs up, just gently massage their sides and back instead.' I watched the class. I loved this morning class. Most of the women had been coming since the beginning and already knew what to do. We had all learned together. 'For those of you with taller dogs who are doing this stretch standing, be sure to have your feet grounded and kneecaps pulling upward and tailbone tucked to protect your lower back. Good, Whitley.'

We ended in *savasana* and I walked around giving gentle massages to the dogs. It always amazed me how much their energy shifted by the end of class. You would think they'd get bored or restless, but they never did. Just calmer and more relaxed.

I decided to bring out the box of dog toys. Sometimes these ladies liked to hang out and socialize for a few minutes and today seemed like one of those days.

Beth Anne had her shih tzu in her arms, holding him like a baby as she approached. He had a blue silk ribbon clip holding his bangs back that matched the one in her ponytail. 'Shakespeare approves of today's class.'

'Yeah, you need to calm down, boy.' I laughed as I stroked his pink freckled belly.

'So,' she glanced around and lowered her voice, 'I did find out that Michael never had a chance to take Cali out of the will, and Selene has no intention of doing so.'

'What are you whisperin' about now?' Violet appeared at her shoulder.

Beth Anne ignored her. 'And Selene confided in Caramel Jessups who confided in Vivi Marks who confided in—'

'Good Lord, Beth Anne, get to the point. We don't have all day for you to recite the gossip chain,' Violet said.

'Caramel?' I said. *Who names their daughter Caramel?*

'Anyway,' Beth Anne shot her a look of exasperation, 'apparently Cali and her brother had a big blowout in the lobby last night, and Selene is upset Cali won't take her medication, especially since Michael died. Selene's worried about her self-harming. Apparently she's done it before.'

I winced at the thought of Cali hurting herself. 'That's awful. Poor girl.' Sounded like even if she wasn't the one who killed Michael, she really needed professional help. What did her and M.J. fight about?

'Selene sure has her hands full with family troubles.' Violet shook her head and rubbed Ghost's ear after he nudged her hand. 'And you all wonder why I'll never get married and have kids.'

'There's good parts, too.' Beth Anne shifted Shakespeare in her arms. I noticed she was unconsciously rocking him. Did she have kids? I didn't think so. She never mentioned any. I suddenly wanted to know more about her. I knew Whitley had a design business that specialized in hotels and restaurants and that her and her husband owned a dozen restaurants in NY and California and various other real estate. And of course, Violet had her makeup line, but I had no idea how Beth Anne had become part of the uber-rich club. She seemed so down to earth I didn't think she'd come from family money, but I could be wrong.

'There's *one* good part,' Violet grinned, 'and I can get that without the bad parts, thank you very much.'

Beth Anne rolled her eyes and turned toward me. 'So, have you found out anything yet?'

Should I tell her? Why not? I suddenly wanted to confide in her. 'Well, Selene is sticking to her story that Cali was with her during the time of Michael's death but I don't know. There's about a ten-minute window where she would've had opportunity. And we know she had motive. But, we also have a new suspect. Apparently that creepy neighbor, Oliver White, and Michael had this ongoing feud over an expensive African mask. They would steal it from each other and M.J. said it's now missing from Michael's art room. I saw a man wearing a wooden mask the night of the party, so we think he used the costume party as a cover to sneak in and steal the mask back, which would put him in the house when Michael was killed.'

Beth Anne gasped and her hand flew to her chest. Then, after a moment, her eyes narrowed. 'You know what? This is perfect. Oliver is having a local art show and auction at his house Friday night. He's invited Carl to enter a sculpture. It's perfect. You and Devon can come as our guests and we can search his house for the mask.'

'Beth Anne,' Violet groaned, 'snooping around a possible murder suspect's house is only a good idea in movies. And even then it usually turns out poorly for the snooper.'

'Yeah.' I shook my head. 'Violet's right, Beth Anne. That could be really dangerous. And besides, Detective Vargas is getting a warrant as we speak to search his house for the mask. So it'll be done the right way, legally.'

Her surgically plumped bottom lip stuck out. It always

fascinated me how these women got their lipstick to stay put through class. 'You two are no fun.'

Between classes, I grabbed my bike out of the storage closet where I'd stashed it. 'Come on, Buddha. Time for some aerobic exercise.' Buddha followed me reluctantly outside and eyed the bike with suspicion as I swung my leg over. 'You'll just have to trust me. It's not that bad.' I held his leash in one hand and started off at his walking pace. We worked up to a slow jog.

I breathed in the fresh, salty air. It was such a gorgeous day with baby blue skies stuffed with white cotton clouds so fluffy they looked like you could pluck a piece off, pop it in your mouth and let it melt on your tongue like sugar.

I guess I should've been paying more attention to the road than the sky. I caught the black car out of the corner of my eye and swerved just in time to avoid getting my leg crushed. As it was, the bumper skimmed my wheel, stopping it dead, and sent me flying over the handlebars. I'd instinctively let go of Buddha's leash so he could jump out of the way.

I hit the perfectly cut grass with an *oof!* then lay there, dazed, staring up at the same white fluffy clouds I'd been admiring before my brush with death disguised as a big hunk of metal on wheels.

Then I felt Buddha's wet nose sniffing my face. 'I'm OK.' *Was I OK?* I ran a mental check over my body, moving my toes and fingers then lifting my feet to rest them on the grass. It tickled my soles. I must have lost my flip-flops mid-flight.

'Oh my heavens, are you all right?' A face suddenly blocked out the fluffy clouds. 'Dear, are you OK? Can you move?' Sissy Berry was leaning over me. Her abandoned golf cart, little white dog and husband sat on the side of the road.

'I think so.' I moaned and tried to sit up. A sharp pain in my right arm immediately let me know putting pressure on it wasn't the smartest move. 'Ouch.' I grabbed my elbow.

'Oh, dear. We should get you to the clinic.'

'No. I'll be fine. I just need some ice.' I used my left arm this time to push myself up. 'Did you see who ran me off the road?'

'Well, some kind of big black car. Dime a dozen around here, I'm afraid.' The lines around her eyes and mouth deepened with worry as she helped me to my feet. 'It sure did look like they were aiming right for you, though.'

I glanced at her and then scanned the area for my shoes. 'I'm sure they were probably just on their cell phone or something,' I said, distracted by the pain and my missing shoes. Though I wasn't sure at all. My gut was telling me it was a warning.

'I suppose,' she said, not looking convinced either. 'Can we give you a ride at least?'

I glanced back at her golf cart and then down at my bike. 'I appreciate it, Mrs Berry, but I think I'm OK now. I just need to find my shoes.' Truth was, I was feeling really shaken up and just wanted to get off the street and out of the view of curious onlookers. Bending down, I ran my hands over Buddha to check for any cuts or signs of pain and then, feeling dizzy, straightened back up. 'He's not hurt,' I reassured myself.

'Here they are,' Mrs Berry called from a few yards away, holding up my dollar store flip-flops in her manicured and diamond-studded hand.

Her husband had climbed out of the cart by this time, his yellow-checkered golf shorts hiked up past his belly button, and was lifting up my bike. He looked so frail. I ignored my arm's protest and went over to take it from him.

'Thank you, Mr Berry. I've got it from here,' I said. Buddha had come over to sniff Bruno at the end of his leash. The little white dog rolled over in submission. I hoped he wouldn't pee.

'That was some somersault, young lady,' he chuckled.

'Yeah, well, when you're as clumsy as I am, you learn how to fall well.' I picked a leaf out of my hair.

He bent down and rubbed Buddha's head with a shaky hand. 'You should report that car to security.' He straightened up and his expression grew serious. 'Black Cadillac, first few letters on the plate were TR6. Sorry, I didn't catch the whole thing.'

'I will, thank you,' I said. Sissy Berry joined us and put my shoes on the ground so I could step back into them. I was now fighting back tears. 'Thank you for . . .' I wanted to say 'caring' but that might sound too personal, so I said, 'stopping.'

For the remainder of the short ride, I kept pressure off my right arm and let the tears fall.

*   *   *

That evening, after making sure the doors were locked, I lay in Devon's bed with the dogs and an ice pack on my elbow. I had the TV on for company but my mind was still trying to figure out who would've run me off the road. Did it have something to do with Michael's case? Did someone overhear me talking about it? I had really tried to be careful. Or . . . what if it had to do with Devon's parents' case? What if someone was trying to warn him by hurting me? What if I was still cursed and the prayer Flavia said hadn't worked? Now I was being ridiculous. But still . . . I reached over and grabbed the little white velvet bag Madame Dutrey had given Devon off the nightstand and tucked it under my pillow.

Buddha and Petey watched me, their ears twitching. Probably wondering if I'd just stashed a delicious treat under my head and not really judging me. 'What? A girl can't be too careful.' Urg. This is exactly why I didn't want to get involved in helping Breezy. Laying here wondering if someone had just tried to run me over on purpose was not my idea of fun.

My phone vibrated on the nightstand. I grabbed it and looked at the number. 'It's your daddy,' I said, resting a hand on Petey's side. He rolled over and stretched out his back legs so I could get at his belly. 'Hey,' I answered, still distracted by my near-death experience with the Cadillac. 'How's it going?'

'Not good.' He sounded drained. 'I'm afraid I've got a bit of bad news.'

EIGHTEEN

'What do you mean she didn't get the warrant?' I stammered. 'I don't understand.'

'Judge Stasio denied it. She thinks he's crooked, gave Oliver White a heads-up on the warrant request and took payment to deny it. She can't prove it but it's happened before with this judge when it comes to Moon Key residents. Money over justice would appear to be his motto. She's not giving up, though. It just may take a bit longer.'

I grabbed Buddha's squeaky shark, which he always decided was appropriate to chew when one of us got on the phone, and tossed it off the bed. 'But if Oliver was warned, he could just hide the mask now. Make it disappear and that's it. We have nothing that puts him in the Beckley home that evening.'

'I'm afraid so.'

That's it. Now, I was just plain mad. 'Want to go to an art show Friday night?'

Oliver White's mansion was every bit as impressive as the Beckleys', only with an air of unapologetic pretentiousness. We'd arrived fashionably late with Beth Anne and Carl, who'd picked us up in their limo – apparently we were the only couple who didn't utilize a limo service regularly – so the party was already in full swing when we were escorted into the grand room. If you could call it a party. It was a pretty subdued atmosphere. Piano music was being played live and there was an underlying drone of quiet conversations going on.

'Carl!' A woman waved with the tips of her fingers and then came over and wrapped herself around Beth Anne's husband like a tiny python in leopard print heels. 'The new sculpture is stunning. I may just bid on it for our own gardens.'

Carl seemed to be keeping very still. His hands stayed in his pockets. He'd apparently had more than one experience of being

prey to powerful women. 'I'm afraid it's too tall for our association to approve but thank you for the sentiment.'

Beth Anne cleared her throat. Loudly. It actually startled me.
'Eloise, may I introduce you to our friends and fellow art lovers.'
Her tone held a quality of steel I'd never heard from sweet little
southern belle Beth Anne before. Was it jealousy? Well, if so it
was nice to know even the uber-rich have to deal with basic
human emotions.

'Oh, hello, Beth Anne.' Eloise slid her slender, lightly freckled
arm off Carl, her red velvet lips imitating a smile as she surveyed
us. I was glad I was wearing Hope's cocktail dress because I'm
sure the woman could tell it was Christian Dior with one flick
of her narrowed hazel eyes. 'Of course,' she sniffed.

'This is Elle Pressley and Devon Burke. They were hoping to
get a large wall piece for their beach bungalow.'

'We are.' I nodded sagely, grabbing Devon's arm when I felt
myself tipping over in Hope's jewel-encrusted Valentino heels.
Who invented these torture devices anyway? I would never get
used to them. Or understand why women spent more on them
than my car was worth. No, that wasn't entirely true. I'd kind of
figured out the answer to that question in the last ten months of
working on Moon Key: because they could.

'Fabulous.' She straightened her back and looked bored
suddenly. 'Well, the pieces are set up for previewing so,' she
waved, 'smaller pieces are in the living room and larger pieces
are out back – go have a look. Auction starts by the pool promptly
at eight.'

I glanced at Beth Anne as I wobbled toward the various art
pieces. Her small jaw was clenched. I'd have to get the scoop
from her on Eloise later.

There was a buffet table set up against the left wall filled with
large silver trays of fruits and cheeses and covered buffet servers
lined up like giant silver beetles. My stomach growled. I noticed
everyone was avoiding the table like it had the plague. Was all
that food going to go to waste? I looked at it longingly. No, I
had to fit in tonight, act like I belonged here. Even if that meant
starving.

I dragged my gaze from the food with a whimper. That's when

I noticed the huge oil painting hanging above the marble fireplace. It was of a thin blond man standing in front of the same fireplace with one elbow leaning on the mantle. It was the most self-serving display I'd ever seen. This had to be Oliver White. At first my mouth just twitched, but the more I stared at it the more ridiculous it became. Who has a life-sized painting of themselves in their own living room? I began to giggle. Beth Anne glanced at me from the conversation she was having with a questioning head tilt.

'Elle?' Devon moved to stand in front of me. 'Do we need to get some air?'

I pressed my lips together, holding in a burst of manic giggling and nodded vigorously.

'We'll be outside,' Devon said to Carl with a smirk. 'We'll be sure to find your sculpture.' He took my hand and led me swiftly through the room and out of the opened sliding glass doors . . . where we ran smack into the real-life version of the painting.

Oliver White, live and in color, dressed fashionably in a pinstripe suit with a pink tie, blond hair swept off his forehead and a chemically whitened smile. 'Welcome,' he said warmly, holding his hand out. 'Oliver White. I don't believe I've had the pleasure.'

Devon shook his hand without hesitation, though I felt his grip tighten on my fingers. 'Devon Burke, and this is Elle Pressley. We were just heading out to take a look at Carl Wilkins' sculpture.'

'Sure, I'd be delighted to show you where it is.' As I endured his dead-fish handshake, he stared at me with bulgy hazel eyes, weirdly the same color as his girlfriend's. I couldn't shake the notion that he was dating himself. 'Have we met before? You look so familiar.'

I began to squirm. 'I . . . I don't think so,' I choked out through a forced smile.

His eyelids clenched for just an instant, a brief crack in his otherwise charming, easy-going manner. It was like watching a venomous snake peek its head out of a hole and take notice of you. It left me chilled as we followed him through backyard to stand in front of an eight- or nine-foot white stone sculpture.

He motioned to the tall piece. 'Here she is. Isn't she a beauty? One of my favorites that Carl's done. My girlfriend, Eloise, really wants to bid on this one, and I'm tempted to let her.'

'Yes, it is remarkable,' I said, having no idea what the two intertwining figures were supposed to represent. Reproduction, maybe? I'd keep my mouth shut in case it was like that Rorschach inkblot test where how you interpreted it told something about you. 'What do you think, honey?' I don't know why I called Devon 'honey' when I was being fake.

Devon shifted his feet. 'Yes. I do like the interplay of the figures and the wave nature. It invokes a certain sense of freedom but at the same time makes a statement about the impermanence of existence. Lovely.'

I nodded, though I felt a giggling spell coming on again. I squeezed his hand. He got the hint. 'I do think it's too large for the association to approve here, though,' he added quickly, repeating Carl's words. 'I think we'll take a look at some smaller pieces. Thank you.'

'Of course. I'll leave you to browse.' He pivoted to leave and then snapped his fingers and turned back, his eyes finding mine. 'I know, didn't I see you at the Beckleys' Halloween party?'

My mind whirled as my mouth dropped open. Did he just admit he was at the party? Out loud? My heart pounded in my ears. My throat dried up. 'I . . . I was there, yes,' I managed.

A ghost of a smile touched his lips but his eyes darkened. 'Thought so. I never forget a pretty face.' He sighed dramatically. 'Shame about Michael's death.'

What was he doing? Was he playing some game with me, like cat and mouse? Taunting me? Does he remember I bumped into him in the hallway while he was wearing the stolen mask? He must. Why else would he just admit being there that night when he wasn't invited? It was a warning. A threat. I crossed my arms protectively over my vulnerable stomach in case he suddenly lunged at me with a butcher knife. 'Yes. A shame.'

He did smile then. It was a slow spread of his mouth that didn't reach his eyes. 'Well, what's done is done. Enjoy yourself tonight, Miss Pressley.' He nodded. 'Mr Burke.' He left us then. I glanced up at Devon. His jaw clenched as he watched Oliver leave.

What's done is done? Did he mean murdering Michael? 'Is it just me or was that a warning?' I whispered. The hairs on my arms stood up.

He nodded once. 'Safe bet he remembers you and knows you

saw him with the mask. Otherwise why risk telling anyone he
was there that night?'

'Should we leave?' I asked, feeling suddenly very uncomfortable and exposed. Asking questions was one thing, being in the
sights of a possible killer was another.

'No. We're here now and we'll not get a second chance to be
in this house. We're going to have to see if he still has the mask.
Him admitting he was at the party that night means he may just
consider himself bulletproof enough to have kept it around. And
it'd be an ego boost for him, a reminder of how smart he is and
what he got away with.'

I clutched my stomach harder. 'Do you really think he's capable
of killing Michael?'

'No doubt.' Devon ran his hands over my arms and pressed
his lips against my forehead. 'We'll have to be very careful.' He
checked his phone. 'We have twenty minutes until the auction
starts and we need to be back out here. M.J. said there are two
rooms where Oliver would most likely have the mask on display.
The house is set up like the Beckleys' with two wings. There's
a large library near the theater over there.' He pointed to the left
of where we were. 'That's one possible place. In the interest of
time we'll have to split up, but I want you to get Beth Anne to
go with you. You two check the library and then come right back
here. I'll check the room in the right wing.'

I didn't know if I could get my feet to move. 'But, but . . .
do you think sneaking around his house is a good idea?'

He nodded, already distracted. 'If someone sees you, just say
you're looking for the toilet.'

Beth Anne was more than excited to be coming on a secret
expedition with me.

'If someone questions us, just say we're looking for the bathroom,' I whispered as we slipped through the unlocked sliding
glass doors. This side of the mansion was quiet and our heels
echoed loudly off the tiled floor. 'Hang on.' Balancing myself
on one leg, I reached down and removed one Valentino heel and
then the other. Spreading my toes on the cool tiles, I sighed with
relief.

'Right. Stealth mode,' Beth Anne giggled, removing her shoes
also. 'I've been here before. The library is amazing. He's got a

glass case full of signed first editions: Ernest Hemingway's *A Farewell to Arms*, George Orwell, Robert Frost.' She sighed. 'Anyway. Yeah, there's a bunch of art in there too that he was showing off to Carl.' She held out her arm and stopped me, then grabbed my hand and pulled me behind a pillar. Holding her finger to her lips, we pressed our bodies against the marble as two women in black pants and white shirts carrying silver trays passed us, talking and laughing. Something on those trays smelled so good, like sweet tomato sauce. Good thing Beth Anne was still holding my hand or in my weakened, hungry state I may have just forgotten about the mask and followed the food.

'OK,' she whispered. 'All clear.'

We stepped out and resumed the trek through the mansion to the library. 'I think you missed your calling,' I whispered to her.

She grinned. 'Does get the blood going, doesn't it?'

Just when I began to wonder if this was a never-ending hallway, Beth Anne said, 'Here we go.' She pushed open the stained-glass French doors and we slipped inside, shutting the doors behind us and flicking on the lights.

'Wow.' I took in the room. Massive bookshelves were stuffed full of various-sized books, sculptures were scattered about the room on pedestals and oil paintings hung on the walls between the floor-to-ceiling bookshelves. 'This is incredible. Like a museum.'

Beth Anne stood beside me, her arms crossed. 'It really is.' I felt her shiver. It was cooler in here. They probably had a separate temperature control so the Florida humidity wouldn't ruin the books. 'So, Oliver admitted to being in Michael's house on the night he was murdered?'

I lowered my voice and shrugged. 'Well, he admitted it to me. I doubt he would admit it if questioned by the police.'

'Right. We need evidence. Let's find that mask then,' she said, moving deeper into the library.

My feet padded silently on the glossy wood floor as I tiptoed to the right side of the room where some of the lighted display cases were set up. Peering into each one of them, I saw frail books with feathery pages, opened to show the signatures.

I was squinting into the glass to read a particular flowery inscription when I heard Beth Anne squeal. 'Elle! Over here.'

My heart fluttered. I was beside her in a few seconds, breathing hard and following her gaze to one of the bookshelves. 'Is that it?' she asked. 'It couldn't be that easy, right?'

I closed my eyes and brought up the memory of the Beckleys' party. The mask tilted down to look at me. I opened my eyes and was staring at the same carved wooden face.

'That's it.' I couldn't believe it. It was just sitting here on a bookshelf. Out in the open. I quickly glanced around. Was this a trap?

'Should we take it?' Beth Anne asked, an edge of excitement in her voice.

'No.' I pulled out my phone with shaking fingers. 'We'll just get a picture of it for Detective Vargas. Then they'll know where to search for it.' I snapped a few photos and then backed up so I could get in the whole bookshelf and then the room. Now I felt like I was holding contraband. We had to get out of here. 'OK, let's get back.'

We pulled open the doors, adrenaline pumping through both our bodies. Beth Anne squeaked. I took an involuntary step back.

Eloise stood there blocking our path, her arms crossed. She glanced into the room behind us. 'Ladies? Can I help you?'

I felt Beth Anne stiffen beside me. I opened my mouth to explain but nothing came out. Luckily Beth Anne was better than I was under pressure. 'Just showing Elle Oliver's collection of rare books. Hope that's all right?'

Eloise pushed her tongue into the side of her cheek but didn't answer. Her eyes just glittered at us behind coal-black lashes.

Beth Anne turned to me. She seemed calm on the outside but I could hear the tension in her higher-than-normal voice. 'Did you know Eloise is a writer?'

'No,' I managed, though my heart was beating so loudly I could barely hear my own voice. Surely Eloise could hear it beating, too?

'She is. Eloise, Elle's a big reader. Maybe you could dig up a signed copy of new your book, *Winding Roads*, for her before she leaves?'

'Oh . . .' Eloise seemed to soften. 'I'm sure I have one or two left over from the signing.' She moved past us, flicked off the light and pulled the doors closed behind her. 'I'll dig one up for you but right now the auction is about to start.'

'Bless your heart. That'd be very generous of you.' Beth Anne smiled and she waved the hand that wasn't holding her shoes. 'Yeah, we were just heading back.'

We found Devon already standing among the crowd that had gathered. I slipped an arm around his waist and whispered in his ear. 'Found it! Took some photos, too.'

He kissed my cheek and then whispered in my ear, 'That'll do nicely. I'll bid on a painting and then we'll be headin' out.'

I breathed in the night air and then let it out in a sigh of relief, feeling particularly proud of myself for managing a successful covert operation without giving in to anxiety. That was, until I happened to glance over at Eloise, who had her hand on Oliver's shoulder, whispering something in his ear. They both turned abruptly and looked straight at us.

I felt Beth Anne clutch my hand. She'd obviously seen them too. 'I think it's time to go,' she whispered.

We all stepped back as casually as possible, slipped deeper into the crowd and then popped out the other side. We hurried along the stone path around the house to the driveway where our limo waited. The whole time I kept waiting for those ninjas to drop down in front of us or for Oliver to grab us from behind.

A fit of giggles gripped me as we slid into the safety of the limo. Beth Anne rested her forehead on my shoulder and joined me, both of us breathing hard. It was either laugh or cry.

'Good grief.' She held her stomach. 'I feel like we've just got caught toilet papering the principal's house.'

Devon and Carl were removing their ties and staring at us sternly, which just made us laugh harder.

'Can I see the photos, Elle?' Devon said, holding out his hand.

'Oh, sure.' I wiped at my eyes and pulled out my phone to give to him. He showed them to Carl, who nodded.

When I caught my breath, I said, 'All that trouble for a wooden mask. I really hope he didn't kill Michael over something like that.'

'I have a feeling their feud went much deeper,' Devon answered.

As we rounded the circle drive to make our exit, I happened to glance up. The four garage doors were open. Inside sat a little red sports car . . . and a black Cadillac.

NINETEEN

M.J. met us at the police station Saturday afternoon with the insurance photos of the mask. We sat in a conference room and waited as Detective Salma Vargas compared the photos M.J. handed her with the ones on my phone from last night.

She nodded and pushed a business card across the table to me. 'All right. Elle, email me these. I'm meeting with a different judge in person later today. I'll share this with Detective Farnsworth and we should be able to do a search tonight.'

'Thank you,' M.J. said with relief. He turned to us. 'Let me buy you two lunch for all your trouble – it's the least I can do. Besides, it'll give me an excuse to check up on Lulu and make sure she's stopping to eat. The woman is a workaholic.'

Devon pushed away from the conference table and stood. 'That's very kind of you, but I told a friend of mine we'd meet him for lunch.'

'Bring him,' M.J. said. 'Please. I feel bad you've put yourselves in danger to help my family.'

Devon glanced at me and I nodded my agreement. It would be nice to see Lulu. 'All right then. Thank you.'

'Devon, can I speak to you a moment in private?' Salma said as we were heading out the door.

I glanced back at them. Salma had a slight smile as she held eye contact with Devon. *Don't react. Was I frowning?* I tried to will my face into a neutral expression.

Devon turned his attention to me then rested a hand on the curve in my back. 'Meet you outside.'

As I waited in front of the station, I tilted my face up to the sun and closed my eyes, pushing away the jealousy that was still trying to take root when it came to Detective Salma Vargas. I'd been avoiding asking Devon about their relationship because I didn't want him to think it bothered me at all but maybe it was time to ask. Maybe it would put a stop to all the painful fantasy scenarios I had in my head.

After a few minutes had passed, I felt a strong arm around my waist and I was twirled around and kissed vigorously. Catching my breath, I opened my eyes. Devon was grinning.

'Good news?' I smirked, leaning back so I could see him.

'She's got it. The subpoena for Seaside Boats' sales records for the year my parents were killed.'

'Oh, Devon, that's fantastic news. I hope that leads straight to the second boat.'

'I hope so too, and hope is something I haven't had for a long time.' He squeezed me in a tight hug and then took my hand. 'Come on – let's go grab Quinn for a celebratory lunch.'

When we arrived, M.J. had already secured us a table by the window. Lulu was standing at the table in black cotton pants and a snug white T-shirt, one hand resting on her lower back. My eyes automatically went to her stomach where I noticed the slight rounding from the life growing there. She was going to be even more adorable when she popped.

'Well, hello, my friends!' She greeted us with an enthusiastic hug and then we introduced her and M.J. to Quinn.

'Hello.' Quinn shook hands with M.J. but his eyes were glued to Lulu. He smoothed down his wavy hair and was speechless for the first time since I'd met him. He held out his hand tentatively.

'Oh, stop, we're not so formal around here,' Lulu laughed, hugging him as well. Did he actually blush? I smiled to myself. 'Sit. Sit. I was just telling M.J. I've got a new shrimp chowder lunch special I'd like for y'all to try if you don't mind. I need some honest opinions.'

'Sure, we'd love to,' I said, taking the chair Devon had pulled out for me beside the window. 'By the way, we got to meet your mother. She was so sweet and very helpful.'

Lulu's smile brightened. 'Yeah, she's a trip, isn't she? Had nothing but good things to say about y'all, too. OK, sit tight, I'll have the soup sent right out.' She whirled and we all watched her flutter around, dropping her magic fairy dust on a few unsuspecting tables on her way back to the kitchen.

M.J. sighed. 'I don't think the baby is going to slow her down one bit.'

'She's in the family way, is she?' Quinn said, surprised and maybe a bit disappointed.

M.J. nodded and pride was written all over his face.

'Yours then?' Quinn seemed to be looking at M.J. with a new respect.

'Yes,' M.J. said. 'I can't believe in eight months I'll be a father.'

'Congratulations.' Quinn held up his water glass. 'Health and a long life to all. *Sláinte.*'

We clinked glasses and Quinn grinned at Devon and added, 'Also a toast to good news. May it lead to the truth.'

'Good news you can share?' M.J. asked curiously.

'I suppose.' Devon's eyes glowed with renewed hope. 'Remember I told you about my parents' deaths? Well, I haven't been convinced it was an accident, and we've just got a way to move forward in the investigation.' He proceeded to explain the significance of the new subpoena to M.J., who listened with rapt attention.

I stared out the window as they talked since I'd heard all the details before. My mind was going back over Michael's murder. I should just leave it alone, especially after the tense night at Oliver White's house, but I couldn't. The need to know what really happened was like an all-consuming fire in my brain. I could barely think of anything else. Now I knew how Devon felt about his parents' deaths.

Well, hopefully, Salma would get the warrant to search Oliver White's mansion tonight and question him. It'd be great if he would just confess, let Breezy off the hook and put this all to rest. I knew that would never happen, though. Then I had a thought. He may not confess to the police but his ego may lead him to confess to me. Just like he did when he boldly admitted to me he was in the Beckley house that night. He thought he was so smart. What if I could get him to confess and record it? There was no way to even try that without putting myself in danger, was there? I would have to get him alone. Then what?

'Elle?' Devon placed a hand on my thigh. 'Where've you gone off to?'

'Oh, sorry.' I turned my attention back to the table. There was a steaming bowl of soup in front of me. 'I'm here. Just worrying about Breezy and fantasizing about how nice it would be if Oliver White confessed.'

M.J. ran his spoon through the thick chowder and sighed. 'Not going to happen. Even if he is guilty, the man is too selfish to confess and give us closure.'

'Sorry about your da,' Quinn said, picking up his own spoon. 'Brutal thing for a family to go through.'

'Thank you.' M.J.'s eyes flashed with pain as he glanced up. Then they softened as Lulu came toward us. 'It is. But Lulu and our baby are all that matter to me now.'

She practically vibrated as she reached our table. 'Have you tried it yet? What do y'all think?' She beamed at us, despite the tendrils of sweat-soaked hair sneaking out from beneath her chef's hat. She obviously loved her job.

We all took a bite and made noises to show our approval. It really was delicious.

As our lunch was winding down, Devon got a text. 'Sorry,' he said, then addressed Quinn. 'Salma would like us to meet her at Seaside Boats in twenty minutes. They're going in.' Quinn nodded. Devon turned to me. 'Elle, do ya mind?'

'Of course not,' I said quickly. 'I can call a cab to get back to the ferry.'

'Nonsense,' M.J. said. 'I'm going back to Moon Key now so you can ride with me.'

Slipping on my sunglasses, I admired the black, cockpit-like interior of the Porsche 911 convertible as M.J. drove us to the ferry. 'Wouldn't have pegged you for a convertible sports car type,' I said.

'No?' M.J.'s lip twitched. 'Well, I'm sad to say it but you're correct. This is a rental. Lulu is a convertible sports car type and loves to cruise the beach with the wind in her hair.'

I could definitely see that. I was struck again by what an odd couple they were, the wild-child free spirit and the conservative. Maybe she was attracted to M.J.'s stability and rational way of looking at the world? They do say opposites attract. Or maybe it was his bank account? Guilt immediately pinched me. No, she didn't seem like the gold-digger type. 'So, how did you and Lulu become friends?'

'Oh.' He turned onto the causeway and I felt the powerful pull of the little car as he accelerated. 'My family's known her for a decade. Back when we met, we were both in our early twenties. I was immediately smitten. She was working as a waitress at the restaurant, but it was called The Crab Café then and the food was not good. We wouldn't have ever gone back but Lulu begged us to the next night. Said she'd have something special for us. Can you imagine refusing Lulu anything?' He chuckled.

'No, I can't,' I said, and meant it.

'Even Mom couldn't resist going back to see how this fire-cracker of a girl was going to fulfill her enthusiastic promise to make the horrible meal up to us.'

He suddenly stepped on the break as a white Mustang veered into his lane. His face flushed as he hit his horn and yelled, 'Idiot!' at the lady on her cell phone. I gripped my bag tighter in anticipation of a confrontation, but she just waved an apologetic hand out the window and M.J. calmed down.

'Sorry. So, anyway, the owner let Lulu cook us up some authentic shrimp gumbo and we were hooked. He also began to let her spend time in the kitchen after that instead of bussing dirty plates in the dining room. It was win-win. Lulu just became more and more a part of our family every time we came back to Florida. Four years ago my parents bought out the restaurant for her. Of course, she's insisting on paying them back.'

'Wow, I know you two have been friends for a long time. What changed that?'

He shrugged. 'Honestly, I don't know. I think she's always known I've been in love with her. I even managed to get up the nerve to ask her out a couple of years back, but I guess the timing was never right. This year, she just looked at me differently and said, *Let's give it a shot.* You could have knocked me over with a feather. But I'm not questioning it. And now the baby.' He grinned at me. 'I am just a blessed man.'

I watched a pod of dolphins gliding through the water below the bridge as we sat in the traffic breathing car exhaust and briny, salty air. 'And she's a lucky girl to be so appreciated.' I wondered if Devon thought that way about me. He did seem to. I guess I was a lucky girl, too.

'Can you keep a secret?' M.J. watched me from behind gold aviator sunglasses. The breeze ruffled his usually perfectly combed hair and made him look like a kid.

Could I? Does keeping a secret mean I couldn't tell Devon? I'd have to play that one by ear. 'Sure, what's up?'

He gripped the steering wheel tighter and nodded, like he was talking himself into something. 'I'm going to propose to Lulu next weekend.'

I twisted in my seat to face him. 'Really? How exciting! When? Where? Do you have a plan?'

'God, I'm so nervous. Yes, I have a plan. The ring is being made as we speak, and I'm going to throw a party on our yacht next Friday with friends and family. I want it to be special but traditional. Down on one knee, all that.'

'You're going to do it in front of everyone?' Well, that was brave. I've seen these things go horribly wrong on TV.

'Do you think she'll say no?' He looked worried suddenly.

'No, no,' I assured him. Though I had no idea. Best that she be the one to break that egg if it was going to happen. 'I think it'll be fine.'

'You and Devon should come. She really likes you, Elle. She doesn't have many girlfriends since she works all the time. Her mom is pretty much it.'

'Oh, well, I really like her, too.' I moved my attention to the vast Gulf waters. I'd never been on a boat before, let alone a yacht, and wondered how my anxiety would handle that. Would I flip out when we started moving away from the shore line and swan dive overboard like a crazy person? Only one way to find out. 'Sure, I'll check with Devon but I'd be honored to be there.'

TWENTY

I had grown to love Sundays. Sundays with Devon meant a lazy morning cuddling in bed, then a leisurely breakfast cooked together, then I'd go down to the shore and do some yoga while the dogs played and he'd go for his run, coming back all hot and sweaty so, of course, we'd have to share a shower. Wasting water in this day and age would be a sin, after all.

Today we'd had an added bonus. Salma had texted Devon that they'd completed the search of Oliver White's house early this morning and found the mask right where we said it would be, and he was now at the station for questioning. We'd high-fived over scrambled eggs. By noon, she'd texted that he'd been released but Farnsworth was seriously considering him a suspect now. That was excellent news for Breezy.

After dinner, we'd dragged some beach chairs down to the sand where the water was gently lapping at our toes, to watch the blue sky morph into streaks of orange, red and pink before the sun did its disappearing act and marked the end of another day. It was chilly this evening and the water was cold, about ten degrees colder in just a few weeks, but refreshing as long as I didn't submerge too much of my foot. I dug my toes into the wet sand and watched a sailboat making its way slowly across the span of water in the distance. Buddha and Petey were sniffing something in the sand a few feet away and then Petey shoved his nose in it, flopped down and began to roll around on his back.

'Ew, Petey! Come here!'

Petey jumped up, shook himself vigorously and hopped over, looking very proud of himself. Buddha ambled along behind him in case I was giving out treats. One sniff told me the object of their attention was indeed a dead fish. I shook my head. 'Yes, you go on and look proud of yourself. You've just earned yourself a nice bubble bath.' I picked up a seashell by my chair and tossed it away from us. Petey let out a bark and raced after it, leaving the smell of dead fish wafting in his wake.

Devon chuckled as I pulled my sweatshirt over my nose. 'He's got a talent for finding dead things, that one.'

Speaking of dead things . . . My mind jerked back to Oliver White. Could he really be Michael's killer? It's hard to know what's in someone's mind and heart. He could've hated him that much that an argument just pushed him over the edge. I still thought Cali was a more likely suspect even though Selene was giving her an alibi. One bonus of going to M.J.'s engagement party on the yacht was that I'd finally get to spend some time around Cali. Surely, as his sister, she would be there. But back to Oliver . . .

'I can't believe Oliver didn't hide the mask after Eloise caught me and Beth Anne in the library. He must've known we'd seen it.'

Devon shrugged. 'People aren't as clever as they'd like to think they are.' He reached over and pulled me onto his lap. 'Piece of advice, love. Don't try to figure out why people do what they do. It will drive you mad.' This wasn't the first time he'd given me that particular piece of advice.

He pushed the unruly waves of hair out of my face and held them back while he kissed my cheek, my nose and the other cheek, finally landing on my mouth. I completely lost all track of time and space as his warm, sweet kisses continued down my neck. Then the persistent sound of a helicopter intruded on my bliss. Squinting, I glanced up. The big metal noise machine was awfully low.

Devon lifted his head with a groan. 'What now?' Then he adjusted me on his lap and squinted at the helicopter now circling the area like a buzzard. 'That's a news'copter. Come on.'

We hurried back up through the soft sand, the dogs running past us and into the house. Devon checked his phone first and his face paled. 'Jaysis.'

'What? What happened?' My chest was hammering and I was having a hard time catching my breath. In the background, Buddha was squeaking his rubber shark, but that was barely registering. Something was wrong.

He looked up but he was looking through me. I could see his mind twisting, trying to wrap around something.

I tented my fingers and held them over my nose and mouth,

now positive by the look on his face that something really bad
had happened. 'Devon?'

'It's Oliver.' He grabbed the remote off the coffee table and
flipped on the flat-screen TV. We sat down in shock and watched
the news show Oliver White's mansion from a bird's-eye view.
The helicopter was shooting live. Devon slowly handed me his
phone and I read the text from Salma: *Oliver White found by
gardener dead in his pool. On our way.*

Beth Anne burst through the French doors ten minutes early
Monday morning, startling Buddha from his pre-class nap. 'Good
God in heaven, Elle! Did you hear about Oliver?' Shakespeare
was turning circles beside her, straining on his copper-studded
leather leash. He was hopped up on her energy like he'd just
smoked a crack pipe full of it. This was going to be a tough
class.

'Yes.' I shook my head and untangled myself from lotus pose.
Standing to accept her hug, I added, 'I can't believe it.'

Her neck and chest were flushed and her ponytail was still
damp from her morning shower. 'We were just in his house. I
mean, he wasn't the nicest person in the world but . . . dead?
What is happening on Moon Key? I'm definitely having our
security system updated. People are dropping like flies.' Reaching
down, she released Shakespeare and he immediately pounced on
Buddha to play. Buddha rolled over on his back as if to say,
'Yeah, yeah, you got me.'

'Well . . .' I bit my lip. Should I share what Salma had told
us, knowing whatever I told Beth Anne would fly through the
gossip chain faster than the speed of light? She did put herself
at risk to help me and Devon find the mask. OK, I'd tell her but
I'd add a disclaimer anyway just to shift the responsibility of
keeping the secret onto her shoulders. 'Don't let this get out, but
Detective Vargas says even though the media is calling it a suicide
and the police have released the house, it looks fishy to them.'

Beth Anne's brown eyes widened, sending her mascara-laden
lashes up to her eyebrows. 'Like someone,' she lowered her voice
to a whisper, 'killed him, too?'

I shrugged. 'Maybe.'

She perched her hands on her slender hips, looking thoughtful.

'The same person that killed Michael Beckley? Maybe a serial killer?'

I bit the inside of my cheek thoughtfully. Serial killer? No, this seemed more personal. 'I don't know. The police were looking at Oliver for Michael's death. So if he didn't do it, why would the real killer off Oliver and eliminate the person who was possibly going to take the blame for it? If Oliver did kill Michael then the suicide would make sense since they were closing in on him. But . . .' The other ladies were starting to filter through the doors and heading our way. 'But if he was murdered, too? Maybe he knew something the killer didn't want him telling the police.'

'Well, I know what Beth Anne is talking about,' Violet said as she unrolled her mat in the front row. 'Those stupid news helicopters kept me up all night. Again.'

'Violet!' Beth Anne whirled on her friend. 'Don't be so insensitive. This is not about your beauty sleep. A man is dead.'

'They're saying it was suicide.' Whitley took her spot next to Violet and unrolled her own mat. Maddox, her greyhound, sniffed the other dogs with his stubby tail wagging. 'Which doesn't make a bit of sense. That man was way too in love with himself to commit suicide.'

'Well, the news said there was a suicide note found.' Beth Anne gave me a knowing look but, to her credit, she didn't share the information I'd given her. Not yet anyway.

Whitley sighed. 'Well, at least the reporters can't camp out on Oliver's street like vultures. Though I did hear two of them tried to dock in the private marina and security caught 'em.'

'We'll have to buy those rent-a-cops a bottle of champagne.' Violet smirked as she stretched out and wiggled her bare toes. 'I'm reading a book about how well men respond to positive reinforcement. Think I'll buy Jarvis a car. He was admiring one of those new Lexus convertibles at the Florence Wine Bar the other night.'

A car? I wanted to ask her if she was serious but managed to keep my mouth shut. Good thing, too, because she apparently was very serious.

'Sounds like someone's getting attached,' Whitley teased her.

She tilted her head thoughtfully toward her friend. 'Oh, God, you're right. No car.'

*   *   *

The class went relatively smoothly considering everyone's lack of sleep last night. Between classes, I checked my phone. There was a group text from M.J. to both me and Devon inviting us to Michael's wake tomorrow evening at the Beckley mansion. *Might help with closure*, he'd added, presumably directed at me since I'd found Michael's body. I'd never been to a wake before. Devon had texted him back already that we'd be honored to be there, but I wasn't so sure I could handle it.

I texted Devon separately: *Will Michael's body be at the wake?* He replied: *It won't. It's just to celebrate Michael's life.* Well, that sounded like a good idea to me.

Darkness had fallen by the time we parked the Jeep in the circle behind the other cars at the Beckley mansion, which was even more impressive with all the landscape lights glowing. As we approached the front porch we could hear a heated argument.

I leaned into Devon. 'Maybe we should wait?'

We paused, but Selene noticed us near the steps and waved us up. 'Please, come on in.'

Awkwardly, we approached Selene and Flavia. Selene was holding a bouquet of white roses protectively in her arms and Flavia was scowling up at her. 'Thank you for coming and ignore my mother, she's just being dramatic.'

'Hello, Flavia.' I waved awkwardly.

'Hello,' she replied but kept her glare locked on Selene. 'What you two think? Is appropriate for boyfriend to bring flowers to dead husband's wake?'

Selene narrowed her eyes. 'He's a good friend, Mother, and flowers are always appropriate.'

'Ack!' She whirled her wheelchair around and threw up her hands. 'I give up.' Then she turned her head so I could see her profile. 'Elle, I have something for you. Come.'

We followed her into the grand room where family and friends were milling about. An enlarged photo of Michael sat on an easel at the back of the room. He had his hands clasped in front of him and was beaming his signature smile at the camera. Happier times. I tried to imprint the photo on my brain. I'd much rather remember him that way. I watched Selene hand off the flowers to a housekeeper and then join the crowd.

'I'm going to go find M.J.,' Devon said, kissing my forehead and leaving me alone with Flavia. His spicy male scent lingered after he'd gone, and I breathed it in for comfort.

Flavia reached into the pocket of her black Mumu, pulled out an evil eye necklace that looked like hers and held it up to me. 'Much bad juju on dis island right now. You wear dis, yes?'

Smiling, I accepted it, slipped it over my head and tucked the creepy blue eye under the neckline of my dress. 'That's so sweet of you to think of me. I will, thank you.'

Lulu bounced toward us. 'Elle, so glad you're here.' She smelled like vanilla and cinnamon when she hugged me. I suddenly wanted a beignet. 'Come on.' She led me over to where M.J. and Devon were standing.

M.J. didn't look good. 'Glad you both could make it,' he said. His voice sounded hoarse and his hand was shaking as it grasped mine. Lulu glanced at him and I could see the worry in her eyes. Her hand went protectively to her stomach.

'Wouldn't miss it,' Devon said quietly. He squeezed M.J.'s shoulder in support.

As the two men began to talk, Lulu threaded her arm through mine and leaned in, whispering, 'I'm really worried about M.J. I heard him break down in the bathroom the other day, and he actually smashed the mirror.'

'Anger is a natural part of the grieving process. I'm sure it'll just take time,' I whispered back. 'At least he has you and the baby, something happier to concentrate on.'

She sighed almost imperceptibly. 'If he didn't have us he would fall apart, for sure.'

Was that doubt? I hoped that she wouldn't say yes to marrying M.J. just to keep him from falling apart. If she did say yes this weekend, I hoped it would be because she loved him and wanted a future with him.

She shook off whatever was bothering her and straightened her shoulders. 'OK, I'm supposed to be eating for two. Let's go grab some food.'

'Girl after my own heart.' I smiled as she led me over to the table full of breads, salads, olives and cheeses, where we greeted some other folks dressed in black, filling their plates. I decided so far I liked wakes way more than art auctions.

Lulu popped a grape in her mouth. 'It's rude not to eat in this house, anyway. *Yiya* will have a fit if any of her *spanakopita* is left over.'

'That would be a sin.' I grabbed a piece of *spanakopita* and then, remembering the little slice of flaky heaven it was, piled on another piece.

Lulu grinned and followed suit. 'Oh, it's on, girlfriend. I can't let you out-eat me. I have a reputation, you know.'

When we returned to where the bulk of the company had gathered, I took the empty seat between Devon and an elderly lady I hadn't met. Selene was in the middle of telling a story about one of Michael's pranks that had everyone chuckling and nodding. The lady next to me held up her glass of red wine in a toast. 'That was Michael. Always trying to make us smile.' She turned to me with a lowered voice while Selene continued the story. 'How did you know him, dear?'

I stopped chewing my stuffed green olive as a flash of Michael hanging from the ceiling rafters lodged itself in my brain. I couldn't shake it. I knew I was staring at her in silence for far too long as her expression was shifting from kindness to worry. Finally I couldn't hold it back; the tears sprang forth and a loud sob escaped.

'I'm sorry,' I croaked as I bolted from the room with my plate. My face burned. I was mortified. Crying and chastising myself, I turned right at the fish tank, my only thought being escape. The problem was I was on autopilot and going the only direction I knew . . . which led me straight to the back kitchen. I dropped my plate on the floor and covered my nose and mouth in horror as I realized I was standing in the kitchen doorway. It was all too real.

Everything came back like it was happening all over again: the smell of the burning cakes; the confusion and then the panic when I realized Michael didn't have a pulse; the sound of my own voice screaming for help. I stared at the space. It didn't seem right that it was now empty. That Michael was actually gone. I felt disorientated and dizzy.

Luckily, Devon, M.J. and Lulu had rushed after me and were now steering me out of the back door and into the fresh night air.

I leaned over and grasped my knees, trying to suck in air as a knot tightened in my chest.

'Oh, Elle, go ahead, get it out, sweetie.' Lulu rubbed my back as Devon pulled me up into his arms, allowing me to wet the front of his shirt with snot and tears.

'I'm so sorry,' I sniffed, accepting a handkerchief from M.J. I wasn't even a part of this family and I had just ruined the whole purpose of Michael's wake. We were supposed to be celebrating his life and remembering the good times. 'I don't know what's wrong with me.'

'I know,' Lulu said. 'Being a human with emotions is such a pesky thing.'

I looked up at her through blurry, swelling eyes and finally smiled. 'It really is.'

She grabbed my hand. 'Come on, we'll just hang out here and enjoy this gorgeous night air for a bit.'

We pulled out the chairs around the patio deck.

'I'll go grab you some water,' Devon said, kissing the top of my head. 'Be right back.'

Selene rushed out as he went in. 'Elle, are you OK?'

My face grew hot. She should be in there telling stories and remembering her husband fondly. But because of me she was out here. 'Yes, I'm so sorry I caused a scene. Oh, God.' I started to stand up. 'I need to clean up that broken plate before someone gets hurt.'

'It's fine.' She came over and gripped my shoulders, looking into my eyes with a sympathetic smile. 'It's already taken care of. It had to be quite a shock to find Michael the way you did. Believe me, the grief hits me at unexpected times, too. It's just how it works.'

'Thank you, Selene. You're too kind, and again, I'm so sorry for your loss.' How strange rich people's lives were. Break something, make a mess and someone else was right there to clean it up. As she gave me one last squeeze and left us, I let my gaze drift to the tall bushes that separated their house from Oliver White's. 'I wonder how Eloise is holding up. Should we go and give her our condolences?'

'She's not there,' M.J. said quietly. 'Cali said she flew out Sunday morning to Germany for a book convention, so I don't even know if she knows Oliver's dead yet.'

'Speaking of Cali, where is she?' Lulu asked. Her eyes blazed like a hot gas fire. 'She should really be here to honor her father today. It's time for her to let go of whatever grudge she has against him.'

'She's here.' M.J. rubbed the bridge of his nose. 'Somewhere. Pouting because Sam left.'

'You know, your mom really should've let Breezy come to the wake.' Lulu crossed her arms over her stomach. 'She knows the poor girl didn't kill Michael.'

'She didn't say anything when Breezy came to the funeral. But until the police clear her, she can't have her coming to the house.' M.J. shrugged. 'She's trying to be fair.'

'Fair? Is it fair that someone who actually cared about Michael can't come to celebrate his life, but that dirt bag trainer can show up with flowers and Selene defends his right to be here?' Lulu swiped at her nose with the back of her hand.

Devon and I shared a glance and then I thought about Sven. Selene said he'd left the party when she went upstairs with Cali, but how do we know that's true? If she left his side at that point, he could've gone anywhere. Including the back kitchen.

M.J. immediately went to her, kneeling on the stone in his dress slacks without hesitation. 'You're absolutely right. Mom should have never let him near the house today. It was tacky and Dad didn't deserve that. Unfortunately I can't do anything about it, but I'll talk to her about Breezy, OK?'

'Yeah, yeah.' Lulu's shoulders fell and she gave him an apologetic smile. 'Sorry, it's these baby hormones. They make me crazy.'

M.J. rested a hand protectively on her belly. I suddenly felt like we were outsiders intruding on a private moment.

'You know, I'm not feeling very well,' I said. 'Do you think it would be rude to duck out early?'

M.J. shook his head and stood. 'Not at all. This is a stressful time and we appreciate you coming.'

We said our goodbyes on the way out and made our way to the Jeep. I heard the rumble of a garage door. Drained from my emotional reaction to being in the kitchen, I was leaning on Devon's arm and not paying much attention. That is, until Cali drove by us in a black Cadillac. Startled, I only caught the first two letters on the license plate: TR.

'I'm telling you, that was the Cadillac that ran me off the road,' I said as Devon cranked up the Jeep.

'You know the Cadillac is the car of choice for wealthy people, right? It holds its value so they are a dime a dozen on this island. And have you seen the way people drive here? I'm sure someone running you off the road was just an accident. If they really wanted to hurt you . . . car versus bike wouldn't be very hard to do.'

I stroked the outline of my new evil eye pendant under my dress. 'So, you don't think it's possible Cali killed her dad and tried to run me over because I've been asking too many questions?'

'Anything's possible.' Devon suddenly wasn't paying attention. His gaze was focused over my shoulder. I turned my head to see what he was staring at as he slowed the Jeep to a crawl.

'Isn't that . . . Eloise?' I asked as we passed Oliver's mansion. It had to be. She was throwing bags in the trunk of the sports car I'd seen in their garage earlier. 'Isn't she supposed to be in Germany?'

Devon glanced at me. 'I guess she came straight back as soon as she heard the news about Oliver . . . or she never left.'

He brought the car to a full stop as a man emerged from the front door, carrying a leather satchel.

'Is that . . . Sven?' But I didn't even have to ask. There was no mistaking the six-foot-seven bulk of man.

TWENTY-ONE

'I never liked that woman.' Beth Anne had her arms crossed, her calm from class fading as I told her about seeing Eloise as we were leaving the Beckleys. 'She's been after Carl since she first laid her beady little eyes on him. She's one of those women that have to take every man within a fifty-mile radius.'

'So, you think she would've cheated on Oliver?'

'I don't have to think, I know.'

'What about with Sven? We also saw him at her house last night.'

'Sven? He's like the Moon Key gigolo. He keeps the bored socialites here happy and they keep him rich.'

So it wasn't just Selene? He could have been having an affair with Eloise, too. Is it just a coincidence that both women he was sleeping with now had dead husbands? I moved Sven to the top of my suspect list.

'Beth Anne, do you think you can find out if Eloise even went to Germany like she told Cali she was doing? And if not, why didn't she go? Devon is going to mention it to Detective Farnsworth to check into, but you know how overworked they are. Who knows when he'll be able to get to it.'

She held up a hand. 'Say no more. I'm on it.' She clipped Shakespeare's leash on and gave me a one-armed hug. 'I'll call you later.'

'Thanks.' As she was leaving, Lulu was coming in the door. Surprised, I went over to greet her. 'Hey! What are you doing here?'

She squeezed me in a tight hug and then bent down to scratch Buddha's ears as he ambled over to sniff her. I noticed she looked tired. 'I picked up some of Breezy's clothes for her from the Beckleys and brought 'em to Novia. Thought I'd stop in and say hi. Do you have time for lunch?'

Disappointed, I said, 'Oh, I have my second class starting in fifteen minutes.' Then I had an idea. 'Why don't you stay and do some yoga with us? It'll be relaxing after all the stress lately and good for the baby. Then we can have lunch afterwards.'

She moved to the side as a few clients started coming in. 'But I don't have a dog.'

I laughed. 'I can't imagine you've followed the rules much in your life.'

Her face melted into a genuine smile and she shook her finger at me. 'You know me too well, Elle. All right, I'll stay.' I noticed her fingernails were bare and manicure-free, too, which made me feel better. Being around all these high-maintenance women was making me question my own priorities way too much.

'Good. I'll just grab you a mat.'

'I do feel better, thanks. Now, I'm starving so you have to eat lots of food with me so I don't feel like a pig. My treat.' She wrapped her arm through mine as we headed to the café.

I laughed. 'Well, at least you have an excuse, but believe me, you don't have to ask me twice. I do not subscribe to the rabbit diet the women on this island are so fond of.'

'See, this is why we're friends. I don't trust anyone who can't appreciate the importance of a tasty meal.'

The place was packed so we had to wait a few minutes for someone to leave before Marisol led us to a table by the window. 'Enjoy, ladies.'

Buddha sniffed the edge of the table to see if there were any treats yet and, finding it lacking, did a few turns and plopped himself down on the cushion between us.

'This place does good business,' Lulu looked around, impressed. 'Maybe I should allow my customers to bring their dogs.'

'You do good business, too,' I said. 'I've seen it packed.'

She waved her hand. 'Yes, it's all good. I'm not complaining. I don't even care about making money as long as I can keep cooking.' She rubbed her stomach. 'Though I don't know how a baby is going to fit into that. I keep some pretty long hours.'

'Thank you,' I said to the waiter as he poured us filtered water and then set some in a bowl next to Buddha. 'A baby will change your life, sure. But you and M.J. will figure it out. At least you have support and a partner. I watched my mom struggle to raise me alone and it was tough for her. And me.'

'I'm sorry, Elle.' She sighed. 'Yeah, my mom had financial support from my father, but that was it. He left us when I was four and the pressure from his family finally got to him. Mom was lonely and it was hard on us. I don't want that for my baby. But . . .' She let her hands fall in her lap and stared out the window. Then she glanced back at me, tears shining in her eyes.

'Oh, what's wrong?' I leaned closer to her as she dabbed at the corner of her eyes with a napkin. It disturbed me to see her upset. 'Lulu?'

She tried to smile. 'I think M.J.'s going to ask me to marry him. I saw a call from a jeweler on his phone and he has this big thing planned on his yacht Friday evening.'

'Oh.' I bit my lip. Should I tell her she's right? 'And that would be a bad thing?'

'I don't know. Maybe in time. It's just that everything's happening so fast. I feel like ever since I watched that little "pregnant" sign appear on that stick I've just been catapulted into this brand-new plan for my life and I kind of feel like I've lost control. Like I don't have a choice anymore. As a woman who's always prided myself on my independence, it's hard to take. I feel like by protecting this baby, I'm betraying myself.' A tear fell then as her face crumpled. 'Maybe even betraying this baby. Oh, Elle, I'm afraid I've made a terrible mistake. My father passed away and I was a mess. It began as him comforting me and one thing led to another . . . it was a mistake. And now . . .'

Wow. That's not how M.J. saw it at all. On one hand, my heart ached for her as she opened up to me. On the other hand, I found myself enjoying the closeness, appreciating her trusting me with these doubts. 'Well, you could have a really long engagement.'

'We could but . . .' She moved her gaze to mine, her fingers playing with the knife restlessly. She licked her lip and I could see the struggle playing out on her face. She wanted to tell me something difficult. She opened her mouth and . . .

'Elle!' Beth Anne appeared at our table, a whirlwind of energy. 'I have the scoop!' She pulled up a chair, tossed her plaid Ralph Lauren handbag on the table and leaned in. I glanced at Lulu – she was shutting down. Opportunity missed. 'So, Eloise had spread the word around that she was going to a book convention in Germany but guess where she was really going? A private little vacation with Sven. They were both still on Moon Key when Oliver died.'

Just then my phone vibrated. It was a text from Devon:

Salma checked the list from the Halloween party. They did not interview Sven. He was gone before the police arrived. Farnsworth is going to try to bring him in for an interview.

'Whoa.' I placed my phone back on the table. 'Apparently Sven *was* gone from the Beckleys' party before the police arrived. Detective Farnsworth is going to track him down for questioning. Could Sven have so much power over these women that they'd help him get rid of their husbands?' I thought about Selene. No, she really seemed to care about Michael and treated Sven as a fling. But he did bring her flowers, which shows an emotional attachment. Maybe, if Sven was the killer, he acted alone.

Beth Anne shrugged. 'I think most of the women know he's just a roll in the hay. Nothing serious, so no. But maybe . . .' Her eyes got that sparkle that they do when she's putting together a plot. 'Maybe Sven starts to get possessive of the women and wants to get rid of the husbands to protect his financial security? So he offs them on his own.'

She might be on to something. 'Or maybe just the husbands who start to protest?'

I moved my gaze to the window, biting the inside of my cheek until the sharp tang of blood made me stop. Breezy only had a little over a week left before they'd officially charge her with Michael's murder. But I wasn't sure I wanted to put myself in danger by poking around trying to expose the real killer, not to mention put my friends in danger.

When I'd asked Devon why he was letting *me* ask so many of the questions in this investigation – since it had become obvious it wasn't just for Breezy's sake – he'd told me the best thing to do when you fall off a horse is to get right back on. At first I was mad. But then I realized it made sense. In his own way he was trying to help me, to make sure everything we went through didn't feed my anxiety and fear. Once fear is allowed to take up residence, it's paralyzing. I'd learned that the hard way. God, I needed this whole thing to be over for Breezy's sake and my sanity. I made my decision and for once it wasn't based on fear.

I turned back to my friends and clutched my hands together on the table. 'Well, there's only one thing to do. Lulu, you have to talk Selene into bringing Sven on the yacht on Friday. She has to make sure he's there so we can figure out some way to get him to talk. Even if we have to confront him directly.'

She shook her head, her springy curls emphasizing her protest. 'I don't know. M.J. won't like that at all.'

'That's why you have to explain to him that we're just doing it to set Sven up – to see if we can figure out if he had any part in the death of these two men. I'll have Devon talk to M.J., too. Between the two of you he should listen.'

'How are you going to get Sven to talk, though?' Beth Anne asked. 'Oh, I know . . . we could get him really plastered. Or maybe you could get hold of some of that truth serum – that's a real thing, right?'

Lulu blinked hard but was nice enough not to squash Beth Anne's idea. Who knew? Maybe if you're rich enough, anything's for sale. 'He's obviously not the sharpest tool in the shed. Surely we could get him to slip up. Maybe we could get him angry enough to blurt out the truth.'

'Or we could seduce him.' Beth Anne bit the red tip of her index fingernail and wiggled her eyebrows.

I sighed. 'We may have to try both. Beth Anne, maybe you could play the part of a bored housewife looking for a little fun,' I said. 'We'll have to play it by ear. But one thing we have to make sure we do is record any interactions with him.'

Lulu still looked doubtful. 'All right. We'll need all the girl power we can get. Are you sure you can make it Friday night, Beth Anne?'

'Of course,' she said, grabbing both our hands. 'I wouldn't miss helping y'all out for the world.'

'Lulu, do you think Cali will be there, too?' I asked.

'She's supposed to be. I overheard her and M.J. have a big blowout over it. He said she will be there or he'll make sure their dad's plan to cut off her inheritance goes through. She said fine but she's not going to act like she's happy to be there . . . along with some choice words I won't repeat. They've really been at each other's throats lately.'

'Yikes.' I wasn't so sure having both the murder suspects on one yacht was a good idea, but it was time to force the situation. Devon would be there for protection and there'd be plenty of other witnesses. What could possibly go wrong?

I rubbed the evil eye pennant under my T-shirt just in case.

TWENTY-TWO

I was pacing the bungalow Thursday evening, waiting to hear back from Lulu. Phase one of our crazy plan was complete. She had talked M.J. into convincing his mother that he was willing to accept Sven and wanted him to be there when he proposed to Lulu. I couldn't believe Lulu had actually talked M.J. into it. He really couldn't refuse that girl anything. But would Selene go for it? And would Sven even be available to go? Maybe he took off with Eloise already. Devon said Farnsworth hadn't gotten around to finding Sven to interview yet. He and Eloise could be living it up in Mexico by now for all we knew.

'You're going to wear a hole through the floor,' Devon said without looking up from the paperwork he was meticulously combing through. Salma had split the workload of sifting through the boat lot's financial records with Devon and Quinn. They'd been going through it for two days, surviving on caffeine judging by the coffee cups piled up around them.

'Urg,' I growled, flopping down on the sofa. 'I'm going crazy. I wish she'd call already.'

Buddha came over and pressed his rubber shark against my knee, repeatedly causing the thing to squeak until my brain was in danger of exploding. 'You win, boy.' I stood. 'I'm taking the dogs down to the beach.' Grabbing my phone, I checked one more time to make sure I hadn't missed her call or text.

A change of scenery did nothing for my anxiety or disposition. I was still pacing, only now I had sand under my feet instead of a hardwood floor. The beautiful weather barely registered. I was a woman obsessed. Finally, at Buddha's insistence by following me and panting, I plopped down in the sand and placed a hand on either side of his head. He lowered himself to sit in front of me, tongue hanging, his keen eyes watching my face.

'You would be an awesome emotional support dog.' I sighed. 'Who am I kidding? You *are* an awesome emotional support dog and I don't know what I'd do without you.' I leaned over and kissed his nose. His tongue caught me right on my eye and I laughed. That only encouraged him and he jumped on me, intent on licking the rest of my face, his paws planted firmly on my chest. 'Ow, ow!' I tried pushing him off but only succeeded in falling backward, which gave him the access he needed. 'OK,' I snorted. 'Off!'

As Petey ran over to see what he was missing, I wiped my drool-soaked face with the back of my hand and pushed myself up before he could get in any licks. Buddha was sitting there squinting at me and panting, looking completely proud of himself.

I dug my phone out of my pocket as I felt it vibrate. Two words from Lulu made my heart skip: *All set.*

M.J. had timed the evening so we'd be on the water for the sunset; therefore we were having cocktails by their pool before we took off. He and Devon were hunched over an iPad when I approached with Devon's rum and coke.

Despite M.J.'s agreement to lure Sven on board and question him, I noticed he was keeping his distance from the man. Selene, on the other hand, couldn't keep her eyes or hands off him. Maybe she didn't just consider him a 'roll in the hay' after all. Beth Anne and Carl were doing their best to chat up Cali, but it didn't look like it was working as Cali had her face buried in her phone, completely ignoring them.

'So, you see, it's an ingenious management system,' M.J. was saying to Devon. 'There are twelve cameras on board so I can check any deck space I need to from here, plus I've already set the air temperature and checked the fuel and alerted the captain we'll be boarding soon, all without stepping foot on her.'

'Her?' I smiled curiously. Glancing at Lulu, I asked, 'Should Lulu be jealous?'

'Jealous? Nah. She's Lulu's namesake. When Dad and I had her built three years ago I christened her the *Voo Deux Queen*, Lulu's childhood nickname.'

Lulu groaned. 'I was mortified and I should've never told you and M.J. about my nickname.' She shook her head. 'You rich people are so strange.'

'What can I say.' M.J. shrugged. 'I was in love.' He leaned over and kissed her cheek. 'Now more than ever.'

'And you can keep an eye on the crew right from this thing at home?' Devon asked. I saw his mouth twitch as M.J. nodded. Then Devon glanced at me and excused himself. I watched him walk away, comforted by the fact that his gun was concealed under the smoky gray jacket. Who knew what we were getting ourselves into tonight.

I glanced nervously at Sven and then back at the yacht. M.J. really did have the most romantic plan, and I felt bad Lulu's doubts were keeping her from enjoying it all. What would she say when M.J. was down on one knee in front of her? Maybe she would know in that moment what her heart truly wanted.

Finally M.J. signaled it was time for us all to move to the yacht: M.J., Lulu, Cali, Selene carrying Chloe – who wore a little sailor outfit – Sven, Beth Anne, Carl and Devon and I. Flavia apparently didn't do boats so she was staying home.

The yacht sure was beautiful. A one-hundred-and-thirty-foot, sleek white Sunseeker with three decks and five cabins. The name *Voo Deux Queen* was elegantly scrolled on her side. Despite my anxiety of being on a yacht for the first time and sharing the experience with a possible killer, I was in awe as I climbed aboard.

'This is like a fairytale,' I said to no one in particular as we climbed the stairs up to the middle deck. A short, thin man in a captain's hat greeted us. M.J. shook his hand, introduced him to us as Captain Bronson and told him we were ready to push off.

Selene released Chloe to sniff around and then led Sven to the bar. Cali joined them, apparently not bothered at all by her mother's boyfriend. She must've really hated her dad. M.J. led the rest of us around the bar and through smoked-glass doors into what he called the main stateroom. It sported mirrored and glossy black walnut walls, a white leather U-shaped sofa, a large flat-screen TV and it smelled like money. He led us over to the left-side balcony and invited us out.

'When it gets dark we can turn on the underwater lights and see the fish swimming around down there. Sometimes even sharks.' He had his arm protectively around Lulu. I felt myself swoon a bit as I looked down and saw that we were actually moving away from the dock. I clutched the crocheted bag I had slung over one shoulder and across my chest so it was always close, knowing I had my anxiety pills in there if I needed them.

'Wow, she sure is quiet,' Devon remarked.

The men began to talk about the engines and other boring things as M.J. led us through the rest of the tour including a state-of-the-art galley, where a chef was cooking something delicious smelling, crew quarters downstairs below the gallery, an on-deck master bedroom plus three other smaller bedrooms, captain's quarters, upstairs and downstairs living rooms with wet bars, three bathrooms, a four-person Jacuzzi, reclining sun pads on the bow and a garage hidden beneath the rear door where a dingy was stashed. And, of course, other toys including deep-sea fishing rods, snorkeling equipment and something on a shelf that caught Devon's eye.

'What are these?' Devon walked over to the shelf and picked up one of two black apparatuses with a mouthpiece and two small handlebars on either side.

'Ah!' M.J. said, smiling and shoving his hands deep into the pockets of his khakis. 'Those would be the Human Gills proto-type, an invention Dad and I've invested in. These beauties allow you to breathe under water just like a fish.' He picked up the other one. 'You see, these filters have holes tinier than water molecules so the oxygen is extracted, compressed and stored here.' He pointed to the small flat area behind the mouthpiece. All you have to do is pop it in your mouth.'

Devon eyed the one in his hand with awe. 'Bleedin' brilliant.'

M.J. nodded. 'Yes, it is. We're going to help them market it, not only for recreational use but to all vessels, including military, as a safety precaution.'

M.J. checked his phone and replaced the Human Gills appa-ratus, suddenly glancing at Lulu nervously. 'I need to check on how our dinner's coming along.' Did he sense Lulu's doubts? I snuck a glance at her. Her eyes were cast downward as she peeled the label off her water bottle. Oh, boy. It was not looking good for M.J. But then she took a deep breath and rested her head on his shoulder. Maybe she was just nervous.

'You all head back to the bow; I'll meet you there.' M.J. pressed a kiss into Lulu's curls and then left us.

As the rest of the party headed back up to the stateroom, I waited as Devon replaced the other Human Gills gadget back on the shelf and followed them. I was about to do the same when

I heard a sharp bark. Whirling around, I saw Angel sitting below the shelf. My hand went to my heart. It looked like I could reach out and pet her and for an instant I moved to. But then she faded a bit as she let out a second sharp bark and one of the Human Gills fell from the shelf. I glanced back but Devon had already turned the corner on the stairs so he didn't see it.

'What is it, girl?' I whispered. In response, she pawed at the gadget on the floor.

I went over and picked it up. 'This?'

She flickered as she barked again.

Sighing, I shoved the thing in my bag. 'Got it. Thanks.' She sneezed and then disappeared. Climbing the stairs, I wondered how sane I could be considering I'd just stolen something on the advice of my deceased dog. The worst part was I was beginning to wonder why I would need it.

As I emerged into the air-conditioned stateroom, I noticed Cali was standing out on the balcony alone. Popping my head outside, I caught Beth Anne's attention and jerked my head in the universal 'come here' signal. She nodded. Devon saw it too and came over with her.

'What's up?'

'Cali's on the balcony alone. I think Beth Anne and I should try to talk to her.'

He stepped into the stateroom and glanced over at Cali. 'All right, then.' He didn't believe Cali was the killer – he really thought it was Sven, so I knew he wasn't worried. He'd reminded me that mentally ill people were more likely to be a victim of crime than the perpetrator, but I still had my doubts. Mostly because she did try to run me down in that Cadillac, I know that wasn't a coincidence.

The wind was a bit biting. I pulled my sweater closed as I flanked Cali on one side and Beth Anne flanked her other side. 'Nice evening,' I said, trying to get a feel for her mood. I'd never been this close to her and it was a bit unsettling. She exuded anger, from her white-knuckled grip on the railing to her clenched jaw muscles flicking up and down under pale skin. Her dark eyes were fixated on the sea but I had a feeling she wasn't seeing it. Her attention was turned inward.

'If you say so,' she said flatly.

'You OK, sugar?' Beth Anne reached out and placed a hand over Cali's.

Cali suddenly turned into Beth Anne and began sobbing on her shoulder.

Whoa! Beth Anne mouthed to me as she stroked Cali's back. 'It'll be OK,' she said out loud over and over until Cali's sobs got further apart and turned into hiccups.

I held my hands up in a helpless gesture to Beth Anne. I had no idea what to do.

'Do you want to talk about it?' Beth Anne asked in her softest Southern tone, the one I'd heard her use to comfort Shakespeare.

Cali threw herself back against the railing, her eyes fixed downward toward the water like she wanted to fling herself overboard. I braced my feet in case we had to grab her and stop her.

But there was no need to worry. She suddenly collapsed onto the deck like a wet noodle and cried, 'It's my fault Dad is dead. I killed him!'

TWENTY-THREE

B eth Anne and I stared at the crumpled mess of girl at our feet and then at each other. I motioned for Beth Anne to keep her talking since Cali obviously felt comfortable with her. While Beth Anne squatted beside her, I reached in and clicked on my phone recorder.

'Cali, tell me what happened,' Beth Anne coaxed, gently pushing the clump of purple bang off the girl's forehead. 'You'll feel better when you get it all out.' She glanced up to make sure I was recording. I nodded. 'Did you . . . did you cut your father's rope, Cali?'

Cali jerked her head up. Her perfect porcelain skin was now blotchy and puffy. Her eyes looked wild. 'No, but I might as well have.'

I kneeled down slowly beside her, my bag opened so it didn't muffle the recording. 'What do you mean, Cali?'

She banged her head against the railing. Beth Anne stuck her hand behind it so she couldn't hurt herself. Cali rubbed her face hard with both hands and then looked at us. So much sorrow there, I found myself tearing up. 'It took a lot to get Dad to lose his cool, you know? I knew I was pushing his buttons. I guess I just wanted him to pay attention to me for once. Whatever kind of attention I could get from him was fine with me. M.J. has always been his favorite. He did everything with him and for him. I was nothing. A disgrace. Something to be locked away and hidden.' These last words came out on a heartbreaking sob. 'He even loved the maid, Breezy, more than he loved me. I pushed his buttons, all right. It felt good, too, to see I could get an emotional reaction from him. Only,' she sniffed, 'when Dad blew up, he really blew up and it took him a while to calm back down. Whoever he got into an argument with in the kitchen that lead to his death, that was because of me. He would never have fought with someone if I hadn't got him all worked up. I hurt everyone I love. That's why Sam left me. She knows she's better off.'

Beth Anne and I sighed at each other and I reached in and turned off the recording. Poor girl. She just wanted her dad's attention and now she felt responsible for his death. As she broke down in sobs again, Beth Anne wrapped an arm around her and pulled her close.

I had one more thing to clear up. 'Cali, can I ask you something? Did you nearly hit me on my bike in that Cadillac?'

She glanced up at me, confused, and shook her head.

Well, there went the rest of my theory. Still, someone with access to that car did. It wasn't my imagination. I went to get Selene. We were in over our heads.

The bonus of Selene rushing to Cali's aid was that it left Sven sitting on the outdoor sofa area alone. I saw Devon heading his way as I followed Selene back through the smoked-glass doors.

'Oh, Cali!' Selene helped her daughter up. She wiped the tears from her cheeks with her thumb and whispered something in Greek. It was touching to see her maternal side. 'Come on, I'll get your medication and you can rest in the bedroom.'

After she led Cali away, Beth Anne and I shared a deep sigh.

She pulled wind-whipped strands of her hair out of her mouth. 'Drink?' she asked, visibly shaken.

'Definitely.' I followed her out to the wet bar. 'Something with rum,' I said to the bartender.

'Make that two,' Beth Anne added. Glancing over her shoulder, she eyed Sven and Devon. Then she moved her gaze to her husband chatting with Lulu and M.J. on the other side of the yacht. 'Hey,' she whispered, 'maybe now would be a good time for me to play the bored housewife?'

We accepted our caramel-colored drinks, stuffed with pineapple, cherries and an umbrella, and I nodded. 'Go on over; I'll get Devon out of there.'

We sashayed casually across like we didn't have a care in the world, sipping our drinks. Beth Anne slid up close to Sven. He seemed startled at first. But then she flipped her tousled hair and batted her eyelashes and he turned toward her, his eyes following her surgically enhanced curves. Devon glanced up at me and I motioned for him to leave them.

He excused himself, coming over to me and taking my hand. Leading me to the railing, he faced me, rested his hands on my hips and leaned in by my ear. 'What's going on?'

'Beth Anne's trying to see exactly how emotionally attached Sven is to Selene.' We both snuck a glance. Beth Anne was holding the straw in her drink as Sven was taking a sip. His lips touched her fingers and she pretended to enjoy it. I grimaced as I imagined how many women's body parts his lips had been on. I'd have to remind Beth Anne to wash her hands.

'I'd say he's not capable of emotional attachment,' Devon grunted.

I snuggled into his chest. 'Some women would say the same about you,' I teased.

'Touché.' He kissed the top of my head. 'What happened with Cali?'

'She broke down. Blames herself for her dad getting in the fight with whoever killed him in the kitchen. Thinks she got him too worked up and angry. She didn't do it.'

'So that leaves Sven.'

We both glanced over at the giant man. I cringed. 'Maybe it's not such a good idea for Beth Anne to be getting his attention.'

Sven was fully turned toward her now. Devon's eyes narrowed. 'I'd say it's a little late for that.'

I couldn't believe he was acting like Beth Anne's husband wasn't twenty feet away. Then again, if you're in the business of killing off husbands, you've got nothing to worry about if one's around. Something was bothering me, though.

Devon tightened his grip on my hips. 'And cue the drama in five . . . four . . . three . . .'

Looking over my shoulder, I saw Selene had emerged from the glass doors and was staring with narrowed eyes at Sven and Beth Anne. Her hands were on her hips and her spine was straight. Finally, plastering on a smile, she smoothed her dark glossy hair and strutted toward them.

Sven looked torn as he noticed Selene coming.

Wow. She looked furious. Wait! That was it. The piece of the puzzle that wasn't fitting. If it wasn't Cali that ran me down in the Cadillac then who else had access to it? Oh my God . . . Selene. Maybe Selene wasn't giving Cali an alibi. Maybe it was the other way around. Could Selene have killed Michael? 'I have to save Beth Anne,' I whispered. Devon released me as I called, 'Beth Anne, you have to come see the dolphins!'

She wisely extracted herself from Sven's presence. 'Oh, I love dolphins,' she was calling as she hopped over little Chloe snoozing on the deck and hurried over to us. 'There are no dolphins, are there?'

'No,' I said, motioning behind us at Selene. 'Only territorial sharks.'

Under different circumstances it would've been a lovely dinner. As it was I barely tasted the food as I studied Selene and tried to remember all my interactions with her. She had seemed genuinely grief-stricken . . . well, unless she was with Sven. Then she seemed . . . stricken by Cupid's arrow. Did she get rid of Michael to be with Sven? Devon seemed to think this was a possibility. Wouldn't it make more sense to just get a divorce, though? He reminded me that nothing about love or murder ever made sense. She didn't do or say anything to give herself away. How were we going to approach the subject with her?

After dinner M.J. led us all to the bridge to watch the sunset. The captain had stopped the *Voo Deux Queen* and anchored her while we ate. I had asked M.J. how far out to sea we were and he said about forty miles. I checked in with my anxiety after hearing that little fact and found I was doing pretty good. Apparently out to sea didn't register, maybe because there were no physical reference points for my mind to freak out about, or maybe it was because I'd always wanted to be a mermaid.

As we all stretched out on the reclining sun pads, we watched the sun begin to sink toward the water and the sky morph into shades of gold and orange. Since I'd been concentrating on Selene I'd almost forgotten why we were all here. One glance at Lulu beside me jogged my memory. She was clutching her stomach and tears were shining in her eyes. She did not look like a woman excited about the prospect of being proposed to. I wanted to warn M.J. but it was too late.

M.J. walked over and took her hand. Gently helping her to her shaky feet, he led her to stand on the deck in front of us. Then he dropped to his knee. It was so perfect, with the breeze lifting her corkscrew curls and the warm, magical sunset backlighting them, I really wished this was going to be a happy ending. I wished it with all my might. I glanced at Selene and

Sven whispering to each other. I doubted M.J. was going to have his happy ending, whether Lulu said yes or not.

Still holding her hands in his, he cleared his throat. 'Lulu, I'm going to keep this short and sweet, like our courtship. I knew you were the only girl for me the first night you waited on our table. You've had my heart since then and, even though it took time for you to let our friendship grow into something more, I am beyond grateful you have. And that we've been blessed with a beautiful gift from our union.' He released her hands, touched her belly softly and then reached in his pocket.

I saw her gaze flick to the horizon. I glanced that way myself and caught the last bit of sun disappearing. When we both looked back at M.J., he was holding out a box with a huge sparkling diamond ring inside. 'Lulu Dutrey, you already have my eternal love; now will you do me the honor of being Mrs Lulu Beckley . . . my wife?'

The tears that had been welling in Lulu's eyes all evening finally cascaded down her face. 'Oh, M.J.' Her voice was hoarse with anguish. I was suddenly sad for them both. 'M.J., I can't do this anymore. I panicked. I didn't think it through. It was an impulse and you deserve the truth.'

M.J. quickly jumped up to his feet and shook his head. 'Lulu, don't do this.'

We all glanced at each other. *What was going on?*

'I'm sorry, M.J. I can't marry you.' She took a step back.

M.J. stepped forward and desperately grabbed her hand. 'Yes, yes, you can. We're going to be so happy together, I promise.'

She was shaking her head and trying to pull her hand out of his grip. 'No, M.J., we won't!'

She finally succeeded in getting her hand loose, grabbed his shoulders and looked into his eyes. 'M.J., I'm sorry, but this baby isn't yours.'

TWENTY-FOUR

There was a collective gasp from everyone . . . everyone except M.J.

He dropped his head and then slowly nodded. 'I know.'

'Lulu!' Selene cried. 'M.J.? What's going on? Whose baby is it?'

Lulu let her hands drop to her sides and faced Selene like a woman staring down a firing squad . . . half terrified and half resigned to her fate. 'Selene, I'm so, so sorry. It . . . it's Michael's.'

'Holy hell,' Devon breathed beside me. I felt my heart drop along with my jaw.

'Whoa,' Beth Anne whispered.

'It was just once. We both knew it was a mistake,' Lulu was trying to explain. 'My dad had just died. I thought I could be with M.J. and at least the baby would grow up with its rightful family. Michael didn't want me to do that. He wanted to tell you the truth.'

So that was probably Lulu who Breezy overheard Michael whispering to on the phone.

Lulu glanced over at M.J. 'I'm so sorry. I never meant to hurt you.'

Selene jumped up, her fists clenched, her chest heaving. 'You mean the baby would grow up with our family *money*, don't you? You. Little. Slut! You seduced my husband for the money, didn't you? Did you kill him?' She launched herself at Lulu with a deep cry of rage.

Wait? What? Selene was accusing Lulu? That didn't make sense.

M.J. jumped in front of Lulu and held out his hand. 'Stop, Mother.'

'You're still defending her?' she cried, her eyes wide with shock.

Sven rose to his feet. Devon stood up, too. I knew they were sensing the situation getting out of control. They were right. An emotional storm was brewing. Its electrical charge was as palpable as a physical storm. We needed to protect Lulu and the baby. I slid off the sun pad and moved in a wide circle to stand next to Lulu. She clutched my hand when she felt me near her. It was damp and shaky. I could tell she wanted to flee but there was nowhere to go. We were all stuck, surrounded by miles and miles of water. Devon stood on the other side of M.J., watching Selene with apprehension.

M.J. looked more determined than ever as he stared at his mother. 'I'm going to raise this baby as mine, Mother. I'm sorry you had to find out it was Dad's. I was hoping that would stay between me and Lulu.'

'You knew?' Lulu squeaked. 'But how? Why didn't you say anything to me?'

'Because I don't care. If this is how God answered my prayers and put us together, so be it.'

Selene was holding her hand on her forehead. 'Are you insane?'

M.J. shrugged. 'Probably. But I will do anything to be with Lulu. She's all that matters to me. Don't try to get in the way of that.' His attention flicked to Sven. 'Any of you.'

Selene's gaze narrowed and moved to Lulu. 'You will be a part of our family . . . over my dead body!' She rushed forward but M.J. was ready for her. He stopped her with a stiff arm and threw her back with force. She tumbled into the sun pads, losing a sandal. Chloe darted under the chair.

Seeing Selene lying there sobbing where she landed, her hair fanned over her face, set Sven off. With a growl, he launched himself at M.J.

M.J. was too fast, though. In a flash, I felt his hand clamp my wrist like a vice. Pain shot through my shoulder as he yanked me in front of him. He pushed my arm up and back behind me. This must be some self-defense move and, holy hell, it hurt. His fishing knife blade pressed into my neck.

I squealed as it bit into my skin. Sven had enough empathy to stop dead in his tracks. The ropey veins in his neck bulged.

What was going on? My brain couldn't process what was happening. Why was M.J. holding me at knifepoint?

'Don't move,' he said into my ear. 'Lulu, I'm sorry, honey. I'm going to fix this.'

Everyone was screaming at him at this point. Lulu had her hands over her mouth, her eyes wide with shock.

I made eye contact with Devon. His expression morphed from surprise to rage to deadly calm.

'M.J.!' Selene cried. 'What are you doing?!'

I noticed Devon going for his gun. Unfortunately M.J. noticed, too.

He slid further behind me so I was between him and Devon. 'Put it on the ground nice and slow. Then kick it over here.' His breath was hot on my neck, his heart beating fast against my back. Our shirts were glued together with sweat despite the chill in the air. When Devon hesitated, he increased the pressure of the blade on my neck. I winced as I felt it poke through. A trickle of warm blood ran down into my shirt. 'Do it now. I really don't want to hurt her but I will.'

Devon pulled out his gun slowly and laid it on the deck with an expletive. Then he stood and kicked it over to M.J., who immediately pushed me across the deck and grabbed the gun.

I fell into Devon's arms, clutching him tight. He stroked my hair, whispering, 'You're all right, love,' I think to reassure himself as much as me.

As M.J. backed up against the bar, pointing the gun at us, Lulu tried to reason with him.

'M.J., put the gun down. You're right. We . . . we belong together. Just put the gun down and I'll marry you. You have my word. I'm sure everyone here is willing to forget this ever happened.'

Emboldened by Lulu's words, Selene pushed herself up and stepped toward her son. 'Oh, for God's sake, give the gun to me, M.J. You're not going to shoot your own mother, are you?'

'I wouldn't be so sure,' I said quietly. As the shock began to wear off, the confusion was lifting. Pieces were clicking into place. His obsession with Lulu . . . the baby. The fact that he already knew he wasn't the father. He said he ran into Selene and Cali coming out of the library after I screamed. That meant he was near the kitchen, too. And if it wasn't Cali or Selene who tried to run me down, it had to be M.J. My own voice sounded far away as I stared at him in disbelief. 'You killed your father.'

The silence that followed was our answer.

'M.J.!' His name was a cry of anguish thrown at him from Lulu. 'Please say that's not true!'

He moved behind the bar, steadying himself with one hand. His face was white. He looked like he was going to be sick. But the gun was still pointed in our direction, ready to fire if anyone made a move toward him.

'Please don't hate me,' he said to Lulu. 'I just got so angry. I went into the kitchen, I was so excited. I told Dad I was going to ask you to marry me. I was confused by his anger at first. He said he couldn't have this lie between us. That's when he told me that the baby wasn't mine. That he had gone to comfort you when your father died a few weeks earlier and you two had made a mistake. That the baby was his. I just saw red. I couldn't let him take you away from me. Let him steal our future together.'

We were all startled by a sudden scream as Selene let out a gut-wrenching cry and fell to her knees, sobbing. Sven kneeled down, trying to comfort her as she rocked back and forth, her face in her hands.

'Oh, M.J.' Lulu wrapped her arms protectively around her stomach. Even in the waning gray light I could see her face pulled taught, stricken with grief. 'What have you done?'

'Did you kill Oliver White, too?' Devon asked gruffly.

M.J. swung his attention to Devon. His jaw tensed but his voice was suddenly flat, emptied of emotion. 'I had to. He saw me, in the kitchen that night arguing with Dad. He didn't say anything to the police because he didn't want to get involved. But when the police started looking at him for Dad's murder, he decided to try to blackmail me. I had to kill him.'

'But they had a suicide note?' Beth Anne sounded confused and defiant. Carl put an arm around her and pulled her protectively closer.

'Which I wrote and printed out on his computer.' M.J. eyed us all and then seemed to come to some sort of decision. I really hoped it didn't have anything to do with us being shark bait. He waved the gun. 'Elle, come here.'

Devon growled, gripping me tighter. 'M.J., I won't let you harm her.'

'I'm not going to harm her if she does what I ask.'

'We don't have a choice,' I whispered to Devon. 'We have to keep him calm.'

Reluctantly Devon released me. 'Be careful.'

On shaky legs, I moved to stand in front of the bar. This close to M.J., I could see the sweat rolling down the sides of his face. His eyes had changed. They were wide like a panicked animal. I glanced at the gun. His hand was the only steady thing about him. He reached beneath him and pulled out a trash bag from the bar. 'Take this and gather everyone's phones.'

It was amazing how that thought made me panic. The little piece of plastic in my purse was an anchor to the rest of the world. A way to call for help. A way to record the killer's confession. Neither of those things were happening now. I took the bag, my gaze glued to the gun.

'Yours first, Elle. Put it in.'

I reached in my bag, dug beneath the Human Gills gadget, making sure M.J. didn't see I'd swiped that, and pulled out my phone.

'Slowly,' he warned. I dropped it in the trash bag. 'Now gather everyone else's.'

My body went through the motions of standing in front of everyone while they threw their phones in the trash bag, but my brain was desperately searching for a way out of this mess.

Beth Anne gripped my hand as she tossed her phone in. Her makeup was streaked from tears but her eyes blazed with anger. 'You OK?'

I nodded.

'No talking!' M.J. yelled.

I turned and moved back toward him. I could swing the bag at him, take him by surprise. Then one of the guys, or all of them, could rush at him. Would they hesitate? Would he get a shot off first? What if he hit Lulu and the baby accidently? No, I couldn't risk it and it didn't matter if I could. Before I reached him, he stopped me.

'Throw the bag overboard.'

With an internal groan, I did what he said. I walked over and dropped it over the railing. There was enough moonlight that I watched it sink into the dark waters.

TWENTY-FIVE

'Now, go into the stateroom,' he said when I forced my legs to walk me back to him. It all seemed so surreal, like I was floating instead of walking. 'Lift the coffee table lid. There's a tackle box in there with a bag of zip ties. Bring those out here.' As I moved behind him, he added, 'Don't try anything funny. I'm sure you care about a few of these people out here and would hate to see them hurt.'

I nodded in understanding and did as he asked. The stateroom was eerily quiet, cool and dark. I wondered where the captain and other two crew members were. Probably down in their private quarters enjoying their evening. After all, the guests were supposed to be celebrating an engagement right now. If only I could signal to them somehow; make some noise to get their attention. The yacht was just too big. As I opened the tackle box and lifted the baggie of zip ties, I noticed a Swiss Army knife poking out from beneath some lures. I slipped it into my bag. It was small, but it was a knife. If anything I wouldn't feel so defenseless.

I looked around at the solemn, scared faces as I emerged back out on the deck. Sven had gathered up a crumpled Selene and helped her to a chair where she quietly sobbed in his arms. Beth Anne and her husband clutched each other tightly next to them and Devon sat stiffly on the other side of Beth Anne. Lulu had moved closer to M.J. – I'm sure not of her own accord – and had her head lowered. I gained strength from Devon, who I could see by the way he was glaring at M.J. was more angry than scared. Was he formulating a plan to get his gun back and stop this madness? I couldn't tell what he was thinking.

'Everyone place your hands together in your lap.' M.J. waved the gun. 'Elle, make sure you pull the ties tight. It's up to you to make sure no one tries anything and gets hurt.'

As if on cue, Sven suddenly jumped up and charged at M.J. The gunshot echoed in the night air. With an *oof!*, Sven dropped to the deck. He rolled over and clutched his neck. Blood poured

from between his fingers. A mewing groan came from his lips.
Then his limp hands dropped beside him and he lay still.

'Nooo!' Selene screamed and jumped up.

'Sit down!' M.J. yelled.

Devon moved to help Sven.

'Devon, don't.' M.J. leveled the gun at him. 'Elle, put the zip
ties on Sven's hands first.'

I looked at him in horror from where I'd reflexively crouched
when the gun shot went off. 'But M.J., he's really hurt—'

'Now!' he yelled. The ocean breeze lifted the smoke away
from the gun. My ears were ringing. My heart was pounding like
a jack hammer. I couldn't move.

'Elle.' Devon's voice penetrated the shock. 'It's OK. Do it.
He won't care now.'

Suddenly we heard yelling and footsteps coming from the
stateroom. M.J. jumped to the side and grabbed Lulu. The captain,
chef and bartender came barreling through the smoked-glass
doors.

'What in the world?' Captain Bronson focused on Sven lying
motionless and bleeding on the deck. Then the chef, who'd
changed into nylon running shorts and was barefoot, grabbed his
arm and pointed silently at M.J. I watched Captain Bronson's
face morph from confusion to shock.

M.J. gripped Lulu's arm and leveled the gun at them. 'Good.
Party's all here. Now you three can take a seat with everyone else.'

I suddenly remembered Cali. As the men complied, I moved
quickly to Sven. *Don't think about the blood. Don't check for a
pulse.* I made myself put the zip tie on quickly and pulled it
tight. Then, turning away just as quickly, I pushed myself up and
moved to Selene.

As I looped the zip tie, I mouthed, *Cali?*

She shook her head slightly. 'Tranquilizers.'

My heart dropped. She wouldn't be any help for a while.
Probably wouldn't even wake up until this was all over. One way
or another. Maybe that was for the best.

I almost broke when I got to Devon. He squeezed my hand
as I took his and whispered, 'I love you.'

'I love you,' I whispered back as I pulled the zip tie, trying
to leave it loose.

'Tighter,' M.J. called.

Dropping my head in defeat, I pulled it tighter.

'Elle, back here. Now.'

Every step toward him felt like an eternity. Lulu was staring at everyone. We made eye contact and I could see the terror in her eyes. She choked on a sob. 'M.J., please!'

He ignored her. When I got close enough he waved me around the bar, where he instructed Lulu to zip tie my hands while he held the gun on us.

'I'm sorry, Elle,' she whispered. Her eyes were swollen now. 'This is all my fault.'

'No, it's not. It's my dad's fault,' M.J. said, growing more agitated by the minute. 'This isn't the way I wanted us to start our future, but we can't change it now. What's done is done. But Lulu.' He waited until she glanced up at him. 'Make no mistake, we will be together. Whether it's in life or death is up to you.'

There was desperation in the way he was looking at her that broke my heart and terrified me at the same time. The look of a man obsessed. It wasn't love. It was possession he wanted. And if there ever was any doubt he'd do whatever it took to have Lulu, it was swept away by that look.

'M.J., you don't have to do this,' I pleaded. 'You don't have to hurt anyone else.'

'But I do. Because everyone needs to get off my yacht.' He grabbed my arm and began to pull me across the deck toward the guardrail. He was muttering under his breath. I lost my footing and stumbled, but he only dug his fingers into my arm harder and dragged me. I got my feet back underneath me and tried to yank my arm free. He pressed the gun against my temple. By the time we reached the guardrail my breathing was shallow and hard. I was gasping like a dying fish for oxygen. Panic was setting in.

'M.J.!' I heard the panic in Devon's voice, too. 'Let her go!'

As the cold metal released from my temple, I saw Devon had pushed himself up to standing. *Please don't. Please don't be a hero*, I pleaded with my eyes. But M.J. wrapped his arm around my throat and pointed the gun at Devon.

'No!' I screamed. Breaking his hold on me, I bent over at the waist and flung myself back as hard as I could. There was a

crack as the back of my head hit M.J.'s face. The impact reverberated through my skull, the pain blacking out my vision for a
moment. I heard his own cry of pain from a distance. Unable to
break my fall with my hands bound, I landed hard on the deck.
I rolled to my side and caught sight of Devon leaping toward us.
His bound hands were in front of him like a battering ram. His
face was twisted in rage. The others were struggling to get to
their feet behind him.

Crack! I heard the shot as Devon's feet left the ground. I
reached out with my fingers. 'Devon!' His forward motion
continued but it was no longer controlled. His head hit the side
of the yacht with a thud and he crumbled like a ragdoll as M.J.
jumped aside.

'Devon!' I scrambled to try and get near him but M.J. grabbed
my hair and pulled me back.

'That'll be enough, Elle.'

'Oh, God. Oh, God. Oh, God,' I whispered. He had to be alive.
The burning sensation in my scalp as M.J. pulled me to my feet
was nothing compared to the pain ripping through my heart. That
pain exploded and numbed me as I waited for any sign of movement from Devon. *Please, please, please be alive.*

The screams of the others barely registered. It was background
noise to my pleas to the universe. Was he breathing? The only
movement so far was a red stain of blood spreading on his
shoulder through his jacket. It didn't look like he'd been hit
anywhere vital, but I could still hear the crack of his head hitting
the side of the yacht. That had to have done some damage.

'Shut up!' M.J. yelled. He pulled a handkerchief out of his
pocket and pressed it against his bloody nose. He glared at me.
'I think you broke my nose, Elle. Not very nice.'

My heart pounded. I waited for him to shoot me next. But
then Lulu approached cautiously. 'M.J.?'

He startled. His eyes tried to focus. Finally he let his attention
settle on her.

She had her hands folded beneath her belly, non-threateningly,
and I could see her bottom lip shaking as she forced a smile.
'M.J., we're on a yacht that can go anywhere in the world, right?'

He blinked, then nodded. 'Yes.'

'So, we can leave. Go anywhere. Somewhere where they'll

never find us. We can just live on the ocean if we want to. Just you and me and . . . our baby.' She reached out and moved his palm to press against her stomach. Her voice only broke once. 'But we can't do that with all this.' She motioned toward Devon crumpled against the railing. 'This blood and bodies in our new home. This has to stop. Let them go. That boat you showed us in the garage – put them on it. Then we can leave. Move on to our future together. You've already taken their cell phones; they have no way to call for help. By the time the Coast Guard finds them, if they find them, we'll be long gone.' She moved a little closer, gaining confidence as he listened. 'It will be the most romantic thing ever. Sailing away to start our new life. Like those old movies where they sail away into the sunset.'

My heart broke. I knew what she was doing. Sacrificing herself for us. I glanced at everyone. Seconds ticked by as we waited to hear our fate from one madman with a gun.

He lowered the blood-soaked handkerchief. His nose was swollen so he sounded like he had a cold when he finally said, 'Lulu, you swear you'll be mine? You won't leave me?'

She licked her lips. Then she turned and glanced around behind her. Picking up the box M.J. had held up to her, she brought it back to him. 'Ask me again.'

M.J.'s eyes lit up with hope. He held the gun on me as he took the ring out of the box and held it up to her. 'Lulu, will you be my wife? Love me no matter what and never leave me?'

She let a slow, seductive smile spread on her lips. 'I will, M.J. I will.'

I saw the victory soften his face as he slipped the ring on her offered hand. Then she leaned in and kissed his lips convincingly, despite the blood still dripping from his nose. Wow, she was good. Part of me wondered if she really did want to be with him. Only a small part, though. The sane part of me knew this was the performance of a lifetime . . . for all our lives.

'For you.' He squeezed her hand and then his gaze skipped over each of us. 'Unfortunately the dingy only holds four.' He glanced at Sven's lifeless body and then at Devon. 'First things first.' He walked over to Sven and waved the gun at Captain Bronson and the other two weary crew members. 'Miguel, Bronson, come over here.' The captain and chef stood and went to him. 'Hold out your hands.' He kept enough distance between himself and the men to keep the gun trained on them as he pulled out his fishing knife and cut the zip ties. 'I'm going to let you go, but if you do anything besides what I tell you I'll shoot you instead. Do you understand?'

They shared a glance and then nodded solemnly.

'Good. Get this body off my ship.'

They stared at him. 'Sir?' Chef Miguel finally said.

'Off. My. Ship,' M.J. repeated. 'Pick him up and toss him overboard.'

Captain Bronson kneeled down slowly and placed two fingers on Sven's neck. He glanced up at Chef Miguel and shook his head. Miguel crossed himself and bent down to take Sven's arm. They worked together to drag his body over to the railing. Selene let out another cry of despair.

'Oh, Mother, knock it off!' M.J. yelled. 'He was a dumb plaything. Nothing more. You should be mourning Dad, not this box of rocks.'

Selene looked up from her hands, rage making her eyes gleam like dark, wet stones. The muscles in her neck popped as a stream of Greek flew from her mouth like missiles.

M.J.'s face turned red and he flung his hand at her with his own barrage of Greek. Then in English, 'What happened to forgiving family no matter what? Or does that only apply to your precious daughter? You're such a hypocrite.' Then he turned his attention to his crew as they struggled to get Sven up and over the railing. When they finally succeeded, a loud splash signaled their success.

M.J. called Lulu over to him. When she obeyed, he slid his hand in hers, eyed the ring on her finger and then seemed anxious. 'OK, get on with it. Throw the second body over.'

Did he mean Devon? My stomach flipped. But, no, Devon wasn't a body. He couldn't be. I watched in horror as the captain bent down and pressed two fingers to Devon's neck. My throat constricted. This wasn't happening. It couldn't be. He glanced up at me and his face paled. He yelled over at M.J., 'This one's alive.'

Alive! I collapsed against the railing in relief, my breath finally coming. Alive. M.J. would have to let him go with us, not throw him in for the sharks. We could get to shore with the small boat. He'd have to hang on. It would take us longer, but it was possible. But then, M.J.'s response registered.

'Not for long.'

I know my heart stopped. My world stopped.

'This man's too weak to swim. We won't be part of murder,' Captain Bronson said, standing up and crossing his arms.

M.J.'s mouth scrunched up in frustration. He marched over and leveled the gun at his mother. 'You will be one way or another. Choose. The man who's already on his way out? Or my mother.'

Selene squeezed her eyes shut and then froze.

'Jesus,' Miguel muttered. He stared from M.J. to the captain. I saw them make their decision. Their shoulders fell as they glanced down at Devon with sympathy. 'Sorry, mate.' Miguel wrapped his hands around Devon's right arm. Swearing under his breath, Captain Bronson kneeled and helped haul Devon to lean against the rail. Devon's head lulled to one side, but he moaned. *He moaned!*

I had to stop this. He was alive. I couldn't lose him. 'Wait!' I yelled, pushing myself off the railing and stumbling toward them. 'Please, let me say goodbye.' They glanced over at M.J. He nodded.

'Devon!' I threw my body against his. The sticky dampness from the blood on his shoulder soaked through my shirt. 'Devon, come back to me,' I whispered in his ear. 'You have to be conscious when you hit the water.' I pressed my mouth against his cool lips, watching his fluttering eyelids. It was now or never. Putting a little space between us, I shoved my hands into my bag. 'Devon, please. Please wake up.'

'OK. Time's up, Elle.'

I pulled out the Human Gills contraption and pressed it into his bound hands as I kissed him one last time. His dark eyelashes fluttered. His eyes cracked open, just enough that I saw the glittering blue life behind them. He was conscious. I glanced down and saw him grip the Human Gills.

'I love you.' I stepped back but made sure I blocked M.J.'s line of sight. Captain Bronson saw what I'd put in Devon's hands and gave me a quick nod. He and Miguel turned Devon around and hoisted him over the railing. Suddenly, he was gone. Disappeared. A loud splash. I fell to my knees in desperation. In grief. In prayer.

'It's time.' M.J. walked over and grabbed Lulu's hand again. 'The dingy only holds four so the women will be going on that. The men, you'll have to make do with the life jackets and hope the Coast Guard finds you before the sharks do.' No one moved. 'Well, let's go, everyone! Before I change my mind.' He straightened his arm and moved it in a sweeping motion, encompassing us all with the gun. 'Get off my yacht!'

TWENTY-SIX

The men were glancing nervously at M.J. as they slipped into life jackets. Beth Anne quietly sobbed as she watched Carl buckle his. M.J. had mercifully cut his zip ties like the other men so he could at least swim. Carl stroked her windblown hair and kissed her forehead silently. The only other sound was a soft whir of hydraulics as the hatch opened to reveal the dingy.

'Get it in the water.' M.J. waved the gun at Captain Bronson. His demeanor was now full of ticks and jerky movements. His mental state was on a downhill slide. We couldn't get away from him fast enough.

Captain Bronson moved wordlessly from the door controls to slide the dingy from its garage and maneuvered it into the water. It made a small splash and then hung on a cable off the end of the yacht, bobbing up and down. The moon had disappeared behind a patch of clouds so the dingy was just a white rectangle in the dark waters.

M.J. ran a rough hand through his hair. 'Get my sister in there first.' I was grateful he'd let us bring Cali along instead of tossing her into the ocean. Mercifully, she was still knocked out. If she'd been awake, she probably would've started a fight with her brother that wouldn't have ended well for her.

We watched nervously as Captain Bronson lifted Cali's sleeping figure off the deck. He threw her over his shoulder like a sack of potatoes and then maneuvered her into the rocking boat.

M.J. still had Lulu's hand clutched tightly in his grip. 'Now, the men get in the water.'

Captain Bronson slipped into the dark ocean, disappearing except for a reflective orange square of life jacket and white oval face in the moonlight. Carl and the other two crew members trudged down the narrow steps onto the back deck. Each of them slipped into the water, joining Captain Bronson with a small splash.

My heart was pounding as I scanned the water. Were there sharks nearby? The blood from Sven's and Devon's gunshot wounds could bring them. I could still feel him in my arms, and I tried to concentrate on that and not him floating alone, surrounded by hungry sharks. Or worse: sinking, too weak to stay afloat, with bound hands and counting on a prototype to stay alive.

'Now the women.'

'M.J., don't you want to cut their zip ties, too?' Lulu's voice was just a whisper in the breeze, but I still heard the heartbreak.

He looked unmoved. 'Not really.' He shoved his mother. She nearly fell down the stairs since she was trying to hold Chloe with bound hands, but managed to hop forward and keep her balance. We watched her kneel and deposit the little shaking, confused dog in the dingy. 'Now!' His rage was bubbling lava that spewed at anyone in his way. I couldn't believe we were leaving Lulu with him. But what choice did we have? I was torn. I had to get in the water so I could find Devon. Maybe we should try to talk M.J. into letting Lulu come with us? No, he'd never let that happen and asking would just aggravate him more. As long as he believed she wanted to be with him, she'd be safe. I hoped she was a good actress.

Beth Anne and I moved quickly down the steps to avoid being 'helped'. We watched as Selene got one leg over the dingy and then fell into the bench seat face first as she tried to get the other one in. I glanced at Beth Anne. Her attention was focused on her husband bobbing in the water.

'Come on,' I whispered, nudging her with my elbow. As I stepped into the dingy, it rocked and I had a hard time keeping my balance without the use of my arms. I grounded my foot to the boat, rooted my right leg and lifted my left leg like I would in tree pose. Who knew yoga would come in handy when your hands are tied and you're being kicked off a yacht by a psychotic killer? I only wobbled a little as I spun and lowered myself on the small bench seat across from Selene and a still-unconscious Cali. Those must have been some heavy tranquilizers.

M.J. came down the stairs and unhooked the cable from the front of the dingy. While he did that, I eyed the center console. It was pretty rudimentary with some knobs and a red pull lever on the side, but I noticed one thing missing.

'M.J., there's no key in the ignition,' I ventured, watching the gun nervously.

'Right,' he said in a clipped manner. 'Afraid I can't take the chance you ladies would make it back to shore. I need a few days to disappear.' With his right foot, he pushed us away from the yacht. 'Happy sailing.'

As he turned and hopped back up the stairs, we watched him grab Lulu's hand once again and yank her back through the doors. Her terrified eyes were the last thing I saw as she glanced back.

'Carl!' Beth Anne called. 'Swim to us!'

The splashing of the men swimming to the dingy was interrupted by the louder motor of the yacht anchor being lifted. The men surrounded the dingy, each holding on to the thin metal rail wrapped around it. We were already drifting away from the yacht. How far had Devon drifted from us?

'How long do you think it'll take the Coast Guard to find us?' Beth Anne asked.

'Depends on when they start looking,' Captain Bronson answered. 'If someone reports us missing when we don't return tonight—'

'We have to find Devon!' I interrupted. I didn't care about anything at the moment except getting Devon out of the water. 'Elle . . .' Beth Anne's voice held mountains of empathy. 'I'm sorry, hon.' She obviously thought he was dead. But I knew better. The world wouldn't make sense without him in it, so he couldn't be gone.

As the yacht's engines revved and it began to move through the water, I shoved my hands in my bag. 'No, you don't understand – he looked at me before they threw him in the water. He was conscious.' *Where is it?*

'Even so, he'd been shot, Elle. He wouldn't be able to tread water in his condition. Especially with his hands tied.'

We all were jostled by the sudden wake as the yacht accelerated and moved away from us.

Aha! I pulled out the knife. 'Give me your hands.'

As I worked the Swiss Army knife to cut the plastic zip ties around Beth Anne's wrists, Captain Bronson said, 'He had the Human Gills. I've tried them out – they work pretty good. If he couldn't stay above water he could be hanging out beneath it.'

'Thank you,' I said, his words stopping the black panic pounding on the doors of my sanity. I would have hugged him if I could.

As her zip ties snapped, Beth Anne let out a sigh of relief and rubbed her wrists. I handed her the knife. As she worked on mine, I eyed the vast ocean around us. How would we ever find him? How far would he have drifted? Or sank? 'Devon!' I shouted.

The water lapped calmly against the dingy in answer. I've always been fond of silence, but at this moment it was not my friend.

As the zip tie snapped and my hands were suddenly free I stood up, my mind narrowing to a single thought. I had to find Devon.

The dingy lurched and rocked back and forth.

'Whoa, whoa, where ya going?' Captain Bronson said.

Pulling my bag over my head and dropping it on the seat, I said calmly, 'I'm going to find Devon.'

I felt Beth Anne grab my hand. 'Elle! You can't go in there. We'll just lose you, too!'

'She's right.' Captain Bronson's voice was calm. A voice of reason. But I had no use for reason right now.

I jumped in the water.

TWENTY-SEVEN

immediately began to shake from cold and fear as my head resurfaced. 'Devon!' I screamed, moving my arms and legs to tread the saltwater. My muscles cramped but I ignored them. 'Devon!' Frantically turning circles, I scanned the area around me. It all looked the same. Miles and miles of flat, dark surface, broken only by tiny ripples in every direction. Something bumped against my toe. I waited. Nothing.

'Elle!' Beth Anne called. 'Get back here!'

I squinted in the moonlight about twenty-five yards ahead. *Something broke the surface. A head? Or a fin?* Adrenaline shot through my body, making me shake more.

'Elle!' I heard one of the men shout as I pushed forward and began to swim toward whatever it was. Devon or a shark or my imagination. It didn't matter. I had to do something. I had to move forward. If I just sat in that dingy I would go mad.

I concentrated on the spot I thought I saw something break the ocean surface, keeping my strokes powerful and steady. The ocean had always been the one place I felt comfort. I counted on that now. It didn't matter if I was right offshore or forty miles out, it was all one place. A place I'd always felt at home. I silently prayed, asking it to please give me Devon back.

I reached the spot and treaded water again. Darkness grew as clouds drifted across the moon. I waited. Splashes broke the silence. I twirled around. They were coming from the direction of the dingy. The men were kicking in the water, swimming, pulling the lifeless dingy in my direction.

I tried to keep my breathing steady but the cold was making my breath come in gasps, especially after the bout of exertion. I suddenly realized it would've been a good idea to borrow one of the life jackets if I was going to be out here.

'Devon!' I called, hearing the desperation in my own voice now. 'Devon!' I screamed until I was hoarse. The screams turned into sobs as I treaded water. My tears dropped and mingled with the ocean.

'Elle!' Beth Anne yelled. The dingy was closing the gap.

Suddenly an object bumped my foot again. I clamped my mouth shut just as something big pulled me under. I'd heard that a shark bite feels like a tug. That your body goes into shock and you don't actually feel pain for a few minutes. It was true. I felt nothing but the cold as my head went under. Nothing but the tug on my leg.

I heard Beth Anne screaming as soon as my head popped out of the water. I gasped for air. The dingy was close enough now that I could reach out and grab it. I heard the hard breathing of the men who'd pulled the boat toward me.

'Elle, get in!' Captain Bronson yelled.

I scanned the water around me, frantically searching for the fin; for my blood pooling on the surface that would soon draw other sharks, if they weren't circling all ready. My body screamed at me. All it wanted to do was lurch forward and scramble up into the dingy but my mind was trying to override that command . . . Something else was happening. I was slowly realizing there was no fin. No blood. I rocked back to float on my back and lifted my foot out of the water. It glowed in the moonlight. Whole. The skin unbroken. Well, that wasn't right. Wait . . .

'Oh, God!' I flipped back over and dove into the water. I went deeper and deeper, my hands searching in front of me. It was like swimming in a pool of starless night. I couldn't see a thing. My lungs felt like they were going to burst from the pressure.

Then it happened. My hand hit something solid. Grabbing on, I pulled with all my might, swimming up until my muscles burned and trembled. I broke the surface. 'Help!' I saw Captain Bronson, Miguel and Carl jump toward me before I was pulled back under.

Suddenly there were hands clutching my arms. My head broke the surface again and I gasped for air.

'We got him!' Carl said. 'You can let go.'

I watched as Captain Bronson and Miguel hauled a limp Devon above the surface right beside me. Carl had his arm around my waist, holding me above water.

Devon lifted his head and his eyes met mine above the Human

Gills gadget. Then he let it drop from his mouth. I let out a cry of happiness and wrapped my arms around him. He was weak, barely conscious, but he was alive.

'Put him in the boat. I'll be fine.'

My arms were almost useless. Captain Bronson ripped his life jacket over his head and slipped it on me as I hung on with one arm. 'I'm not sure if that was the bravest or the dumbest thing I've ever seen anyone do,' he chuckled.

'Both.' Beth Anne shook her head but grinned at me as she helped the men get Devon inside the dingy. I watched as she used the penknife to cut the zip ties on his hands. He was trying to say something but he was too weak.

'Just rest,' she told him. Removing his wet jacket, she wrapped her sweater around his shoulders.

'Thanks, Beth Anne,' I said. *Now what?* 'Now we need to find a way to get him to the hospital.' In the distance, the yacht was just a grouping of orange and yellow dots.

'Think we can flag down that helicopter?' Miguel asked with a touch of tired humor.

We all turned our heads to the west. He was right. The thumping sound of the blades was beginning to reach us as the spotlight wove in and out of the clouds.

There was some shuffling in the dingy and then Selene said, 'We can. With these!'

I peered over the edge of the dingy and saw her holding a flare. Hope bloomed. Everyone began to cheer.

'Yes!'

'Hang on, Devon,' I whispered. 'We're almost home.'

TWENTY-EIGHT

The Coast Guard helicopter reached us first, fairly quickly after we'd shot off the first stress flare. Two crewmen were lowered down with a rescue basket.

'He needs immediate medical attention!' Yelling over the thumping and roaring, I pointed at Devon slumped against the seat. 'Please!'

While they worked on strapping Devon into the basket, the helicopter hovered above. There was so much noise and commotion, I didn't even notice the Clearwater Police boat approaching.

The lights washed over us and I turned to see Salma and Quinn waving from it. Lifting a tired arm, I waved back.

We let the helicopter go so they could rush Devon to the hospital faster while we all climbed on board the police boat. It was cramped but doable.

Quinn grabbed me by the life jacket when I climbed in and helped me sit down on the bench seat. 'Jaysis, Elle, you all right?'

I fell into his arms, shaking from the cold and adrenaline. The tears finally came as he squeezed me and whispered, 'There, there, you're safe now.'

There was so much excitement on the small boat with people talking all at once. Finally I pulled myself together enough to sit up, though the physical exhaustion made me want to just collapse and sleep for a week.

'Yeah. I'm fine, sorry.' I finally offered him a small smile in exchange for his kindness. 'Just worried about Devon now.'

He rubbed his beard thoughtfully then assured me, 'No need, he's a tough one.'

'But, he was shot . . . again. And half-drowned. Wait. How . . . How did you guys find us so quickly?'

'You can thank Devon for that.' Salma stepped over feet and legs to sit on the other side of me as the boat took off back toward shore. She pulled an iPad out of a leather case. 'Devon called Quinn before you guys left on the yacht – told him to get me and Breezy and head to the Beckleys. Said we needed to watch and record what was happening on the yacht and we could do that from M.J.'s iPad. He was worried about Sven and hoped we could record it if he said anything incriminating. Imagine our surprise when it was M.J. Beckley we should've been watching. Anyway, Breezy talked Flavia into letting us in and knew where M.J. kept the iPad. Technology is amazing, isn't it?'

It was almost too good to be true. 'So you saw everything? Recorded everything?'

'Yes.' She nodded. 'As soon as M.J. pulled the gun on you all we jumped in the boat. We had the yacht coordinates on here so that wasn't the hard part. It was just you were so far out. Time was against us.'

I suddenly remember the man we left behind. I wasn't his biggest fan but surely someone would need closure. Maybe even Selene. 'What about Sven? Will his body be recovered?'

She blew out a deep breath. 'We'll send a dive team out here to try but . . .' She shook her head sadly.

The wind was whipping wet pieces of hair against my cheek and eye. I pushed them aside and stared at the strip of city lights coming into view. 'He's still got Lulu.'

Salma put her hand on my knee. 'The Coast Guard is looking for him. They'll find him, don't worry.'

What I was worried about was what he'd do to Lulu if they found him. Would he go through with his threat that they'd be together no matter what? In life or death. Rubbing the evil eye pendant through my shirt, I closed my eyes and sent up a prayer to the universe, the stars, the saints and whatever gods were listening to keep Lulu and the baby safe.

'What's going on?' Cali was finally semi-conscious beneath a blanket. Selene pulled her closer and Chloe licked her ear from her perch on Selene's lap. 'Go back to sleep, Cali. It's all over now. We're safe.' Selene had stopped crying but she was white as a ghost and her flat tone suggested shock. I imagined it would take her a while to recover from M.J.'s actions. Could she forgive him like she forgave Cali? I highly doubted it. Murder was a lot different than betraying your family with tabloid gossip. I felt sorry for her, and I wouldn't take all the money in the world to be in her shoes right now.

Salma took statements from everyone as we made the hour-and-a-half trek back to shore. About twenty minutes in she'd received a radio call from the Coast Guard. Devon was on the ground and en route to the hospital.

'He's going to be fine,' she said, offering me a rare smile. 'You did good.' I saw it clearly then: the love she had for Devon. In that moment of raw relief, it was unmasked. Then she turned away quickly to finish taking Captain Bronson's statement.

Selene insisted on going right back home instead of getting checked out at the hospital. That was fine with me. I could get Devon's Jeep and go check on the dogs before I headed to the hospital to be with Devon.

The first one to greet us as we all piled off the police boat at the dock was Athena. Her yipping echoed through the night air, and I smiled despite my fatigue. Flavia's cries of relief could be heard right behind her as Breezy wheeled her toward us.

'Thank you, thank you for bringing my daughter home safe!' she cried, clutching Selene's hands and then her face. Athena and Chloe had their own reunion party as Selene collapsed on her knees, resting her head in her mother's lap and letting fresh tears fall.

'I can't believe it, Mom,' she kept whispering. 'My little boy.'

The men helped to get Cali into the house as Beth Anne and I locked arms, leaning on each other, and followed behind them.

'Elle,' Flavia called to me as she stroked Selene's head in her lap. Moonlight reflected in her eyes, which were swimming in tears. 'You are OK?'

With effort, I smiled and pulled the evil eye pendant from my still-damp shirt. Everyone needs to believe in something. I could give her this. 'I am. Thank you.'

She nodded sagely and gave her attention back to her broken daughter.

TWENTY-NINE

'Where do you think you're going?' A hand reached out and grabbed mine. Devon's voice was groggy, his eyes still closed.

I slid back into the chair I'd held vigil in beside his hospital bed all morning and grinned at him, gripping his hand. Emotion overwhelmed me as his eyes fluttered open for the first time since he'd come out of surgery to repair the damage to blood vessels and muscle inflicted on his shoulder by the bullet.

He turned his head slowly and our eyes met. His voice was a raspy whisper. 'Jaysis, it's bloody good to see you, Elle.'

I felt like I would lift off the chair like a balloon as relief flooded my body. 'You, too. How are you feeling?'

His lips were pale but his eyes were bright. 'Like I'm on some really good painkillers.'

'Ah. That would be morphine.' I lifted myself out of the chair, carefully making sure I didn't touch his bandaged shoulder, and gently kissed his lips. 'Welcome back.' We held hands, intertwining them tighter as I lowered myself back into the chair, ignoring my stiff back and legs. 'You know, you really have to stop getting yourself shot.'

He shifted in the bed and then winced. 'Agreed. What happened? Is everyone all right?'

'What do you remember?'

His gaze drifted behind me as he tried to recall. 'I . . .' He blinked and then squinted. 'What is all that? Did somebody die then?'

I glanced behind me at the mounds of balloons and flowers and food. 'That is mostly from Breezy's family, their way of saying thank you for clearing Breezy of the murder charges. I think they'll be bringing us homemade food for the next year.'

Devon cracked a smile and his chest rose as he chuckled. Then he sighed. 'I remember bits and pieces. Getting shot. Hitting the water. Coming to a few times beneath the water. Being terrified of what was happening to you . . .' He squeezed his eyes shut and squeezed my hand at the same time. When he spoke again, emotion had thickened his voice. 'I remember hearing you shouting for me. I can't believe I didn't see that comin' with M.J. I'd been so distracted with my parents' case. How were we rescued? Did they catch him? Is Lulu safe?'

I shook my head. I'd been trying to stay positive about Lulu. I kept telling myself that M.J. loved her, that he'd never hurt her. But then I remembered the look on his face and how it wasn't love but obsession. He would have her at any cost and he'd already killed to prove that. *Don't cry.* 'I haven't heard anything yet. Of course, my phone is at the bottom of the Gulf.'

His eyes closed as he blew out a deep breath. He forced them back open. 'But you're safe.'

'And you're safe,' I whispered back. Stroking his hair, which was stiff from the dried salt water, gratitude washed over me. This time I couldn't stop the flood of tears. Sniffing, I wiped my eyes with my sweater sleeve.

His eyes cracked open and met mine. Such an intense blue. Sparkling. Alive. Full of love. 'Maybe that wee bag from Madame Dutrey did help protect me. Either that or I've got a guardian angel.' He squeezed my hand once more and then drifted off.

I smiled, thinking about my dog, Angel, and how she was the reason he'd had the Human Gills to keep him alive. 'You have no idea,' I said quietly.

It took the Coast Guard four days to find the yacht. Devon got the call on his new iPhone from Salma as we were having our last dinner with Quinn, which consisted of various plates of food Novia had been bringing me at the Pampered Pup the last two days. The dogs were at our feet under the table. They hadn't left our side since Devon came home from the hospital on Monday, even insisting on sleeping in the bed with their favorite toys. We were such pushovers.

I watched his face as he nodded and then chuckled. 'She's a feisty one, for sure. Thanks for lettin' us know.' He seemed to be enjoying a private joke as he put the phone on the table and adjusted the sling on his injured arm.

'Well?' Quinn said. 'Are you gonna keep us in the dark then?'

Devon shook his head slowly and then blew out a deep breath.

'Seems like Lulu had managed to drug M.J. with the tranquilizers Selene had left in the bedroom and tie him up by their second day at sea. But he'd disabled the GPS and radios so she had no choice but to wait to be rescued. She's fine . . . well, as fine as a lass can be goin' through somethin' like this. The babe's fine, too. M.J.'s in custody and being shipped back to Florida to face murder, kidnapping and various other charges.'

I sat back in the chair and took in a shuddering breath; my first full breath in days. A rush of warmth filled my body. It was over. Lulu was safe. M.J. was in custody and wouldn't hurt anyone again. Devon reached over and squeezed my hand at the same time as Buddha popped his big head onto my lap with his squeaky shark planted firmly in his jaws.

I smiled at Devon and stroked the soft indent between Buddha's eyes. 'I'm all right, you two.' And I was. 'Though I guess I'll be trusting Buddha's judgment from now on. You know he growled at M.J. when he went to help me after I fell at the spa.' He deserved an ear scratch for that. 'Sorry for not listening to you, boy.'

Devon held something under the table and Buddha left my leg and dropped his shark to gulp it down. 'That's a good dog.'

'You will be the one cleaning that up off the floor later,' I teased him.

Despite the danger we'd all been in, something precious had come from it. Bonds of friendship had formed between us from the high pressure situation that wouldn't have been possible in day to day life. Lulu felt like my sister now, and I couldn't wait to give her a hug and see for myself that she and the baby were OK. Beth Anne was no longer an intimidating rich client but a dear friend that I knew, despite our socio-economical differences, was the same as me on the inside, where it mattered. Devon and I now had a bond that allowed me to stop worrying about his past relationship with Salma – even though I knew without a doubt now how she felt about him – and just be grateful for every second I had with him. I guess almost losing someone you love makes you realize how fragile life is. How much it has to be appreciated. Even Quinn felt more like a brother than someone I'd just met a few weeks ago.

When I looked at Quinn, a tiny secret smile was nestled in his beard as he watched us.

'OK, spill it,' I said.

He glanced from me to Devon and then reached for his beer. 'Well, I was a bit bored while waiting for this bloke to get his sorry arse out of a hospital bed. So, first . . . Elle, I fixed your car. She'll run as good as a car with 230,000 miles can run.'

My cheeks burned. 'Oh, Quinn, thank you! I don't know what to say.'

He held up a hand. 'No need to say anything but that. I've seen the way people drive those golf carts here – can't have you ridin' a bike.' After a generous swig from his Guinness bottle, he eyed Devon with a bit more reserve. 'Also, I finished goin' through all the bleedin' paperwork. I think I found the second boat.'

I watched Devon lean slowly forward, his eyes growing wide with surprise and then hope. Finally he nodded and grinned at us both. 'Right then. Let's finish our meal and you can show me.'

'Since my time is up, you two will have to come to Dublin to celebrate when the dirtballs are locked up for good,' Quinn said, stabbing a chunk of spicy pork.

Devon glanced at me and put down his fork. He must have seen the fear that gripped me, closing my throat, because he reached over and gently squeezed my hand. 'That'd be grand.' Then he winked and gave me that killer smile of his, the one that melted me and made me feel like I could do anything as long as he kept looking at me like that. 'We'll work on it . . . together.'

Later that evening, we were snuggled beneath the sheets with the dogs pinning us down on both sides. Petey was dreaming already, his legs twitching like he was chasing something in his sleep. Devon had his good arm wrapped around me as he flipped through some photos he'd downloaded from his camera to the laptop, and I was enjoying the feel of his bare chest beneath my cheek as I watched him.

'Well, that's a bit strange,' he muttered to himself.

'What is?' I asked, snuggling closer.

He clicked on the keyboard, enlarging the photo he was looking at and tapped on the screen. 'Sort of looks like a little brown dog sittin' in front of you, but I don't remember a dog there not in costume.'

I lifted my head up and stared at the photo. The subject of the picture was obviously Ghost in his William Wegman costume, but you could also see me sitting on the side and Devon was right . . . a little brown dog-shaped form sat in front of me. 'Can you blow it up more?'

He did and we watched as the form grew larger but less clear. Plus, you could see my shoe on the other side of it.

'Well, that's obviously one of Pricilla Moon's Yorkies.' I grinned up at him. Yes, I was teasing him, but I also wanted to see his reaction when I brought up the spirit dogs. I'd like to be able to tell him about Angel one day without him thinking I was off my rocker.

'Pricilla Moon, the billionaire heiress who bought this island because her dogs weren't welcomed in the restaurant?'

'Yes,' I said, still watching him closely.

He glanced back at the photo and then down at me. 'Aren't her dogs . . . long gone?'

I was enjoying his confusion. I smiled. 'Yes.'

'Huh.' He zoomed the photo back out and stared at it thoughtfully. 'Ma believed in spirits, you know. Said she saw one in a castle one day when she was a wee girl.'

I pulled the bulk of his arm tighter around my shoulder. 'I would've really liked your mom.'

'She would've liked you, too.' He kissed the top of my head. 'Elle, have you given any thought to finding your da?'

The question was startling and stirred up all sorts of emotions, the dominant one being anger. *Had I?* 'No, actually. Why would I want to? He abandoned Mom and me. Obviously he doesn't want anything to do with us.'

He closed the laptop. 'Just a thought. If you change your mind I'd be glad to help you find him.'

I moved the laptop to the nightstand for him. Buddha grunted to let me know he didn't appreciate the jostling. I scratched his foot in apology and then snuggled back into the warmth and safety of Devon's arms. 'I appreciate it, but I don't think I'll change my mind.'

As I drifted off to sleep, my mind was set free to speculate about my biological father. Did I have his green eyes? Did he ever think about me and wonder what I'd become? What about my ancestry? I could be Irish. I had the hair and skin for it. What if I had grandparents that were still alive? Maybe I would change my mind.

I let out a contented sigh. Until then, I had all I needed right here in this bed.